THE FIRE ENGINE THAT DISAPPEARED

MAJ SJÖWALL ◆ PER WAHLÖÖ

Translated from the Swedish by Joan Tate

VINTAGE BOOKS
A Division of Random House
New York

Library of Congress Cataloging in Publication Data

Sjöwall, Maj, 1935-
The fire engine that disappeared.

Translation of Brandbilen som försvann.
I. Wahlöö, Per, 1926-1975, joint author. II. Title.
[PZ4.S61953Fi9] [PT9876.29.J63] 839.7'3'74 76-42997
ISBN 0-394-72340-6

Manufactured in the United States of America

THE
FIRE ENGINE
THAT
DISAPPEARED

1

The man lying dead on the tidily made bed had first taken off his jacket and tie and hung them over the chair by the door. He had then unlaced his shoes, placed them under the chair and stuck his feet into a pair of black leather slippers. He had smoked three filter-tipped cigarettes and stubbed them out in the ashtray on the bedside table. Then he had lain down on his back on the bed and shot himself through the mouth.

That did not look quite so tidy.

His nearest neighbor was a prematurely retired army captain who had been injured in the hip during an elk hunt the previous year. He had suffered from insomnia after the accident and often sat up at night playing solitaire. He was just getting the deck of cards out when he heard the shot on the other side of the wall and he at once called the police.

It was twenty to four on the morning of the seventh of March when two radio police broke the lock on the door and made their way into the apartment, inside which the man on the bed had been dead for thirty-two minutes. It did not take them long to establish the fact that the man almost certainly had committed suicide. Before returning to their car to report the death over the radio, they looked around the apartment, which in fact they should not have done. Apart from the bedroom, it consisted of a living room, kitchen, hall, bathroom and wardrobe. They could find no message or farewell letter. The only written matter visible was two words on the pad by the telephone in the living room. The two words formed a name. A name which both policemen knew well.

Martin Beck.

It was Ottilia's name day.

Soon after eleven in the morning, Martin Beck left the South police station and went and stood in the line at the

1

state liquor store in Karusellplan. He bought a bottle of Nutty Solera. On the way to the subway, he also bought a dozen red tulips and a can of English cheese biscuits. One of the six names his mother had been given at baptism was Ottilia and he was going to congratulate her on her name day.

The old people's home was large and very old. Much too old and inconvenient according to those who had to work there. Martin Beck's mother had moved there a year ago, not because she had been unable to manage on her own, for she was still lively and relatively fit at seventy-eight, but because she had not wanted to be a burden on her only child. So in good time she had ensured herself a place in the home and when a desirable room had become vacant, that is, when the previous occupant had died, she had got rid of most of her belongings and moved there. Since his father's death nineteen years earlier, Martin Beck had been her only support and now and again he was afflicted with pangs of conscience over not looking after her himself. Deep down, inwardly, he was grateful that she had taken things into her own hands without even asking his advice.

He walked past one of the dreary small sitting rooms in which he had never seen anyone sitting, continued along the gloomy corridor and knocked on his mother's door. She looked up in surprise as he came in; she was a little deaf and had not heard his discreet tap. Her face lighting up, she put aside her book and began to get up. Martin Beck moved swiftly over to her, kissed her cheek and with gentle force pressed her down into the chair again.

"Don't start dashing about for my sake," he said.

He laid the flowers on her lap and placed the bottle and can of biscuits on the table.

"Congratulations, Mother dear."

She unwound the paper from the flowers and said:

"Oh, what lovely flowers. And biscuits! And wine, or what is it? Oh, sherry. Good gracious!"

She got up and, despite Martin Beck's protests, went over to a cupboard and took out a silver vase, which she filled with water from the washbasin.

"I'm not so old and decrepit that I can't even use my legs," she said. "Sit yourself down instead. Shall we have sherry or coffee?"

2

He hung up his hat and coat and sat down.

"Whichever you like," he said.

"Then I'll make coffee," she said. "Then I can save the sherry and offer some to the old ladies and boast about my nice son. One has to save up the cheerful subjects."

Martin Beck sat in silence, watching as she switched on the electric hotplate and measured out the water and coffee. She was small and fragile and seemed to grow smaller each time he saw her.

"Is it boring for you here, Mother?"

"Me? I'm never bored."

The reply came much too quickly and glibly for him to believe her. Before sitting down, she put the coffee pot on the hotplate and the vase of flowers on the table.

"Don't you worry about me," she said. "I've got such a lot to do. I read and talk to the other old girls, and I knit. Sometimes I go into town and just look, though it's awful the way they're pulling everything down. Did you see that the building your father's business was in has been demolished?"

Martin Beck nodded. His father had had a small transport business in Klara and where it had once been, there was now a shopping center of glass and concrete. He looked at the photograph of his father that stood on the chest of drawers by her bed. The picture had been taken in the mid-twenties, when he himself had been only a few years old and his father had still been a young man with clear eyes, glossy hair with a side-part, and a stubborn chin. It was said that Martin Beck resembled his father. He himself had never been able to see the likeness, and should there be any, then it was limited to physical appearance. He remembered his father as a straightforward, cheerful man who was generally liked and who laughed and joked easily. Martin Beck would have described himself as a shy and rather dull person. At the time the photograph had been taken, his father had been a construction worker, but a few years later the depression came and he was unemployed for a couple of years. Martin Beck reckoned that his mother had never really got over those years of poverty and anxiety; although they were much better off later on, she had never stopped worrying about money. She still could not bring herself to buy anything new if it were not absolutely necessary, and

3

both her clothes and the few bits of furniture she had brought with her from her old home were worn by the years.

Martin Beck tried to give her money now and again and at regular intervals he offered to pay the bill at the home, but she was proud and obstinate and wished to be independent.

When the coffee had boiled, he brought the pot over and let his mother pour it. She had always been solicitous toward her son and when he had been a boy she had never even allowed him to help with the dishes or make his own bed. He had not realized how misdirected her thoughtfulness had been until he had discovered how clumsy he was when it came to the simplest domestic chore.

Martin Beck watched his mother with amusement as she popped a sugar lump into her mouth before taking a sip of the coffee. He had never seen her drinking coffee "on the lump" before. She caught his eye and she said:

"Ah well, you can take a few liberties when you're as old as I am."

She put down her cup and leaned back, her thin freckled hands loosely clasped in her lap.

"Well," she said. "Tell me how things are with my grandchildren."

Nowadays, Martin Beck was always careful to express himself in nothing but positive terms when he talked to his mother about his children, as she considered her grandchildren cleverer, more brilliant and more beautiful than any other children. She often complained that he did not appreciate their merits and she had even accused him of being an unsympathetic and harsh father. He himself thought he was able to regard his children in a quite sober light and he presumed they were much like any other children. His contact with sixteen-year-old Ingrid was best, a lively, intelligent girl who found things easy at school and was a good mixer. Rolf would soon be thirteen and was more of a problem. He was lazy and introverted, totally uninterested in anything to do with school and did not seem to have any other special interests or talents either. Martin Beck was concerned about his son's inertia, but hoped it was just his age and that the boy would overcome his lethargy. As he could not find anything

4

positive to say about Rolf at the moment and as his mother would not have believed him if he had told her the truth, he avoided the subject. When he had told her about Ingrid's latest progress at school, his mother said quite unexpectedly:

"Rolf's not going into the police force when he leaves school, is he?"

"I don't think so. Anyhow, he's hardly thirteen. It's a little soon to begin worrying about that sort of thing."

"Because if he wants to, you must stop him," she said. "I've never understood why you were so stubborn about becoming a policeman. Nowadays it must be an even more awful profession than it was when you first began. Why did you join the police force, anyway, Martin?"

Martin Beck stared at her in astonishment. It was true she had been against his choice of profession at the time, twenty-four years ago, but it surprised him that she brought the subject up now. He had become a Chief Inspector in the Homicide Squad less than a year ago and his conditions of work were completely different from those that had existed when he had been a young patrolman.

He leaned forward and patted her hand.

"I am all right now, Mother," he said. "Nowadays, I mostly sit at a desk. But of course, I've often asked myself the same question."

It was true. He had often asked himself why he had become a policeman.

Naturally he could have replied that at the time, during the war years, it was a good way of avoiding military service. After a two-year deferment because of bad lungs, he had been declared fit and no longer exempt, which was quite an important reason. In 1944 conscientious objectors were not tolerated. Many of those who had evaded military service in the way he had, had since changed occupation, but he himself had been promoted over the years to Chief Inspector. That ought to mean that he was a good policeman, but he was not so sure. There were several instances of senior posts in the police being held by less good policemen. He was not even certain he wanted to be a good policeman, if that involved being a dutiful person who never deviated one iota from the regulations. He remembered something Lennart Kollberg had once said a

5

long time ago. "There are lots of good cops around. Dumb guys who are good cops. Inflexible, limited, tough, self-satisfied types who are all good cops. It would be better if there were a few more good guys who were cops."

His mother came out with him, and they walked together in the park a bit. The slushy snow made it difficult to walk and the icy wind rattled round the branches of the tall bare trees. After they had slipped about for ten minutes, he accompanied her back to the porch and kissed her on the cheek. He turned around on his way down the slope and saw her standing there waving by the entrance. Small and shrunken and gray.

He took the subway back to the South police station in Västberga Allé.

On the way to his office, he glanced into Kollberg's room. Kollberg was an Inspector as well as Martin Beck's assistant and best friend. The room was empty. He glanced at his wristwatch. It was half-past one. It was Thursday. It required no profound thoughts to know where Kollberg was. For a brief moment Martin Beck even considered joining him down there with his pea soup, but then he thought of his stomach and desisted. It was already disturbed by the far too numerous cups of coffee his mother had pressed on him.

On his blotter there was a brief message about the man who had committed suicide that same morning.

His name was Ernst Sigurd Karlsson and he was forty-six years old. He was unmarried and his nearest relative was an elderly aunt in Borås. He had been absent from his work in an insurance company since Monday. Influenza. According to his colleagues at work, he was a loner and as far as they knew he had no close friends. His neighbors said he was quiet and inoffensive, came and went at definite times and seldom had visitors. Tests on his handwriting showed that it had indeed been he who had written Martin Beck's name on the telephone pad. That he had committed suicide was perfectly evident.

There was nothing else to say about the case. Ernst Sigurd Karlsson had taken his own life, and as suicide is not a crime in Sweden, the police could not do very much more. All the questions had been answered. Except one. Whoever had written out the report had also asked this

6

question: Had Chief Inspector Beck had any connection with the man in question and could he possibly add anything?

Martin Beck could not.

He had never before heard of Ernst Sigurd Karlsson.

2

As Gunvald Larsson left his office at the police station in Kungsholmsgatan, it was half-past ten at night and he had no plans whatsoever for becoming a hero; insofar as it was no great deed to go home to Bollmora, shower, put on his pajamas and go to bed. Gunvald Larsson thought about his pajamas with pleasure. They were new, bought that same day, and most of his colleagues would not have believed their ears if they had heard what they had cost. On his way home, he was to carry out a minor duty which would hardly set him back more than five minutes, if that. As he thought about his pajamas, he struggled into his Bulgarian sheepskin coat, put out the light, slammed the door and left. The decrepit elevator which went up to their department went wrong as usual and he had to stamp twice on the floor before it could be persuaded to get going. Gunvald Larsson was a large man, 6 feet 2 inches in his stockings, weighing over 200 pounds, and it was noticeable when he stamped his feet.

It was cold and windy outside, with gusts of dry, swirling snow, but he had only a few steps to get to the car and did not need to worry about the weather.

Gunvald Larsson drove across Väster bridge, glancing indifferently to his left. He saw the City Hall with the yellow light thrown onto the three golden crowns on the spire at the top of the tower, and thousands upon thousands of other lights which he could not identify. From the bridge, he continued straight to Hornsplan, turned left onto Hornsgatan and then turned right by the Zinkensdamm subway station. He drove only about 500 yards southward along Ringvägen, then braked and stopped.

There are as good as no buildings there, despite the fact that it is still in central Stockholm. On the west side of the street, Tantolunden, a hilly park, spreads out, and to the east there is a rocky knoll, a parking lot and a gas station. It is called Sköldgatan and is not really a street at all, but rather, a bit of road which for some incomprehensible reason has remained since, with doubtful zeal, the planners devastated this city district, as well as most of the others, depriving them of their original value and obliterating their special character.

Sköldgatan is a winding bit of road, less than 300 yards long, which connects Ringvägen with Rosenlundsgatan and is largely used by a few taxi drivers or occasional lost police cars. In the summer, it is something of an oasis with its luxuriant roadside foliage, and despite the heavy traffic on Ringvägen and the trains thundering along the line only 50 yards away, the older generation of the district's unhappy children, with bottles of wine, bits of sausage and greasy packs of cards, can operate relatively undisturbed in the undergrowth. No one is to be found voluntarily there in the winter.

On this particular evening, the seventh of March, 1968, however, a man was standing freezing among the bare bushes on the south side of the road. His attention was not entirely what it ought to have been and was only partly directed toward the one dwelling house in the street, an old wooden, two-story building. A short while earlier, the lights had been on in two of the windows on the second floor and the sounds of music, shouting and occasional peals of laughter had been heard, but now all the lights in the house were out and the only thing to be heard was the wind and the hum of the traffic far away. The man in the bushes was not standing there of his own free will. He was a policeman and his name was Zachrisson and he was wishing heartily that he was elsewhere.

Gunvald Larsson got out of his car, put up his coat collar and pulled his fur cap down over his ears. Then he strode straight across the wide road, past the gas station, and slogged on through the slushy snow. The highway authorities clearly did not think it worth their while wasting road salt on this useless bit of roadway. The house lay about 75 yards farther on, slightly above road level and at a sharp angle to it. He stopped in front of it, looked around and said quietly:

"Zachrisson?"

The man in the bushes shook himself and came up to him.

"Bad news," said Gunvald Larsson. "You've got two more hours. Isaksson is off sick."

"Hell!" said Zachrisson.

Gunvald Larsson surveyed the scene. Then he made a disgruntled grimace and said:

"It'd be better if you stood up on the slope."

"Yes, if I want to freeze my ass off," said Zachrisson misanthropically.

"If you want a decent view. Has anything happened?"

The other man shook his head.

"Not a damned thing," he said. "They had some sort of party up there a while back. Now it looks as if they're lying up there sleeping it off."

"And Malm?"

"Him too. It's three hours since he put his light out."

"Has he been alone all the time?"

"Yes, seems so."

"Seems? Has anyone left the house?"

"I haven't seen anyone."

"What have you seen, then?"

"Three people have gone in since I came. A guy and two dames. They came in a taxi. I think they were in on that party."

"Think?" said Gunvald Larsson inquiringly.

"Well, what the hell is one to think. I haven't got . . . "

The man's teeth were chattering so that he had difficulty in speaking. Gunvald Larsson inspected him critically and said:

"What haven't you got?"

"X-ray eyes," said Zachrisson dismally.

Gunvald Larsson was inclined to severity and had little understanding for human weaknesses. As an officer, he was anything but popular and many people were afraid of him. If Zachrisson had known him better, he would never have dared behave as he had, that is, naturally; but not even Gunvald Larsson could wholly ignore the fact that the man was exhausted and cold, and his condition and ability to observe would hardly improve over the next few hours. He realized what ought to be done but did not plan to drop the matter for that reason. He grunted irritably and said:

9

"Are you cold?"

Zachrisson gave a hollow laugh and tried to scrape the icicles off his eyelashes.

"Cold?" he said with dull irony. "I feel like the three men in the burning fiery furnace."

"You're not here to be funny," said Gunvald Larsson. "You're here to do your job."

"Yes, sorry, but—"

"And one part of that job is keeping warm and properly dressed and moving your flat feet occasionally. Otherwise, you may be left standing there like a goddamn snowman when something happens. And then perhaps it won't be so funny . . . afterward."

Zachrisson began to suspect something. He shivered awkwardly and said apologetically:

"Yes, of course, that's okay, but—"

"It's not at all okay," said Gunvald Larsson angrily. "I happen to have to take the responsibility for this assignment and I prefer not to be messed about by some bungler in the ordinary force."

Zachrisson was only twenty-three years old and an ordinary policeman. At the moment he belonged to the Protection Section in the Second District. Gunvald Larsson was twenty years older and an Inspector in the Stockholm Homicide Squad. When Zachrisson opened his mouth to reply, Gunvald Larsson raised his large right hand and said harshly:

"No more jaw, thanks. Get off to the station in Rosenlundsgatan and have a cup of coffee or something. In precisely half an hour, you're to be back here, fresh and alert, so you'd better get a move on."

Zachrisson went. Gunvald Larsson looked at his wristwatch, sighed and said to himself, "Greenhorn."

Then he turned right around, walked through the bushes and began climbing up the slope, muttering and swearing under his breath because the thick rubber soles of his Italian winter shoes could not get a grip on the icy stones.

Zachrisson had been right in that the knoll did not offer any shelter whatsoever against the mercilessly biting north wind, and he himself had been right when he had said that this was the best observation point. The house lay directly in front and slightly below him. He could not help observing anything that happened in the building and its immediate surroundings. The windows were all wholly or partly covered with frosted ice and no lights were showing behind them. The only sign of life was the smoke from the chimney, which hardly had time to be colored by the cold before it was torn to shreds by the wind and rushed away in great cottonwool blobs up into the starless sky.

The man on the knoll automatically moved his feet from side to side and flexed his fingers inside his sheepskin-lined gloves. Before becoming a policeman, Gunvald Larsson had been a sailor, first as an ordinary seaman in the navy, later on cargo ships in the North Atlantic, and many wintry watches on open bridges had taught him the art of keeping warm. He was also an expert on this sort of assignment, though nowadays he preferred to and usually did only organize them. After he had stood on the knoll for a while, he was able to make out a flickering light behind the window farthest to the right on the second floor, as if someone had struck a match to light a cigarette or look at the time, for instance. He glanced automatically at his own watch. It was four minutes past eleven. Sixteen minutes since Zachrisson had left his post. By this time, he was presumably sitting in the canteen at Maria police station, filling himself with coffee and grumbling to the off-duty uniformed policemen, a short-lived pleasure, for in seven minutes the man would have to be on the march back again. If he did not want to be in for the bawling out of the century, thought Gunvald Larsson grimly.

Then he thought for a few minutes about the number of people who might be in the house at that particular moment. There were four apartments in the old building, two on the first floor and two on the second floor. Up on the left lived an unmarried woman in her thirties, with three children, all with different fathers. That was more or less all he knew about the lady and that was enough. Below her, to the left on the first floor, lived a married couple, old people. They were about seventy and had lived there for almost half a century, in contrast to the upper apartments, which changed tenants rapidly. The husband drank and, in spite of his venerable age, he was a regular customer in the cells at Maria police station. To the right on the second floor lived a man who was also well known, but for more criminal reasons than just Saturday-night

11

boozing. He was twenty-seven and already had six different sentences of varying lengths behind him. His crimes varied from drunken driving, breaking and entering, to assault. His name was Roth and it was he who had thrown a party for his one male and two female buddies. Now they had turned off the record-player and the light, either to sleep or else to continue the festivities in some other way. And it was in his apartment that someone had struck a match.

Below this apartment, at the bottom right, lived the person whom Gunvald Larsson was watching. He knew what this person's name was and what he looked like. On the other hand, oddly enough, he had no idea why the man had to be watched.

It had come about in this way: Gunvald Larsson was what the newspapers in exalted moments refer to as a murder-scout, and as at this particular moment there was no special murderer to scout for, he had been loaned to another department to be responsible for this assignment, on top of his own duties. He had been allocated a scratch collection of four men and given simple directions: Ensure that the man in question does not disappear and that nothing happens to him and note whom he meets.

He had not even bothered to ask what it was all about. Drugs, presumably. Everything seemed to be about drugs these days.

Now the watch had gone on for ten days and the only thing that had happened to the man in question was a tart and two half-bottles of liquor.

Gunvald Larsson looked at his watch. Nine minutes past eleven. Eight minutes left.

He yawned and raised his arms to start beating them round him.

At that precise moment the house exploded.

3

The fire began with an ear-splitting bang. The windows in the right-hand first floor apartment were blown out and most of the gable seemed to be torn off the house, as

12

simultaneously long ice blue flames shot through the broken panes. Gunvald Larsson was standing on the top of the hillock with his arms stretched out, like a statue of the Saviour, paralytically staring at what was happening on the other side of the road. But only for a moment. Then he rushed, slipping and swearing, down the stony slope, across the street and up toward the house. As he ran, the flames changed color and character, became orange and licked greedily upward along the boards. He also got the impression that the roof had already begun to sag above the right-hand part of the house, as if part of the actual foundations had been jerked away. The apartment on the first floor had been in flames for several seconds and before he reached the stone steps outside the front door, it was burning in the room above as well.

He flung open the door and at once saw that it was too late. The door to the right in the hall had been torn off its hinges and was blocking the stairs. It was blazing like a giant log and the fire had begun to spread up the wooden staircase. A wave of intense heat blew back against him and he staggered, scorched and blinded, backward down the outer steps. From inside the house came desperate screams of human beings in pain and terror. So far as he knew, there were at least eleven people in the building, helplessly barricaded inside this veritable death-trap. Presumably some of them were already dead. Tongues of flame were shooting out of the first floor windows as if from a blowtorch.

Gunvald Larsson glanced swiftly around to see if there were any ladders or other aids. There was nothing in sight.

A window was thrown open on the second floor and through the smoke and flames he thought he could make out a woman, or rather a girl, who was screaming shrilly and hysterically. He cupped his hands around his mouth and yelled:

"Jump! Jump to the right!"

She was up on the windowsill now, but hesitating.

"Jump! Now! As far out as you can! I'll catch you."

The girl jumped. She came hurtling through the air straight at him and he managed to catch the falling body with his right arm between her legs and his left arm round her shoulders. She was not all that heavy, perhaps 100 or

110 pounds and he caught her expertly, without her even touching the ground. The moment he caught her, he swung right around so that he was protecting her from the roaring fire, took three steps and put her down on the ground. The girl was hardly more than seventeen. She was naked and her whole body was shaking as she screamed and tossed her head from side to side. Otherwise, he could see nothing wrong with her.

When he turned around again, there was another person at the window, a man wrapped in some sort of sheet. The fire was burning more fiercely than ever, smoke seeping out along the length of the ridge of the roof, and on the right-hand side the flames had begun to come through the tiles. If that blasted fire department doesn't come soon, thought Gunvald Larsson, getting as close to the fire as he was able. There were cracks and creaks from the burning woodwork, and showers of mercilessly burning sparks fell on his face and over his sheepskin coat, where they slowly burned their way in and were extinguished in that expensive material. He shouted as loudly as he could to make himself heard above the roar of the fire.

"Jump! As far out as you can! To the right!"

At the same moment as the man jumped, the fire caught the piece of cloth he was wrapped in. The man let out a penetrating scream as he fell, trying to tear off the burning sheet. This time the descent was not so successful. The man was considerably heavier than the girl, and he twisted around, hitting Gunvald Larsson's shoulder with his left arm and then thudding on to the uneven cobblestones with his shoulder first. At the last moment, Gunvald Larsson managed to get his huge left hand under the man's head, thus saving him from cracking his skull open. He laid the man down on the ground, tore away the burning sheet, at the same time irreparably burning his own gloves. The man was naked too, except for a gold wedding ring. He was groaning horribly, chattering gutturally in between times like an imbecile chimpanzee. Gunvald Larsson rolled him a few yards away and let him lie in the snow more or less out of the way of the burning timbers that were falling. As he turned around, a third person, a woman in a black bra, jumped from the now blazing apartment up on the right. Her red hair was alight and she fell much too near the wall.

14

Gunvald Larsson rushed in among the burning planks and woodwork and dragged her away from the immediate danger zone, extinguished the fire in her hair with snow and left her lying. He could see that she was badly burned and she was shrieking shrilly, twisting like a snake with the pain. She had obviously also fallen badly, for one leg lay stretched out at a highly unnatural angle to her body. She was slightly older than the other woman, perhaps about twenty-five, and was red-haired, between her legs too. The skin on her stomach was remarkably undamaged and looked pale and slack. Her face, legs and back were most damaged, as well as across her breasts, where the bra had burned into her skin.

When he raised his eyes toward the second floor apartment for the last time, he saw a ghostly figure burning like a torch, and in a pathetic spiral it sank out of sight, its arms raised above its head. Gunvald Larsson presumed that he was the fourth member of the party and realized that he was already beyond human help.

The attic was now in flames too, as well as the roof beams beneath the tiles. Thick smoke was billowing up and he heard sharp cracks from the burning woodwork. The windows farthest to the left on the second floor were flung open and someone shouted for help. Gunvald Larsson rushed over and saw a woman in a white nightgown leaning over the windowsill, a bundle pressed to her chest. A child. Smoke was pouring out of the open window, but clearly it was not yet burning in the apartment, at least not in the room the woman was in.

"Help!" she cried desperately.

As the fire was not yet so fierce in this part of the house, he was able to stand quite near the wall, almost immediately below the window.

"Throw the child," he shouted.

The woman immediately flung down the child, so unhesitatingly that he was taken by surprise. He saw the bundle falling straight at him, and at the last moment flung out his arms and caught it directly in his hands, much like a soccer goalkeeper catching a free kick. The child was very small. It whimpered a bit, but did not cry. Gunvald Larsson remained standing with it in his arms for a few seconds. He had no experience of children and could not even remember with any certainty ever having to hold one

15

before. For a second he wondered whether he had been too rough and had crushed it. Then he moved away and put the bundle down on the ground. As he stood there bending over, he heard running steps and he looked up. It was Zachrisson, panting and scarlet in the face.

"What?" he said. "How . . . ?"

Gunvald Larsson stared at him and said:

"Where the hell's the fire truck?"

"It should be here . . . I mean . . . I saw the fire from Rosenlundsgatan . . . so I ran back and telephoned . . ."

"Run back then, for God's sake, and get the fire truck and the ambulance here . . ."

Zachrisson turned about and ran.

"And the police!" yelled Gunvald Larsson after him.

Zachrisson's cap fell off and he stopped to pick it up.

"Idiot!" yelled Gunvald Larsson.

Then he returned to the house. The whole of the right-hand side was now a roaring inferno and the attic floor looked as if it were on fire. Much more smoke than before was pouring out through the window, where the woman in the nightgown was now standing with yet another child, a fair-haired boy of about five, wearing flowered blue pajamas. The woman flung down the child just as swiftly and unexpectedly as before, but this time Larsson was more prepared and caught the boy safely in his arms. Strangely enough, the boy did not seem at all frightened.

"What's your name?" he shouted.

"Larsson."

"Are you a fireman?"

"For God's sake, push off now," said Gunvald Larsson, putting the child down on the ground.

He looked up again and was hit on the head by a tile. It was red-hot and although his fur cap deadened the blow, everything went black before his eyes. He felt a burning pain in his forehead and blood pouring down his face. The woman in the nightgown had disappeared. Presumably to fetch the third child, he thought, and at that moment the woman appeared at the window with a large porcelain dog, which she at once threw out. It fell to the ground and smashed to pieces. The next second, she herself jumped. That did not go so well. Gunvald Larsson was standing directly in line and fell in a heap on the ground,

16

the woman on top of him. He hit the back of his head and his back, but at once heaved the woman off and began to get up. The woman in the nightgown looked unhurt, but her eyes were glazed and staring. He looked at her and said:

"Haven't you got another child?"

She stared at him, then hunched up and began to whimper like a hurt animal.

"Get over there and look after the other two," said Gunvald Larsson.

The fire had now caught the whole of the second floor and flames were already shooting out the window from which the woman had jumped. But the two old people were still in the left-hand first floor apartment. It had obviously not begun to burn in there yet, but they had not given any sign of life. Presumably the apartment was full of smoke, and it was also only a matter of minutes before the roof would fall in.

Gunvald Larsson looked around for a tool and saw a large stone a few yards away. It was frozen into the ground, but he forced it loose. The stone weighed at least forty to fifty pounds. He raised it above his head with straight arms and flung it with all his strength through the middle of the window farthest to the left in the first floor apartment, shattering the window frame in a shower of splinters of glass and wood. He hauled himself up onto the sill, leaned against a blind which gave way and a table which fell over and landed on the floor in the room, where the smoke was thick and suffocating. He coughed and pulled his woolen scarf up over his mouth. Then he tore down the blind and looked round. The fire was roaring all around him. In the flickering reflections from outside, he saw a figure huddled in a shapeless heap on the floor. The old woman, obviously. He lifted her up, carried the slack body over to the window, took her under the arms and carefully let her down to the ground, where she at once sank into a heap against the foundation wall. She appeared to be alive, but hardly conscious.

He took a deep breath and returned to the apartment, tore down the blind on the other window and smashed the windows with a chair. The smoke lifted slightly, but above him the ceiling was now bulging and orange tongues of flame were beginning to appear around the hall door. It did not take him more than fifteen seconds to find the man. He had not managed to get out of bed, but he was alive and was coughing weakly and pitifully.

Gunvald whipped off the blanket, slung the old man over his shoulder, carried him right across the room and climbed out in a cascade of falling sparks. He coughed hoarsely and could hardly see for the blood running down from the wound in his forehead, mixing with the sweat and tears.

With the old man still over his shoulder, he dragged the old woman away and laid them both down beside each other on the ground. Then he examined the woman to see if she were breathing. She was. He hauled off his sheep-skin coat and brushed a few sparks off it. Then he used it to cover the naked girl, who was still screaming hysterically, and led her away to the others. He took off his tweed jacket and swept that around the two small children, and gave his woolen scarf to the naked man, who at once wound it round his hips. Finally he went over to the red-haired woman, lifted her up and carried her over to the assembly place. She smelled revolting and her screams cut to the quick.

He looked over at the house, which was now blazing all over, burning wildly and uninhibitedly. Several private cars had stopped near the road and bewildered people were just getting out of them. He ignored them. Instead he took off his ruined fur cap and pressed it down over the forehead of the woman in the nightgown. He repeated the question he had put to her a few minutes earlier:

"Haven't you got another child?"

"Yes . . . Kristina . . . her room's in the attic."

Then the woman started weeping uncontrollably.

Gunvald Larsson nodded.

Bloodstained, soot-streaked, drenched with sweat and his clothes torn, he stood among these hysterical, shocked, screaming, unconscious, weeping and dying people. As if on a battlefield.

Above the roar of the fire came the primeval wail of the sirens.

And then suddenly everyone came at once. Water trucks, fire ladders, fire engines, police cars, ambulances, motorcycle police, and fire department officers in red sedans.

18

Zachrisson.

Who said: "What . . . how did it happen?"

And at that moment the roof fell in and the house was transformed into a cheerfully crackling beacon.

Gunvald Larsson looked at his watch. Sixteen minutes had gone by since he had stood, frozen, up on that hill.

4

On the afternoon of Friday, the eighth of March, Gunvald Larsson was sitting in a room at the police station in Kungsholmsgatan. He was wearing a white polo sweater and a pale gray suit with slanting pockets. Both hands were bandaged and the bandage around his head reminded him very strongly of the popular picture of General von Döbeln during the battle of Jutas in Finland. He also had two bandage patches on his face and neck. Some of his brushed-back fair hair had been singed away, as had his eyebrows, but his clear blue eyes looked just as blank and discontented as ever.

There were several other people in the room.

For instance, Martin Beck and Kollberg, who had been called there from the Homicide Squad in Västberga, and Evald Hammar who was their superintendent and until further notice considered responsible for the investigation. Hammar was a large, heavily built man and his thick mane of hair had by now turned almost white in the course of duty. He had already begun to count the days until he retired, and regarded every serious crime of violence as persecution of himself personally.

"Where are the others?" asked Martin Beck.

As usual, he was standing to one side, fairly near the door, leaning with his right elbow against a filing cabinet.

"What others?" asked Hammar, well aware of the fact that the composition of the investigation team was entirely his affair. He had sufficient influence to be able to second any individual member of the force he wanted and was used to working with.

"Rönn and Melander," said Martin Beck stoically.

19

"Rönn is at South Hospital and Melander at the site of the fire," said Hammar shortly.

The evening papers lay spread out over the desk in front of Gunvald Larsson and he was rustling angrily among them with his bandaged hands.

"Damned hacks," he said, shoving one of the papers over toward Martin Beck. "Just look at that picture."

The picture took up three columns and portrayed a young man in a trench coat and a narrow-brimmed hat, a troubled look on his face, standing poking with a stick in the still-smoking ruins of the house in Sköldgatan. Diagonally behind him, in the left-hand corner of the picture, stood Gunvald Larsson, staring foolishly into the camera.

"You perhaps don't come out to your best advantage," said Martin Beck. "Who's the guy with the walking stick?"

"His name is Zachrisson. A greenhorn from the Second District. Absolute idiot. Read the caption."

Martin Beck read the caption.

The hero of the day, Inspector Gunwald Larsson (1) made a heroic contribution during last night's fire by saving several people's lives. Here he can be seen examining the remains of the house, which was totally destroyed.

"Not only do the blasted bunglers not even know the difference between right and left," mumbled Gunvald Larsson, "but they . . ."

He did not say anything more, but Martin Beck knew what he meant, and nodded thoughtfully to himself. The name was spelled wrong too. Gunvald Larsson looked at the picture with distaste and pushed the paper away with his arm.

"And I look moronic too," he said.

"There are snags about being famous," said Martin Beck.

Against his will, Kollberg, who detested Gunvald Larsson, squinted down at the scattered newspapers. All the pictures were equally misleading and every front page was decorated with Gunvald Larsson's staring eyes underneath glaring headlines.

Heroic deeds and heroes and God knows what else, thought Kollberg, sighing dejectedly. He was sitting hunched up in a chair, fat and flabby, his elbows on the desk.

"So we find ourselves in the strange position of not knowing what happened?" said Hammar severely.

"Not all that strange," said Kollberg. "I personally hardly ever know what's happened."

Hammar looked critically at him and said:

"I mean we don't know whether the fire was arson or not."

"Why should it be arson?" asked Kollberg.

"Optimist," said Martin Beck.

" 'Course it was damned well arson," said Gunvald Larsson. "The house blew up practically right in front of my nose."

"And are you certain the fire began in this man Malm's room?"

"Yes. As good as."

"How long had you had the house under observation?"

"About half an hour. Personally. And before that, that fathead Zachrisson was there. Hell of a lot of questions, by the way."

Martin Beck massaged the bridge of his nose between his righthand thumb and forefinger. Then he said:

"And are you certain no one went in or out during that time?"

"Yes, I'm damned sure of that. What happened before I went there, I don't know. Zachrisson said that three people had gone in and no one had come out."

"Can one rely on that?"

"Don't think so. He seems unusually dumb."

"You don't mean that, do you?"

Gunvald Larsson looked angrily at him and said:

"What the hell's all this about anyhow? I'm standing there and the miserable house catches fire. Eleven people were trapped inside and I got eight of them out."

"Yes, I've noticed that," said Kollberg, glancing sideways at the newspapers.

"Is it quite certain that it is a question of only three people killed in the fire?" Hammar asked.

Martin Beck took some papers out of his inside pocket and studied them. Then he said:

"It seems so. That man Malm, another called Kenneth

21

Roth who lived above Malm, and then Kristina Modig, who had a room in the attic. She was only fourteen."

"Why did she live in the attic?" asked Hammar.

"Don't know," said Martin Beck. "We'll have to find that out."

"There's a hell of a lot more we've got to find out," said Kollberg. "We don't even know that it was just those three who were killed. And also, all that about eleven people is just a supposition, isn't it, Mr. Larsson?"

"Who were the people who got themselves out, then?" said Hammar.

"First of all, they didn't get themselves out," said Gunvald Larsson. "I was the one who got them out. If I hadn't happened to have been standing there, not a damned one of them would have got clear. And second, I didn't write down their names. I had other things to do at the time."

Martin Beck looked thoughtfully at the big man in bandages. Gunvald Larsson often behaved badly, but to be offensive to Hammar must be due to either megalomania or a stroke.

Hammar frowned.

Martin Beck shuffled through his papers and said as a diversion:

"I've at least got the names here. Agnes and Herman Söderberg. They are married, sixty-eight and sixty-seven years old. Anna-Kajsa Modig and her two children, Kent and Clary. The mother is thirty, the boy five and the girl seven months. Then two women, Clara Berggren and Madeleine Olsen, sixteen and twenty-four, and a guy called Max Karlsson. How old he is, I don't know. The last three didn't live in the house, but were there as guests. Probably at Kenneth Roth's, the one who was killed in the fire."

"None of those names means anything to me," said Hammar.

"Nor me," said Martin Beck.

Kollberg shrugged his shoulders.

"Roth was a thief," said Gunvald Larsson. "And Söderberg a drunk and Anna-Kajsa Modig a whore. If that makes you any happier."

A telephone rang and Kollberg answered. He pulled a

22

notepad toward him and took a ballpoint pen out of his top pocket.

"Oh, yes, it's you is it? Yes, get going."

The others watched him in silence. Kollberg put down the receiver and said:

"That was Rönn. This is the position: Madeleine Olsen probably won't survive. She's got eighty per cent burns plus concussion and a multiple fracture of the femur."

"She was red-haired all over," said Gunvald Larsson.

Kollberg looked sharply at him and went on:

"Old man Söderberg and his old woman are suffering from smoke poisoning, but their chances are passable. Max Karlsson has thirty per cent burns and will live. Carla Berggren and Anna-Kajsa Modig are physically uninjured, but both are suffering from severe shock, as is Karlsson. None of them is fit to be interrogated. Only the two kids are perfectly all right."

"So it might be an ordinary fire, then," said Hammar.

"Balls," said Gunvald Larsson.

"Shouldn't you go home to bed?" said Martin Beck.

"You'd like that, wouldn't you, eh?"

Ten minutes later, Rönn himself appeared. He goggled at Larsson in astonishment and said:

"What in the world are you doing here?"

"You may well ask," said Gunvald Larsson.

Rönn looked reproachfully at the others.

"Have you lost your mind?" he said. "Come on, Gunvald, let's go."

Gunvald rose obediently and walked over to the door.

"One moment," said Martin Beck. "Just one question. Why were you shadowing Göran Malm?"

"Haven't the slightest idea," said Gunvald Larsson, and left.

An astonished silence reigned in the room.

A few minutes later, Hammar grunted something incomprehensible and left the room. Martin Beck sat down, picked up a newspaper and began reading it. Thirty seconds later, Kollberg followed his example. They sat like this, in sullen silence, until Rönn returned.

"What did you do with him?" said Kollberg. "Take him to the zoo?"

"What d'you mean," said Rönn. "Do with him? Who?"

"Mr. Larsson," said Kollberg.

"If you mean Gunvald, he's in South Hospital with concussion. He is not allowed to speak or read for several days. And whose fault is that?"

"Well, not mine," said Kollberg.

"Yes, that's just what it is. I've a damned good mind to punch you one."

"Don't stand there yelling at me," said Kollberg.

"I can do better than that," said Rönn. "You've always behaved like a clod to Gunvald. But this just takes the cake."

Einar Rönn was from Norrland, a calm, good-natured man, who never normally lost his temper. During their fifteen-year acquaintanceship, Martin Beck had never before seen him angry.

"Oh, well, then, it's just as well he's got *one* buddy, anyhow," said Kollberg, sarcastically.

Rönn took a step toward him, clenching his fists. Martin Beck rose swiftly and stood between them, turning to Kollberg and saying:

"Stop it now, Lennart. Don't make things any worse."

"You're not much better yourself," said Rönn to Martin Beck. "You're both a couple of stinkers."

"Hey, now, what the hell . . . ." said Kollberg, straightening up.

"Calm down, Einar," said Martin Beck to Rönn. "You're quite right, we should have seen that there was something wrong with him."

"I'll say you should," said Rönn.

"I didn't notice much difference," said Kollberg nonchalantly. "Presumably one has to be at the same high intellectual level to . . . "

The door opened and Hammar came in.

"You all look very peculiar," he said. "What's up?"

"Nothing," said Martin Beck.

"Nothing? Einar looks like a boiled lobster. Are you thinking of having a fight? No police brutality, please."

The telephone rang and Kollberg snatched up the receiver like a drowning man grasping the proverbial straw.

Slowly, Rönn's face resumed its normal color. Only his nose remained red, but it was usually red anyway.

Martin Beck sneezed.

"How the hell should I know that?" said Kollberg into the telephone. "What corpses anyhow?"

24

He flung down the receiver, sighed and said:

"Some idiot at the medical labs who wanted to know when the bodies can be moved. Are there any bodies, for that matter?"

"Have any of you gentlemen been to the site of the fire, may I ask?" said Hammar acidly.

No one replied.

"Perhaps a visit for study purposes would do no harm," said Hammar.

"I've got a bit of desk work to do," said Rönn, vaguely.

Martin Beck walked toward the door. Kollberg shrugged his shoulders, rose and followed him.

"It must simply be an ordinary fire," said Hammar stubbornly, and to himself.

5

The site of the fire was now barricaded off to such an extent that no ordinary mortal could catch a glimpse of anything more than uniformed police. The moment Martin Beck and Kollberg got out of the car, they were accosted by two of them.

"Hey you, where are you two off to?" said one of them pompously.

"Don't you see you can't park there like that," said the other.

Martin Beck was just about to show his identification card, but Kollberg warded him off and said:

"Excuse me, officer, but would you mind giving me your name?"

"What business is it of yours," said the first policeman.

"Move along, then," said the other. "Otherwise there might be trouble."

"Of that I'm certain," said Kollberg. "It's just a question of for whom."

Kollberg's bad temper was reflected very clearly in his appearance. His dark blue trench coat was flapping in the wind, he had not bothered to button up his collar, his tie hung out of his righthand jacket pocket and his battered old hat was perched on the back of his head. The two policemen glanced at each other meaningfully. One of them took a step nearer. Both had rosy cheeks and round blue eyes. Martin Beck saw that they had decided that Kollberg was not sober and were just about to lay hands on him. He knew Kollberg was in a state to make mincemeat of them, both physically and mentally, in less than sixty seconds and that their chances of waking up next morning without a job were very great. He wished no one ill that day, so he swiftly drew out his identity card and thrust it under the nose of the more aggressive of the two policemen.

"You shouldn't have done that," said Kollberg, angrily.

Martin Beck looked at the two policemen and said placidly:

"You've got a lot to learn. Come on, now, Lennart."

The ruins of the fire looked melancholy. Superficially, all that was left of the house were the foundations, one chimney stack and a huge heap of charred boards, blackened bricks and fallen tiles. Over everything hung the acrid smell of smoke and burned matter. Half a dozen experts in gray overalls were crawling about, carefully poking in the ashes with sticks and short spades. Two great sieves had been set up in the yard. Hoses still snaked their way along the ground, and down on the road there was a fire engine. In the front seat sat two firemen playing rock, scissors, paper.

Ten yards away stood a long dismal figure, a pipe in his mouth and his hands thrust deep down in his coat pockets. This was Fredrik Melander of the Homicide Squad in Stockholm and a veteran of hundreds of difficult investigations. He was generally known for his logical mind, his excellent memory and immovable calm. Within a smaller circle, he was most famous for his remarkable capacity for always being in the toilet when anyone wanted to get hold of him. His sense of humor was not nonexistent, but very modest; he was parsimonious and dull and never had brilliant ideas or sudden inspiration. Briefly, he was a first-class policeman.

"Hi," he said, without taking his pipe out of his mouth.

"How's it going?" said Martin Beck.

"Slow."

"Any results?"

"Not exactly. We're being very careful. It'll take time."

"Why?" asked Kollberg.

"By the time the fire engine got here, the house had collapsed and before the extinguishing work got going, it was almost burned out. They poured on gallons of water and put the fire out pretty quickly. Then it got colder later on in the night and it all froze together into one great slab."

"Sounds mighty cheerful," said Kollberg.

"If I've got it right, then they have to sort of peel off that heap, layer by layer."

Martin Beck coughed and said:

"And the bodies? Have they found any yet?"

"One," said Melander.

He took his pipe out of his mouth and pointed with the stem toward the right-hand part of the burned-out house.

"Over there," he said. "The fourteen-year-old girl, I guess. The one who slept in the attic."

"Kristina Modig?"

"Yes, that's her name. They're leaving her there overnight. It'll soon be dark and they don't want to work except in daylight."

Melander took out his tobacco pouch, carefully filled his pipe and lit it. Then he said:

"How're things going with you, then?"

"Marvelously," said Kollberg.

"Yes," said Martin Beck. "Especially for Lennart. First he almost had a fight with Rönn ... "

"Really," said Melander, raising his eyebrows slightly.

"Yes. And then he almost got taken in for drunkenness by two policemen."

"Oh, yes," said Melander tranquilly. "How's Gunvald?"

"In the hospital. Concussion."

"He did a good job last night," said Melander.

Kollberg regarded the remains of the house, shook himself and said:

"Yes, I have to admit that. Hell, it's cold."

"He didn't have much time," said Melander.

"No, exactly," said Martin Beck. "How could the house burn out at such a rate in such a short time?"

"The fire department reckon it's inexplicable."

"Mmm," said Kollberg.

He glanced over at the parked fire engine and picked up another train of thought.

"Why are those guys still here? The only thing that could burn here now is the fire engine, isn't it?"

"Extinguishing the embers," said Melander. "Routine."

"When I was small, a funny thing happened once," said Kollberg. "The fire station caught fire and burned down and all the fire engines were destroyed inside, while the firemen all stood outside staring. I don't remember where it was."

"Well, it wasn't quite like that. It happened in Uddevalla," said Melander. "To be more exact on the tenth of—"

"Oh, can't one even have one's childhood memories left in peace," said Kollberg irritably.

"How do they explain the fire, then?" Martin Beck asked.

"They don't explain it at all," said Melander. "Waiting for the results from the technical investigation. Just like us."

Kollberg looked around despondently.

"Hell, it's cold," he said again. "And this place stinks like an open grave."

"It is an open grave," said Melander solemnly.

"Come on, let's go," said Kollberg to Martin Beck.

"Where to?"

"Home. What are we doing here, anyway?"

Five minutes later they were sitting in the car on their way south.

"Didn't that clod really know why he was tailing Malm?" asked Kollberg, as they passed Skanstull bridge.

"Gunvald, d'you mean?"

"Yes, who else?"

"I don't think he knew. But one can never be certain."

"Mr. Larsson is not what you'd call a great brain, but . . ."

"He's a man of action," said Martin Beck. "That has its advantages, too."

"Yes, of course, but it's a bit much to stomach that he had no idea what he was up to."

"He knew he was watching a man and perhaps that was enough for him."

"How did it come about?"

"It's quite simple. This Göran Malm had nothing to

28

do with the Homicide Squad. Someone else had caught him and had him up for something. They tried to get him remanded in custody and it didn't work. So he was released, but they didn't want him to vanish. As they were up to their necks with work, they asked Hammar for help. And he let Gunvald organize the tailing job, as an extra duty."

"Why just him?"

"Since Stenström died, Gunvald has been considered the best at that sort of job. Anyhow, it turned out to be a stroke of genius."

"Insofar as?"

"Insofar as it saved eight people's lives. How many do you think Rönn would have got out of that death-trap? Or Melander?"

"You're right, of course," said Kollberg heavily. "Perhaps I ought to apologize to Rönn."

"I think you ought to."

The lines of cars going south were moving very slowly. After a while, Kollberg said:

"Who was it wanted him shadowed?"

"Don't know. Larceny department I suppose. With three hundred thousand breaking-and-entering and theft cases a year, or whatever it is, those boys hardly have time to run downstairs to eat their lunch. We'll have to find out all that on Monday. That's easily done."

Kollberg nodded and let the car creep forward another 10 yards or so. Then they had to stop again.

"I suppose Hammar's right," he said. "It's quite simply an ordinary fire."

"Well, it did begin to burn suspiciously quickly," said Martin Beck. "And Gunvald said that—"

"Gunvald's a fool," said Kollberg. "And he's always imagining things. There are lots of natural explanations."

"Such as?"

"Some sort of explosion. Some of those people were thieves and had a mass of high-explosives at home. Or cans of gasoline in the wardrobe. Or cylinders of gas. That Malm can't have been any great shakes if they let him go. It seems crazy that anyone should risk eleven people's lives to get rid of him."

"If it turns out to be arson, then there's nothing to show that it was Malm they were after," said Martin Beck.

29

"No. That's true," said Kollberg. "This is not one of my best days, is it?"

"Not exactly," said Martin Beck.

"Oh, well, we'll see on Monday."

At that, conversation ceased.

At Skärmarbrink, Martin Beck got out and took the subway. He did not know which he loathed more, the overcrowded subway or crawling along in traffic. But going by subway had one advantage. It was quicker. Not that he had anything to hurry home for.

But Lennart Kollberg had. He lived in Palandergatan and had a fine wife called Gun, and a daughter who was just six months old. His wife was lying on her stomach on the rug in the living room, studying a correspondence course of some kind. She had a yellow pencil in her mouth and alongside the open papers lay a red eraser. She was wearing an old pajama top and was idly moving her long naked legs. She looked at him with her large brown eyes and said:

"Jee-sus, you look gloomy."

He took off his jacket and threw it into a chair.

"Is Bodil asleep?"

She nodded.

"It's been a damned awful day," said Kollberg. "And everyone keeps jumping on me. First Rönn, of all people, and then two imbecile cops in Maria."

Her eyes glittered.

"And it wasn't your fault at all?"

"Anyhow, now I'm off duty until Monday."

"I'm not going to beat you," she said. "What d'you want to do?"

"I want to go out and eat something hellish good and have five doubles."

"Can we afford that?"

"Yes. Hell, it's only the eighth. Can we fix a sitter?"

"I expect Åsa will come."

Åsa Torell was a policeman's widow, although she was only twenty-five. She had lived with a colleague of Kollberg's called Åke Stenström, who had been shot dead on a bus only four months earlier.

The woman on the floor drew down her strong dark eyebrows and rubbed energetically at her papers.

30

"There's an alternative," she said. "We can go to bed. It's cheaper and more fun."

"Lobster Vanderbilt's fun too," said Kollberg.

"You think more about food than love," she complained. "Although we've only been married two years."

"Not at all. Anyhow, I've an even better idea," he said. "Let's go and eat first and have five doubles and then go to bed. Call Åsa up now."

The telephone had a twenty-foot extension cable and was already on the rug. She stretched out her hand and pulled it toward her, dialed a number and got a reply.

As she talked, she turned over on her back, drew up her knees and placed the soles of her feet on the floor. The pajama top slid up a bit.

Kollberg looked at his wife, thoughtfully regarding the broad patch of thick raven-black hair which spread over the lower half of her abdomen and reluctantly thinned out between her legs. She was looking up at the ceiling as she listened. After a while she drew up her left leg and scratched her ankle.

"Okay," she said, putting down the receiver. "She's coming. It'll take her an hour to get here, won't it? Have you heard the latest, by the way?"

"No, what?"

"Åsa's going to train to be a policewoman."

"Christ," he said absently. "Gun?"

"Yes."

"I've thought of yet another solution, even better than the last one. First we go to bed and then we go and eat and have five doubles and then we go to bed again."

"But that's almost brilliant," she said. "Here on the rug?"

"Yes, call up Operakällaren and order a table."

"Look up the number, then."

Kollberg riffled through the telephone directory as he unbuttoned his shirt and undid his belt; he found the number and heard her dialing it.

Then she sat up, pulled the pajama top over her head and flung it away across the floor.

"What are you after? My vanished chastity?"

"Exactly."

"From behind?"

"However you like."

She giggled and began to turn, slowly and pliably, standing on all fours with her legs wide apart and her dark head down, her forehead pressed against her forearms.

Three hours later, over the ginger sherbert, she reminded Kollberg about something he had not thought about since he had seen Martin Beck disappearing in the direction of the subway station.

"That awful fire," she said. "Do you think it was deliberate?"

"No," he said. "I can't believe that. There must be some limit."

He had been a policeman for more than twenty years and should have known better.

6

Saturday came with sun and bright clear light.

Martin Beck woke slowly, with an unusual feeling of contentment. He lay still, his face burrowed into the pillow, and he tried to hear whether it was late or early in the morning. He heard a blackbird in the trees outside the window and heavy drops falling with irregular splashes into the slush on the balcony. Cars driving past and a subway train braking at the station farther away. His neighbor's door slamming. Gurgling in the water pipes and suddenly, in the kitchen on the other side of the wall, a crash which made him open his eyes immediately. Rolf's voice:

"Oh hell!"

And Ingrid:

"You're so damned clumsy."

And Inga hushing them.

He put out his hand for cigarettes and matches, but had to get up on his elbow and dig out the ashtray from under a heap of books. He had lain reading about the battle of Tsushima until four in the morning and the ashtray was full of cigarette butts and dead matches. When he could not be bothered to get up and empty it before going to sleep, he usually hid it under a book to avoid hearing Inga's prophecies about how one fine day they would all wake up burned to death as a result of his smoking in bed.

His watch said half-past nine, but it was Saturday and he was off duty. Off duty in two ways, he thought contentedly, feeling a twinge of self-reproach. He was going to be alone in the apartment for two days. Inga and the children were going with Inga's brother to his cottage in Roslagen, and staying there until Sunday evening. Martin Beck was of course also invited, but as a weekend alone at home was a rare pleasure which he did not particularly want to forego, he had pleaded work to avoid having to go with them.

He finished his cigarette before getting up and then took the ashtray with him to the toilet and emptied it. He skipped shaving and pulled on his khaki trousers and corduroy shirt. Then he put the book about Tsushima back on the bookshelf, rapidly transformed the bed back into a sofa and went out into the kitchen.

His family were sitting around the table, eating breakfast. Ingrid got up and fetched a cup for him from the cupboard and poured some tea.

"Oh, Daddy, you can come too, can't you?" she said. "Look what a marvelous day it is. It's not such fun when you don't come."

"Can't, I'm afraid," said Martin Beck. "It'd be great fun, but—"

"Daddy has to work," said Inga acidly. "As usual."

Again he felt a twinge of conscience. Then he thought that they would have more fun without him, as Inga's brother always took Martin Beck's presence as an excuse to bring out the liquor and get drunk. Inga's brother in a sober state was certainly nothing much to write home about and drunk he was almost unbearable. He had, however, one positive feature and that was that on principle he never drank alone. Martin Beck's thoughts continued in that direction and arrived at the conclusion that he was really doing a good deed by lying and staying at home, as his absence would force his brother-in-law to remain sober.

He had just come to this advantageous conclusion when his brother-in-law rang the doorbell, and five minutes later

33

Martin Beck was able to begin celebrating his coveted free weekend.

It was just as successful as he had hoped. Inga had in fact left food in the icebox for him, but he went out all the same and shopped for dinner. Among other things, he bought a bottle of Grönstedts Monopole cognac and six strong beers. Then he devoted the rest of Saturday to putting down the deck of the model of the *Cutty Sark*, which he had not had time to touch for several weeks. For dinner he ate cold meatballs, fish roe and camembert on pumpernickel bread, and he drank two beers. He also drank some coffee and cognac and watched an old American gangster film on television. Then he got his bed ready and lay in the bathtub reading Raymond Chandler's *The Lady in the Lake*, every now and again taking a sip of cognac which he had placed within reach on the toilet seat.

He felt very well and thought about neither work nor his family.

When he had finished his bath, he put on his pajamas, switched off all the lights except the reading lamp on his desk, and went on reading and drinking cognac until he felt sleepy and dopey and went to bed.

He slept late on Sunday, then sat in his pajamas, working on his model ship, and did not dress until afternoon. In the evening, when the family had returned, he took Rolf and Ingrid to the movies and saw a film on vampires.

It was a successful weekend and on Monday morning he felt quite rested and energetic, and at once took up the question of just who Göran Malm had actually been and what he might have had on his conscience. He spent the morning in the offices of various colleagues at the police station and paid a brief visit to the court. When he returned to relate the results of his investigations, there was no one there to tell, for they had all gone for lunch.

He called up the South police station and to his surprise was put straight through to Kollberg, who was ordinarily the first out to lunch, especially on Mondays.

"Why aren't you out to lunch?"

"I was just about to go," said Kollberg. "Where are you, anyhow?"

"I'm in Melander's room. Come over here and eat instead, then I know where I've got you. When Melander

34

and Rönn put in an appearance, we can take a slightly closer look at Göran Malm. If Melander can possibly drag himself away from the site of the fire. Anyhow, I've found out quite a bit about Malm."

"Okay," said Kollberg. "I'll just get hold of Benny and instruct him, so to speak."

"If that's possible," he added.

Benny Skacke was their newest recruit. He had joined the Homicide Squad two months earlier, to replace Åke Stenström. Stenström had been twenty-nine when he died and had been regarded as a toddler by his colleagues, especially Kollberg. Benny Skacke was two years younger.

Martin Beck took out Melander's tape recorder and as he waited for the others, he played back the tape he had borrowed from the court. He took a piece of paper and made notes as he listened.

Rönn arrived on the dot of one, and fifteen minutes later Kollberg jerked open the door and said:

"Well, let's have it."

Martin Beck handed over his chair to Kollberg and placed himself by the filing cabinet.

"It was about car thefts," he said. "And trading in stolen cars. During last year, the number of undetected car thefts rose so much that there's reason to believe that one, or several larger well-organized gangs were occupied with the selling of stolen cars. And presumably also smuggling them out of the country. Malm was probably some kind of cog in the machine."

"A large cog or a small one?" asked Rönn.

"Small, I should think," said Martin Beck. "Even very small indeed."

"What had he done that he'd got caught?" said Kollberg.

"Wait a moment, and I'll start from the beginning," said Martin Beck.

He took up his notes and put them down beside him on the cabinet; then he began to speak, easily and fluently.

"At about ten o'clock on the night of the twenty-fourth of February, Göran Malm was stopped at a roadblock some two miles north of Södertälje. It was an ordinary routine traffic check and he was heading in that direction by chance. He was driving a Chevrolet Impala, 1963 model. The car seemed okay, but as it turned out that

Göran Malm was not the owner, they compared the registration number with the current list of stolen cars. The number was indeed there, but according to the list belonged to a Volkswagen and not to a Chevrolet. It appears that the car was given a false number and by mistake, or by chance, it was a hot number. At the first interrogation, Malm said that he had been loaned the car by the owner, who was a friend of his. This owner's name was Bertil Olofsson. That name was given by Malm and it was on the name plate of the car too. It turned out that this Olofsson was not unknown to the police. In actual fact, he had for some time been suspected of just this kind of car racket. A few weeks before Malm was caught, they had managed to find quite a bit of evidence against Olofsson, but then they couldn't get hold of him. He has still not been found. Malm maintained that Olofsson had loaned the car to him because he did not need it for a while, as he was to go abroad. When the boys who suspected Olofsson, and had already begun to look for him, heard this about Malm and that the police had got him by chance, they tried to have him remanded in custody. They were convinced that Malm and Olofsson were in some way or other accomplices. When they failed —well, he wasn't remanded in custody, as you will shortly hear—they put Gunvald, with Hammar's gracious consent, on to tail Malm. They hoped in this way to get at Olofsson, who in his turn then might reveal the gang. If there was such a gang. And if Olofsson and Malm, in that case, belonged to it."

Martin Beck crossed the floor and stubbed his cigarette out in the ashtray.

"Well, that's about it," he said. "No, it's not. The registration certificate and the license were forged, of course, very skillfully, by the way."

Rönn scratched his nose and said:

"Why did they let Malm go?"

"Insufficient evidence," said Martin Beck. "Wait till you hear it."

He bent over the tape recorder.

"The prosecution pleaded that Malm should be remanded in custody as suspected of receiving. The motivation being that Malm might complicate the investigation if he was free."

He switched on the tape recorder and let the spool run on quickly.

"Here it is. Prosecution's interrogation of Malm."

P: Well, Mr. Malm, you have heard my case before the court regarding this evening, that is, the twenty-fourth of February, this year. Will you now please tell us in your own words what happened?

M: Well, it was just like what you said. I was driving along the Södertälje road and there was a police car there, one of those police roadblocks and I stopped of course and ... and when the police saw the car wasn't mine, they took me to the police station.

P: Oh, yes. Well, Mr. Malm, how did it happen that you were driving about in a car which wasn't yours?

M: Well, I was going to go down to Malmö to see a buddy of mine and as Berra had——

P: Berra? That's Bertil Olofsson, is it?

M: Yes, that's right. Berra, or Olofsson, had loaned me his car for a couple of weeks. I was going to go down to Malmö anyhow. So I took the chance of going when I had a car so that I didn't have to go by train. It's cheaper too. Well, so I took the car and drove. How was I to know the car was hot?

P: How did it come about that Olofsson loaned you his car for such a long time just like that? Didn't he need it himself?

M: No, he was going abroad, he said, so he didn't need it.

P: Oh, yes, so he was to go abroad. How long was he to be away?

M: He didn't say.

P: Were you thinking of using the car all the time until he came back?

M: Yes. If I wanted to. Otherwise I was to put it in his parking lot. He lives in one of those buildings where a parking lot sort of goes with the apartment.

P: Has Olofsson come back home yet?

M: Not as far as I know.

P: Do you know where he is?

M: No. Perhaps he's still in France or wherever it was he was going to.

P: Mr. Malm, have you a car of your own?

M: No.

37

P: But you have had one, haven't you?

M: Yes, but a long time ago.

P: Did you often borrow Olofsson's car on other occasions?

M: No, only this once.

P: How long have you known Olofsson?

M: About a year.

P: Did you often meet?

M: Not often. Sometimes.

P: What do you mean by sometimes? Once a month? Once a week? Or how often?

M: Well, perhaps about once a month. Or twice.

P: So you knew each other quite well, then?

M: Well, fairly.

P: But you must have known each other quite well if he loaned you his car just like that.

M: Yes, of course.

P: What was Olofsson's profession?

M: What?

P: What did Olofsson do for a living?

M: I don't know.

P: Don't you know after having known him for at least a year?

M: No. We never talked about it.

P: What do you yourself do for a living?

M: Nothing special now . . . not just at the moment, that is.

P: What do you usually do?

M: Different things. Depends on what one can get.

P: What did you do last?

M: I was a car sprayer in a garage in Blackeberg.

P: How long ago was that?

M: Well, last summer. Then the garage shut down in July and I had to leave.

P: And then? Have you looked for other work?

M: Yes, but there wasn't any.

P: How have you managed financially without work for, let's see, nearly eight months?

M: Well, it hasn't been too good.

P: But you must have got money from somewhere, mustn't you, Mr. Malm? You have your rent to pay and a man must eat.

M: Well, I had a bit saved up and I've borrowed a bit here and there and so on.

P: What were you going to do in Malmö, anyhow?

M: Look up a buddy of mine.

P: Before Olofsson offered to lend you the car, you were to go by train, you said. It's quite expensive to go by train to Malmö, as you said yourself. Could you afford that?

M: We-ell . . .

P: How long had Olofsson had that car? The Chevrolet?

M: I don't know.

P: But you must have noticed what car he had when you first met?

M: I didn't think about it.

P: Mr. Malm, you've worked with cars quite a bit, haven't you? You were a car sprayer, you said. Isn't it strange that you didn't notice what make of car your friend had? Wouldn't you have noticed if he had changed his car?

M: No, I didn't think about it. Anyhow, I never saw much of his car.

P: Mr. Malm, wasn't it in fact so that you were going to help Olofsson sell that car?

M: No.

P: But you knew that Olofsson traded in stolen cars, didn't you?

M: No, I didn't know that.

P: No more questions.

Martin Beck switched off the tape recorder.

"Unusually polite prosecutor," said Kollberg, yawning.

"Yes," said Rönn, "and ineffective."

"Yes," said Martin Beck. "So then they let Malm go and Gunvald undertook to watch him. They hoped to get at Olofsson through Malm. It's very probable that Malm worked for Olofsson, but taking Malm's standard of living into consideration, he can't have got much for his pains."

"He was a car sprayer too," said Kollberg. "People like that are useful when you're handling stolen cars."

Martin Beck nodded.

"This Olofsson," said Rönn. "Can't we get hold of him?"

"No, he's still not been traced," said Martin Beck. "It's highly possible that Malm was telling the truth during his interrogation when he said that Olofsson had gone abroad. He'll appear no doubt."

Kollberg thumped his fist irritably on the arm of his chair.

"I just don't understand that Larsson fellow," he said, glancing sideways at Rönn. "I mean, how can he maintain he didn't know why he was watching Malm?"

"He didn't need to know, did he?" Rönn asked. "Don't start knocking Gunvald again now."

"For Christ's sake, he must have known that he had to keep his eyes open for Olofsson. Otherwise there wasn't much point in tailing Malm."

"Yes," said Rönn tranquilly. "You'll have to ask him when he's better, won't you?"

"Huh," said Kollberg.

He stretched himself so that the seams of his jacket creaked.

"Oh, well," he said. "That car business is not our headache, anyhow. And thank God for that."

7

On Monday afternoon, it looked as if Benny Skacke, for the first time in his life in his capacity as a member of the Homicide Squad, would have to solve a murder on his own.

Or at least a case of manslaughter.

He was sitting in his office at the South police station, busy with a task set for him by Kollberg before going to Kungsholmsgatan. That is, he was listening for the telephone and was sorting reports into different files. This sorting process was slow, for he read carefully through every report before filing it. Benny Skacke was ambitious and painfully conscious of the fact that even if he had learned everything there was to learn about investigation into murder at the police training college, he had not really had any opportunity of putting his knowledge into practice. In expectation of a chance of showing his hidden talents in this field, he tried in every way to acquire a share in his older colleagues' experiences. One of his methods was to listen in on their conversations as often as possible, something which was already driving Kollberg crazy. Another was to read old reports, which he was in the act of doing when the telephone rang.

It was a man in the reception department in the same building.

"I've a person here who says he wants to report a crime," he said, somewhat nonplussed. "Shall I send him up, or—"

"Yes, do that," said Assistant Inspector Skacke immediately.

He replaced the receiver and went out into the corridor to let in his visitor. Meanwhile he wondered what the man in reception had been about to say when he was interrupted. Or? Perhaps—"or shall I tell him to go to the proper police?" Skacke was a sensitive young man.

His visitor came slowly and unsteadily up the stairs. Benny Skacke opened the glass doors for him and involuntarily fell back a step at the acrid smell of sweat, urine and stale liquor. He went ahead of the man into his office and offered him the chair in front of his desk. The man did not sit down at once, but remained standing until Skacke himself had sat down.

Skacke studied the man in the chair. He looked between fifty and fifty-five, was scarcely more than 4 feet 5 inches and very thin, weighing not more than about 100 pounds. He had thin, ash-blond hair and faded blue eyes. His cheeks and nose were covered with red veins. His hands were trembling and a muscle in his left eye was twitching. His brown suit was spotted and shiny and the machine-knitted vest under his jacket had been darned with wool of another color. The man smelled of liquor but did not appear to be drunk.

"Well, you want to report something? What's it about?"

The man looked down at his hands. He was nervously rolling a cigarette butt between his fingers.

"Do smoke if you want to," said Skacke, pushing a box of matches across the desk.

The man picked up the box, lighted his butt, coughed dryly and hoarsely and raised his eyes.

"I've killed the missis," he said.

41

Benny Skacke stretched out his hand for his notepad and said in a voice which he considered calm and authoritative.

"Oh, yes. Where?"

He wished that Martin Beck or Kollberg had been there.

"On the head."

"No, I didn't mean that. Where is she now?"

"Oh. At home. Number 11 Dansbanevägen."

"What's your name?" asked Skacke.

"Gottfridsson."

Benny Skacke wrote the name down on the pad and leaned forward with his forearms resting on the desk.

"Can you tell me how it happened, Mr. Gottfridsson?"

The man called Gottfridsson chewed his lower lip.

"Well," he said. "Well, I went home and she began nagging and going on so. I was tired and couldn't be bothered to answer back so I told her to shut up, but she just went on and on at me. Then I saw red and took her by the throat and she began to kick and yell and so I bashed her over the head several times. Then she fell down and after a while I got scared and tried to bring her round but she just lay there on the floor."

"Didn't you call a doctor?"

The man shook his head.

"No," he said. "I thought she was already dead so there wasn't no point in getting a doctor."

He sat in silence for a moment. Then he said:

"I didn't mean her no harm. I just got annoyed. She shouldn't have gone on so."

Benny Skacke rose and fetched his coat from the hanger by the door. He was not sure what he ought to do with the man. As he pulled on his coat, he said:

"Why did you come here instead of going to the district police station? It's quite near."

Gottfridsson got up and shrugged his shoulders.

"I thought ... I thought a thing like this ... murder and all that, so ... "

Benny Skacke opened the door into the corridor.

"You'd better come with me, Mr. Gottfridsson."

It took only a few minutes to get to the block where Gottfridsson lived. The man sat in silence, his hands shaking violently. He went ahead up the stairs and Skacke took the key away from him and opened the front door.

They went into a small, dark hall with three doors, all shut. Skacke looked inquiringly at Gottfridsson.

"In there," said the man, pointing to the left-hand door.

Skacke took three steps across the floor and opened the door.

The room was empty.

The furniture was shabby and dusty, but seemed to be in its right place and there was no sign of a struggle of any sort. Skacke turned around and looked at Gottfridsson, who was still standing by the outer door.

"There's no one here," he said.

Gottfridsson stared at him. He raised his hand and pointed as he slowly came into the doorway.

"But," he said. "She was lying there."

He looked around in confusion. Then he walked straight across the hall and opened the kitchen door. The kitchen was also empty.

The third door led to the bathroom and there was nothing remarkable there either.

Gottfridsson ran his hand through his thinning hair.

"What?" he said. "I saw her lying there."

"Yes," said Skacke. "Perhaps you did. But she obviously wasn't dead. How did you come to that conclusion, anyhow?"

"I could see," said Gottfridsson. "She wasn't moving and she wasn't breathing. And she was cold. Like a corpse."

"Perhaps she just seemed dead."

It occurred to Skacke that perhaps the man was pulling his leg and had invented the whole story. Perhaps he had no wife at all. Also, both the death of his presumed wife, and her resurrection and disappearance appeared to leave the man singularly unmoved. He eyed the floor where the dead woman, according to Gottfridsson, had lain. There was no trace of either blood or anything in particular.

"Well," said Skacke. "She's not here now. Perhaps we should ask the neighbors."

Gottfridsson tried to dissuade him.

"No, don't do that. We're not on very good terms. Anyhow, they're not at home at this time of day."

He went into the kitchen and sat down on a wooden chair.

"Where the devil is the woman," he said.

At that moment, the outer door opened. The woman who came into the hall was short and plump. She was wearing a coverall apron and a cardigan, and had tied a checked scarf around her head. She was carrying a string bag in one hand.

Skacke could not immediately find anything to say. Neither did the woman say anything. She walked swiftly past him into the kitchen.

"Oh, yes, so you dared come back, did you, you clod?"

Gottfridsson stared at her and opened his mouth to say something. His wife dumped the string bag on the kitchen table with a bang and said:

"And who's that creature? Now, it's no good you bringing your boozing pals here, you know that. You boozers can go somewhere else."

"Excuse me," said Skacke uncertainly. "Your husband thought you'd had an accident and—"

"Accident," she snorted. "Accident, my foot."

She swung around and looked at Skacke with hostility.

"I just thought I'd scare him a bit. Coming home like that and beginning to fight after being out boozing several days. There has to be a limit."

The woman took off her scarf. She had an insignificant bruise on her jaw, but otherwise there did not appear to be anything wrong with her.

"How do you feel?" said Skacke. "You're not hurt, are you?"

"Poof!" she said. "But when he knocked me down, I thought I'd just lie there and pretend to have fainted."

She turned to the man.

"You were a bit scared, weren't you?"

Gottfridsson glanced embarrassedly at Skacke and mumbled something.

"Who are you, anyhow?" asked the woman.

Skacke met Gottfridsson's eyes and said curtly: "Police."

"Police!" cried Mrs. Gottfridsson.

She put her hands on her hips and leaned over her husband, who was cowering on the kitchen chair, a miserable expression on his face.

"Have you gone crazy?" she cried. "Bringing the fuzz here! What was that for, may I ask?"

44

She straightened up and looked angrily at Skacke.

"And you. What sort of policeman are you? Pushing your way in here onto innocent people. Aren't you supposed to show your badge at least before you come barging in on honest folk?"

Skacke hurriedly got out his identity card.

"An assistant, eh?"

"Assistant Inspector," said Skacke bleakly.

"What did you think you'd find here, then, eh? I've not done nothing wrong and neither has my husband either."

She placed herself beside Gottfridsson and protectively laid her hand on his shoulder.

"Has he got a warrant or anything, that he can come tramping like this into our home?" she asked. "Has he shown you anything, Ludde?"

Gottfridsson shook his head but said nothing. Skacke took a step forward and opened his mouth, but was immediately interrupted by Mrs. Gottfridsson.

"Well, just you be off with you, then. I've half a mind to report you for breaking-and-entering. Off you go now, before I get angry."

Skacke looked at the man, who was stubbornly staring down at the floor. Then he shrugged his shoulders, turned his back on the pair and returned somewhat shaken to the South police station.

Martin Beck and Kollberg had not yet returned from Kungsholmsgatan. They were still in Melander's office and had again played back the tape on the Malm case, this time for Hammar, who had looked in during the afternoon to ask whether they had got anywhere.

The smoke from Martin Beck's cigarettes and Hammar's cigar lay like fog over the room, and Kollberg had added to the air pollution by lighting a bonfire of dead matches and empty cigarette cartons in the ashtray. Rönn worsened the situation even more by opening the window and letting in the most polluted city air in the whole of northern Europe. Martin Beck coughed and said:

"If we're going to consider the arson theory at all, then everything is made much more difficult by all the witnesses being in the hospital and not available for questioning."

"Yes," said Rönn.

45

"I don't think it was arson, now," said Hammar. "But we mustn't draw any hasty conclusions until Melander has finished at the site of the fire and the labs have had their say."

The telephone rang. Kollberg stretched out his hand for the receiver and simultaneously put an empty matchbook onto the glowing heap in the ashtray. He listened for about half a minute.

"What?" he said, with unfeigned surprise, and the others immediately reacted.

He stared absently at Martin Beck and said:

"I've a hell of a surprise for you gentlemen. Göran Malm was not killed in the fire."

"What do you mean?" said Hammar. "Wasn't he in the house?"

"Oh, yes, he was practically burned into the mattress. That was the autopsy man himself. He says that Malm was stone dead before the fire even started."

8

The head nurse in Gunvald Larsson's ward sounded stern and unshakable.

"I can't help that," she said. "I don't mind how important it is. The most important thing is that Mr. Larsson gets better and he won't if you keep phoning and upsetting him. He must have absolute quiet, and that's doctor's orders. I said the same thing to Mr. Kollerberg, who called just now and was very rude. There's no point in phoning until tomorrow at the earliest. Goodbye."

Martin Beck was left with the receiver in his hand. Then he shrugged his shoulders and replaced it.

He was sitting in his office in the South police station. It was half-past eight in the morning, Tuesday, and neither Kollberg nor Skacke had put in an appearance yet. Kollberg appeared to be on the go already anyhow, and so might appear at any moment.

Martin Beck lifted the receiver again, dialed the number of the Maria police station and asked for Zachrisson. He was not there, but was coming on duty at one o'clock.

Martin Beck opened a new pack of Floridas, lit one and stared out of the window. It was not exactly a scintillating panorama that lay spread out before his eyes. A dismal industrial area and a motorway, of which all lanes leading into the city center were crammed with shining vehicles jerking along at a snail's pace. Martin Beck loathed cars and only in cases of extreme necessity put himself behind the wheel of one. He did not like the temporary police station in Västberga and was looking forward to the day when the extension to the old police station in Kungsholm was finished and all the scattered departments would again be contained under one roof.

Martin Beck turned his back on the lugubrious view, clasped his hands behind his neck and stared at the ceiling as he pondered.

When, how and why had Göran Malm died and what was the connection between his death and the fire? One handy theory was that someone had first killed Malm and then set fire to the place to hide any traces. But in that case, how had any possible murderer succeeded in getting into the house without being seen by Gunvald Larsson or Zachrisson?

Martin Beck heard Skacke walk past outside the door with swift purposeful strides and a moment later Kollberg also appeared. He crashed his fist on Martin Beck's door, thrust his head inside, said hello and then vanished again. When he came back, he had taken off his overcoat and jacket and loosened his tie. He sat down in the visitor's chair and said:

"I tried to have a chat with Gunvald Larsson on the phone, but it didn't work at all."

"I know," said Martin Beck. "I tried too."

"On the other hand, I have spoken to that Zachrisson," said Kollberg. "I called him at home this morning. Gunvald Larsson went to Sköldgatan at about half-past ten and Zachrisson left just after that. He says that the last sign of life he saw from Malm's apartment was the light going out at a quarter to eight. He also said that apart from Roth's three guests, he saw no one go either out or in through the front entrance all the evening. But one doesn't really know whether he was keeping his eyes open all the time. He could have stood there dozing."

"Yes, I suppose so," said Martin Beck. "But it seems

pretty incredible that anyone should have had the luck to get both into the house and then out again without being seen."

Kollberg sighed and rubbed his chin.

"No—that does undoubtedly seem pretty unbelievable," he said. "What do we do now?"

Martin Beck sneezed three times and Kollberg blessed him each time. Martin Beck thanked him politely.

"As far as I'm concerned I'm going to go and talk to the pathologist," he said.

Someone knocked on the door and Skacke came in and stood in the middle of the floor.

"Well, what do you want?" said Kollberg.

"Nothing," said Skacke. "I just thought I'd find out if there was anything new on the fire."

When neither Martin Beck nor Kollberg replied, he went on hesitantly:

"I mean, if I could do anything . . ."

"Have you eaten?" said Kollberg.

"No," said Skacke.

"In that case, you can get us some coffee for a start," said Kollberg "Three mazarin cupcakes for me. What d'you want, Martin?"

Martin Beck got up and buttoned up his jacket.

"Nothing," he said. "I'm going out to the Forensic Institute right now."

He put the pack of Floridas and the matches into his pocket and telephoned for a taxi.

The pathologist who had carried out the autopsy was a white-haired professor of about seventy. He had been a police doctor since Martin Beck's early days as a patrolman, and Martin Beck had also had him as a lecturer at police college. Since then, they had worked together on a large number of cases and Martin Beck had great respect for the man's experience and knowledge.

He knocked on the door of the pathologist's office at the Forensic Institute in Solna, heard the rattle of a typewriter inside and opened the door without waiting for a reply. The professor was sitting typing over by the window with his back to the door. He finished what he was doing, and pulled the paper out of the machine before turning around and seeing Martin Beck.

"Hi," he said. "I was just sitting here writing a preliminary report for you. How're things?"

Martin Beck unbuttoned his coat and sank into the visitor's chair.

"So-so," he said. "This fire is somewhat mystifying. And I've got a cold. But not quite ready for an autopsy."

The professor looked searchingly at him and said:

"You ought to go to a doctor. It's all wrong that you keep getting these colds all the time."

"Oh, doctors," said Martin Beck. "With due respect to your honored colleagues, but they haven't yet learned to cure common colds."

He took out his handkerchief and emphatically blew his nose.

"Well, now, let's have it," he said. "It's Malm I'm interested in first and foremost."

The professor took off his glasses and put them down on the desk in front of him.

"D'you want to see him?" he said.

"Preferably not," said Martin Beck. "I'll be quite happy with what you can tell me."

"I must say he doesn't look like much," said the pathologist. "Neither do the other two. What is it you want to know?"

"How he died."

The professor took out his handkerchief and began to clean his glasses.

"I'm afraid I can't tell you that," he said. "I've already told you most all of it. I've been able to establish that he was dead when the fire started. He was lying on his bed, obviously fully dressed, when the fire broke out."

"Could death have been caused by violence?" asked Martin Beck.

The pathologist shook his head.

"Unlikely," he said.

"Weren't there any wounds or injuries on the body?"

"Yes, naturally. A number. The heat was very intense and he was lying in the fencing position. His head was full of cracks, but they had occurred after death. There were also some bruises and contusions, presumably from falling beams and other objects, and his skull had burst from inside from the heat."

Martin Beck nodded. He had seen fire victims before

49

and knew how easy it was for a layman to think that injuries had occurred before death.

"How did you come to the conclusion that he was dead before the fire began?" he said.

"First, there was no sign that the circulation was functioning when the body was first exposed to the fire. Then there was no trace whatsoever of either soot or smoke in his lungs and bronchial passages. Both the other two had flakes of soot in their respiratory organs and also clear blood clots in the membranes. As far as they are concerned, there is no doubt that they did not die until after the outbreak of the fire."

Martin Beck rose and went across to the window. He looked down onto the road outside where the highway department's yellow vehicles were spreading road salt over the almost wholly melted gray slush. He sighed, lit a cigarette and turned his back on the window.

"Have you good reason to believe that he was killed in some way?" asked the professor.

Martin Beck shrugged.

"I find it difficult to believe that he died of natural causes just before the house burned down," he said.

"His internal organs were quite healthy," said the pathologist. "The only unusual thing about him was that the carbon monoxide count in his blood was a bit high, when one considers he hadn't breathed in any smoke."

Martin Beck stayed on for another half-hour before returning to the city. As he got off the bus at Norra Bantorget and breathed in the polluted air at the bus terminal, he thought that presumably there was not a single city dweller who did not suffer from chronic carbon monoxide poisoning.

He pondered for a while on the significance of what the pathologist had said about the carbon monoxide count in the dead man's blood, but then dismissed the matter. Then he walked on down toward the subway's even more poisonous layers of air.

9

On the afternoon of Wednesday, the thirteenth of March, Gunvald Larsson was for the first time given permission to get out of bed at South Hospital. With some difficulty, he squeezed into the dressing gown the hospital had produced and with a displeased frown regarded his reflection in the mirror. The dressing gown was several sizes too small and its color had faded into obscurity. Then he looked down at his feet. They were inserted into a pair of black wooden-soled shoes, which either had been made for Goliath or had been intended as a sign to hang outside some clog-maker's.

· His change lay in a pigeonhole in his bedside table, so he hunted out a few coins and headed straight for the nearest patients' telephone, dialed the police station's number, absentmindedly pulling at the sleeve of the objectionable garment. It wouldn't move an inch.

"Yes," said Rönn. "Well, it's you, is it? How are you?"

"Fine. How the hell did I land up here?"

"I took you. You were quite nutty."

"The last thing I remember was sitting looking at a picture of Zachrisson in the paper."

"Well," said Rönn. "That was five days ago. How are your hands?"

Gunvald Larsson looked at his right hand and flexed his fingers experimentally. The hand was very large and covered with long fair hairs.

"Seems okay," he said. "Only a few small bandages."

"Well, that's a good thing."

"Must you begin every sentence with 'Well,' " said Gunvald Larsson, irritably.

Rönn did not reply to that.

"Well, Einar?"

"Well, what is it?" said Rönn, with a slight laugh.

"What are you laughing at?"

"Nothing. What d'you want?"

"At the back on the left of the middle drawer of my desk, there's a purse of black leather. Inside are my spare keys. Drive out to Bollmora and fetch my white dressing gown and white slippers, will you? The dressing gown is hanging in the wardrobe and the slippers are in the hall, just inside the door."

"Well, I think I might do that."

"On the chest-of-drawers in my bedroom, there's an N.K. shopping bag with some pajamas in it. Get that too, will you?"

"Do you want these things at once?"

"Yes. The fools here won't let me out until the day after tomorrow at the earliest, and they've given me a grayish-brown, grayish-blue thing which is ten sizes too small and a pair of clodhoppers that look like coffins. How're things otherwise?"

"Well, not so bad. Quite quiet."

"What're Beck and Kollberg doing?"

"They're not here. They've retreated to Västberga."

"Fine. How's the case going?"

"Which case?"

"The fire, of course."

"That's closed."

"What d'you mean?" shouted Gunvald Larsson. "What the hell are you saying? Closed?"

"Yes, it was an accident."

"Accident?"

"Yes, more or less ... you see, the investigation on the site was finished this morning and—"

"What the devil do you mean? Are you drunk?"

Gunvald Larsson was talking so loudly that the ward nurse came sailing down the corridor.

"No, you see, that creature Malm—"

"Mr. Larsson," said the nurse, warningly. "This will not do."

"Shut up," said Gunvald, out of habit.

The nurse was about fifty, a slightly plump lady with a determined chin. She looked icily at her patient and said sharply:

"Replace the receiver immediately. It is evident that you have been allowed to get up much too soon, Mr. Larsson. I shall speak to the doctor immediately."

"Well, I'll come as soon as I can," said Rönn on the telephone. "I'll bring the reports with me so that you can see for yourself."

"Off back to bed now, Mr. Larsson," said the nurse.

Gunvald Larsson opened his mouth to say something, but stopped.

"So long, then," said Rönn.

"So long," said Gunvald Larsson, gently.

"Off back to bed, I said," said the nurse. "Didn't you hear what I said, Mr. Larsson?"

She did not take her eyes off him until he had closed the door of his room.

Gunvald Larsson stamped angrily over to the window. It faced north and he could see almost all of the Södermalm district. When he focused sharply, he could even see the top of the soot-covered chimney which remained on the site of the fire.

"What the hell is all this about?" he said to himself.

And shortly after that:

"They must have gone mad, Rönn and the whole lot of them."

Steps approached in the corridor.

Gunvald hurriedly got into bed and tried to look well behaved and innocent.

A perverse project.

A mile and a half away, Rönn put down the telephone receiver and, beaming, tapped his red nose with his right forefinger, as if trying to stop himself bursting out laughing. Melander, who was sitting opposite him banging away on his ancient typewriter, looked up, took his pipe out of his mouth and said:

"What's so funny?"

"Gunvald," said Rönn, gurgling with supressed laughter. "He's getting better now. You should have heard his voice when he was talking about the clothes they've given him. And then a nurse came along and began to bawl him out."

"What did he think about Malm and all that?"

"He was furious. Ranted and raved."

"Are you going up to see him?"

"Well, I expect so."

Melander pushed a clipped-together report across the desk and said:

"Take this with you, then . . . then he'll be pleased."

Rönn sat in silence for a moment. Then he said:

"Will you chip in with ten kronor for some flowers?"

Melander pretended not to hear.

"Five then," said Rönn, a mintue later.

Melander busied himself with his pipe.

"Five," said Rönn, obstinately.

Without the slightest change of expression, Melander got out his wallet, studied the contents, holding it so that Rönn could not see inside the bill compartment. Finally, he said:

"Can you change a ten-kronor bill?"

"I expect so." ·

Melander looked blankly at Rönn. Then he took out a five-kronor bill and placed it on top of the report file. Rönn pocketed the money, picked up the papers and walked toward the door.

"Einar," said Melander.

"Well?"

"Where are you going to buy the flowers?"

"Don't know."

"Don't go to the stall outside the hospital. You just get swindled there."

Rönn left. Melander looked at his watch and wrote:

Case closed. No further measures necessary. Stockholm, Wednesday, 13th March, 1968, 14:30 hours.

He pulled the paper out of the typewriter, took out his fountain pen and completed the report with his totally illegible signature. It was small and cramped and Kollberg used to say it looked like three dead midges from the previous summer. Then he put the report in the letter basket for duplicating, straightened out a paperclip, took out another pipe and began scratching inside it.

Melander was very thorough with his reports. He worked on them in his own way and made quite sure that everything was put down on paper. It was part of his system. It was easier to remember details if one had once and for all formulated them clearly and lucidly. He never forgot anything that he had seen in writing. Generally speaking, he never forgot anything else either.

The fire in Sköldgatan had occupied him for exactly five days, from Friday afternoon until two minutes ago. As he had been under no obligation to work on Saturday and

Sunday, he was now looking forward to four consecutive days off. Hammar had already agreed, as long as nothing unforeseen occurred. Was it too early to go out to their summer cottage on Värmdö? Hardly. He could begin to paint indoors while his wife covered the kitchen shelves with shelving-paper. The cottage was the apple of his eye. He had inherited it from his father, who had also been a policeman, a sergeant in Nacka to be more precise, and the only trouble was that he himself did not have any children to leave it to in his turn. On the other hand, his childlessness was entirely voluntary, a decision he and his wife had come to partly for convenience and partly after careful financial planning. At the time, it had been impossible to foresee that police pay would rise so rapidly, and in addition he had always been conscious of the risk involved in the profession he had chosen, and he acted accordingly.

He finished cleaning out his pipe, filled it and lit it. Then he got up and went to the toilet. He hoped that the telephone would not ring while he was still within earshot.

As an examiner of crime sites, Fredrik Melander perhaps had at this stage more routine work to do than any other still active policeman in the country. He was forty-eight years old and had received his early training from men like Harry Söderman and Otto Wendel. During his years with the Homicide Squad, to which he had applied after the centralization of police forces in 1965, he had seen hundreds of crimes and sites of every imaginable kind. The overwhelming majority had been extremely distasteful. But Melander was not primarily a man to fall victim of his emotions. He had the capacity to keep a chilly distance from his work, for which many of his colleagues envied him but of which he himself was quite unconscious.

So what he had seen in Sköldgatan had neither disturbed his psyche nor to any noticeable degree affected him emotionally.

The work at the site of the fire had demanded patience and system. It had been primarily a matter of finding out how many people had died. They had found three bodies, which were identified as the corpses of Kristina Modig, Kenneth Roth and Göran Malm. All three were severely burned. Malm partly charred. His body was found last,

55

after they had worked their way down to the bottom layer of the remains of the fire. The Modig girl was lying in the west part of the house, which had been least damaged, comparatively speaking. Both the men were found in the totally destroyed eastern part, where the fire had appeared to have started. Kristina Modig was barely fourteen, still going to school. Kenneth Roth was twenty-seven and Göran Malm forty-two. Both the latter had criminal records and neither appeared to be in regular employment. Most of this had been known beforehand.

The second stage of the investigation aimed at finding the answers to two questions: What were the causes of death, and How had the fire arisen?

The answer to the first question lay with the pathologist at the Forensic Institute. The question of the cause of the fire was Melander's headache, apart from the fact that he had never had a headache.

At his disposal he had several experts from the fire department and the Forensic laboratories, who did not produce much joy for him at first. Their main contribution to the investigation was to frown heavily and acquire puzzled expressions.

Melander had several hundred photographs taken. As each dead person was found and exposed, Kristina Modig the day after the fire, Kenneth Roth on Sunday and Göran Malm not until Monday afternoon, he had them photographed from every imaginable angle and then he sent the remains away for the autopsy.

They were not especially tidy corpses, but as the fire had not lasted very long and the human body consists of 90 per cent liquid, they were far from cremated, so the medical experts had quite a lot to work with.

The first reports did not contain any surprises either.

Kristina Modig had died of carbon monoxide poisoning. She had been wearing a nightgown and had been lying in bed. Everything pointed to the fact that she had died in her sleep. Particles of soot had been found in her respiratory organs and bronchial passages.

The circumstances for Kenneth Roth were the same, apart from the fact that he was not dressed and had been conscious at the time. During his attempts to save himself, he had been very severely burned. He too had breathed in

the suffocating smoke and had soot in his throat, bronchial tubes and lungs.

But this was not the case with Göran Malm.

There were other, more striking differences, too. Malm
had indeed died lying in his bed, but as far as could be
made out, he had been fully dressed. Much pointed to the
fact that he had not only been wearing underclothes,
trousers and jacket, but also socks, shoes and an overcoat.
The body was severely charred and was lying in the
so-called fencing position, a phenomenon caused by the
muscles contracting after death because of the heat. Everything pointed to the fact that the fire had started in his
apartment, but nothing to the fact that he had been
conscious of it or made any attempt to save himself.

As far as the cause of the fire was concerned, Melander
had already had a private theory when he had spoken to
Martin Beck and Kollberg on Friday afternoon. It would
not, however, have occurred to him to mention it. The fire
had begun with some sort of explosion and then spread
very swiftly and violently. Deep down, Melander believed
the explosion had been caused by an ember fire, a glowing
fire without flames, which had perhaps gone on for hours
before the temperature had risen to such an extent that
the windows had blown out. At that stage, Göran Malm
may well have already been dead for several hours and
most of the contents of the apartment melted down or
charred, as well as the surfaces of the floors, ceilings and
walls. The extreme violence of the "explosion" which
Gunvald Larsson thought he had seen would in that case
have been due to the fire blazing up to full strength all
over the apartment simultaneously with the first window
blowing out and oxygenated air from outside streaming in.
Then, naturally, there might be secondary explosions of
gas pipes, explosives or inflammable liquids such as gasoline or spirits. A fire of this kind could be caused by
practically anything, a dropped cigarette, a spark from a
stove, a forgotten iron, a toaster, some fault in the electric
wiring; there were hundreds of possibilities and most of
them seemed quite plausible. But there was one hitch in
this reasoning, however, and it was for this reason perhaps
that Melander kept his thoughts to himself. If the fire had
gone on for so long that both the contents of the apartment and Malm personally had become charred, then the

heat should have been noticeable in the apartment above, in which four people had been at the time. On the other hand, there was nothing to contradict the supposition that those people had been asleep or under the influence of drink or drugs. And to question them was not his affair. Whichever way it was looked at, there were still many obscure points.

At half-past one on Tuesday, Melander returned to the site of the fire after a frugal lunch outside a hotdog stand on Ringvägen, to find a motorcycle orderly there waiting for him with a brown envelope in his hand. The envelope contained a brief message from Kollberg.

Preliminary telephone report from autopsy on Malm. Death from carbon monoxide poisoning before the fire started. No trace of soot in lungs or respiratory passages.

Melander read through the note three times. Then he raised his eyebrows slightly and calmly began to fill his pipe. He knew what he had to look for. And where the activity should be carried out.

It was not long before he found what he was looking for.

With endless caution, everything that five days earlier had been in Göran Malm's apartment kitchen had now been exposed. Among these, they had found a small old-fashioned iron gas stove, with two burners and four feet. It had stood on a linoleum-covered drainboard, but when the latter had been burned away, the gas stove had fallen through the wooden board. The floorboards and the cross-beams had also been destroyed and the remains of the half-melted gas stove lay in a hollow about 30 inches below the original floor level. The gas stove was severely distorted, but the taps to both rings were of brass and had suffered rather less than the rest. Both taps were turned off; they were of the type that locked with a spigot in a notch in the collar so that they should not be turned on by mistake, for instance by an involuntary blow or by some piece of clothing catching in them. The stove had been connected to the mains by a rubber tube. Of this practically nothing remained, but there was enough left so that it could be established that it had been red and about half an inch in diameter. It had been fastened to a mouth-

58

piece, which in its turn was fastened to the pipe itself. As a safety measure, this mouthpiece was equipped with a quarter-inch guard through which the tube was threaded, and behind the guard there ought to have been an open clamp of galvanized metal held together with the aid of a nut and bolt. The reason for this arrangement was so that the rubber tube was not accidentally torn away from the mouthpiece. As a further safeguard, there was a main tap adjusted to the mouthpiece between the clamp and the guard. This tap was open and the clamp, which should hold the rubber tube to the guard, was not in its place. Its absence had no natural explanation, for even if the actual rubber had been destroyed by the heat, the clamp, or at least the remains of it, should still be around the mouthpiece, for technically speaking it could not be pushed over the guard, provided the bolt had not been loosened.

It took Melander and his men nearly three hours to find the clamp. It was indeed of galvanized metal and lay exactly 7 feet 3 inches away from the mouthpiece of the gas pipe. It was not very distorted and both the nut and the bolt were in place. The bolt, however, was hanging on the last two threads, which indicated that someone had unscrewed the bolt so that the clamp was sufficiently open to come free of the guard. Beside the guard, they found an object which at first sight appeared to be a crooked nail, but on closer examination turned out to be a screwdriver with its handle burned off.

Melander now turned his attention in another direction.

Inside the apartment, there had been two sources of heating, a tiled stove and a small iron stove, and in both cases the flues had been shut.

The hall door had been totally destroyed, as well as the door frame, but the lock remained. The key was on the inside, the bit in fact melted into the mechanism, but still a clear witness to the fact that the door had been locked from the inside, and in addition double-locked.

When they had got that far, it began to grow dark and Melander, with considerably revised theories, headed for his own minutely well-ordered apartment in Polhemsgatan, where dinner would be waiting for him, followed by peaceful hours in front of the television, and to crown everything, ten hours' dream-free sleep. As he stepped over the threshold, he saw that his wife had already laid the kitchen table and the food was ready. Baked beans and fried Falu sausages. His slippers were in their place by the armchair in front of the television set and the bed seemed to be standing there waiting for its lord and master.

Not so bad, thought Melander.

His wife was a parsimonious, ugly, coarsely built woman, 5 feet 10 inches tall, with flat feet and large pendulous breasts. She was five years younger than he and was called Saga. He thought that she was very beautiful and had thought so for more than twenty-two years. In actual fact, she had not changed much during that time, weighing now, as then, 160 pounds naked and taking size 12 shoes, and her nipples were still small and pink and cylindrical, like a rubber on the end of a new pencil.

When they had gone to bed and turned out the light, he took her hand and said:

"Darling."

"Yes, Fredrik?"

"That fire was an accident."

"Are you sure?"

"Yes, pretty well."

"How nice. I love you."

Then they went to sleep.

Next morning, Melander studied the windows in Göran Malm's apartment. Naturally, the panes themselves had gone, as had the frames, but the window-catches remained among the ashes, bits of tile, splinters of glass and other rubbish. Some of them were still hanging from several charred windowposts. All of them had been properly fastened from the inside. Most of the house's eastern gable had been blown out and shattered to pieces by the explosion, but fragments of that wall were not quite so charred as the rest of the building.

He found two more objects.

First, a piece of the wooden frame of Malm's gable window. Along the whole of the edge was a sticky yellowish-gray coating. He had no doubt whatsoever that this was the remains of masking tape.

Second, a ventilator which had been let into the gable wall. The ventilator was plugged with cotton and the remains of a towel.

With that the case was clear. Göran Malm had committed suicide. He had locked the door and shut all the windows, closed the flues and plugged the ventilators. He had also plugged the cracks in the windows with masking tape. So that it should be as swift and painless as possible, he had loosened the clamp holding the gas pipe to the mouthpiece and pulled off the rubber tube. Then he had opened the main tap and gone and lain down on his bed. The gas had rushed out swiftly through the relatively wide pipe, he had become unconscious within a few minutes and died within less than a quarter of an hour. The carbon monoxide in his blood was caused then by gas poisoning, and in all likelihood he had already been dead a couple of hours when the fire started. During all that time, gas had been streaming out of the main pipe. The apartment had been transformed into a veritable bomb, the least spark sufficient to cause the desolating gas explosion and set the house alight.

Melander's last measure on the site was to examine the battered gas meter and check the clock's position, thus acquiring further evidence that his theory was correct.

Then he drove to Kungsholmsgatan and produced his results.

The facts were indisputable.

Hammar was delighted and did not even try to hide it.

Kollberg thought, "I told you so" and then said so, after which he immediately made preparations to return to the relative calm of Västberga.

Martin Beck looked thoughtful, but accepted the facts and nodded in confirmation.

Rönn sighed with relief.

The investigation was declared complete and the case closed.

Melander himself was content.

Technically speaking there was only one unanswered question, he thought. But there were hundreds of imaginable answers to that, and to sort them out until the right one appeared was not only unnecessary but also almost impossible.

As he left the toilet, he heard the telephone ringing somewhere near, probably in his own office, but he ignored it. Instead he went into the cloakroom to fetch his overcoat, and thus began his well-earned four-day holiday.

Ten minutes later, the red-haired Madeleine Olsen died. Twenty-four years old and after five and a half days of hellish suffering.

10

Gunvald Larsson was not backward in asking the unanswered question which Melander had had in his thoughts.

He was now draped in his own dressing gown and for the first time was wearing his new pajamas. His feet were thrust into his white slippers.

He was standing by the window, trying to avoid looking at the flowers that Rönn had brought with him, an abominably composed bouquet of carnations, tulips and a mass of greenstuff as filler.

"Yes, yes," he said angrily, waving the papers he had received from Rönn. "Even a child could understand that."

"Well," said Rönn.

He was sitting in the visitor's chair, now and again glancing with modest pride at his flower arrangement.

"But even if the apartment was as full of gas as a May Day balloon, then something must have damned well ignited it, right?"

"Well . . . "

"Well, what?"

"Well, almost anything can cause an explosion in a gas-filled room."

"Almost anything?"

"Yes, the slightest spark is enough."

"But the spark itself has damned well got to come from somewhere, hasn't it?"

"I had a case with a gas explosion once. A guy who had turned on the gas taps and committed suicide. Then along came a tramp and rang the doorbell and the spark from the battery sent the house sky-high."

"But in this case it so happens that no tramp did come along and ring Malm's doorbell."

"Well, but there are perhaps hundreds of explanations."

"There can't be. There's only one explanation, and no one has bothered to find it out."

"It's impossible to find it. Everything is destroyed. Just think, a short circuit in a switch or a cable that's badly insulated is enough to make a spark."

Gunvald Larsson said nothing.

"And during the fire, the whole electrical system was shot to hell," said Rönn. "Every fuse blew. No one can prove that one fuse went earlier than the others, for instance."

Gunvald Larsson still said nothing.

"An electric alarm clock or a radio or a TV set," Rönn went on. "Or a spark suddenly falling out of either of the stoves."

"But the flues were closed?"

"A spark might fall all the same," said Rönn stubbornly. "In the chimney flue, for instance."

Gunvald Larsson frowned with displeasure and stared fixedly out over the bare trees and wintry roofs.

"Why should Malm kill himself anyhow?" he asked suddenly.

"He was down and out. Had no money and knew the police were after him. That he wasn't remanded in custody didn't mean that he was safe. He'd have probably been taken in again as soon as Olofsson appeared."

"Hm," said Gunvald Larsson, reluctantly. "Yes, that's true."

"His domestic circumstances were terrible too," said Rönn.

"Alone and an alcoholic. A criminal record. Divorced twice. Had kids, but hadn't paid their maintenance for years. Was just about to be sent to a work camp for alcohol offenses."

"Uhuh."

"And then he had some sort of illness. Had been in the bin several times."

"Do you mean he was a bit nutty?"

"He was manic-depressive. Had severe depressions when he drank or was faced with any kind of reverse."

"Yes, that's enough. That's enough."

"Well, he had tried to kill himself before," went on Rönn relentlessly. "At least twice."

"But that still doesn't explain where the spark came from."

Rönn shrugged. There was a moment's silence.

"A few minutes before the bang, I saw something," said Gunvald Larsson, thoughtfully.

"What?"

"Someone struck a match or lit a lighter on the floor above. Above Malm's apartment."

"But the explosion occurred in Malm's place, not up there," said Rönn.

He polished his nose with a folded handkerchief.

"Don't do that," said Gunvald Larsson, without looking at him. "You just make it redder than ever."

"Sorry," said Rönn.

He put away his handkerchief, thought for a moment and then said:

"Though the house was old and badly built, Melander says that there ought to have been some gas in the apartment above too, even if the concentration wasn't fatal."

Gunvald Larsson turned round and glared at Rönn.

"Who interrogated the survivors?"

"No one."

"No one?"

"No. They had nothing to do with Malm. Anyhow, there's nothing that points to it."

"How do you know that?"

"Well . . ."

"Where are they all now?"

"They're still in the hospital. Here, I think. Except the children. They were taken care of by the children's department."

"And they're going to survive? The adults, I mean?"

"Yes, except that Madeleine Olsen. She hasn't much chance, but the last I heard was that she hadn't died yet."

"Then the others could be questioned?"

"Not now. The case is closed."

"Do you yourself believe this business about it being an accident?"

Rönn looked down at his hands. At long last he nodded.

"Yes. There's no other explanation. Everything is corroborated."

64

"Yes. Except about that spark."

"Well, that's true. But it's impossible to prove anything about that."

Gunvald Larsson pulled a fair hair out of one of his nostrils and gazed at it thoughtfully. Then he went across to the bed and sat on it, folded the papers Rönn had brought with him and slung them onto the bedside table, as if in that way he was also closing the case on his own behalf.

"Are you being discharged the day after tomorrow?"

"Seems so."

"Then you'll have another week off, I presume?"

"Presumably," said Gunvald Larsson absently.

Rönn looked at his watch.

"Well, I'd better be off. My boy's got a birthday tomorrow and I've got to buy him a present."

"What are you going to get him?" asked Gunvald Larsson, without interest.

"A fire engine," said Rönn.

The other man stared at him as if he had said something extremely obscene.

"He wants one," Rönn went on, unmoved. "It's no bigger than that, and it costs thirty-two kronor."

He raised two fingers to show the size of the fire engine.

"Oh, yes," said Gunvald Larsson.

"Well—er—so long, then."

Gunvald Larsson nodded. Not until Rönn had his hand on the door handle did he say anything.

"Einar?"

"Yes?"

"Those flowers—did you pick them yourself? Off some grave or other?"

Rönn gave him a hurt look and left.

Gunvald lay down on his back, clasped his huge hands behind his head and gazed up at the ceiling.

The next day was Thursday, the fourteenth of March to be more exact, and there was no visible sign whatsoever that it was spring, which according to the almanac was arriving. On the contrary, the wind was colder and more biting than ever and out at the South police station, squalls of fine-grained frozen snow rattled against the windowpanes. Kollberg was sitting gulping coffee out of a paper cup and stuffing himself with sweet rolls, scattering crumbs all over Martin Beck's desk. Martin Beck himself was drinking tea, in the vain hope that it would be better for his stomach. It was half past three in the afternoon and Kollberg had devoted the greater part of the day to grumbling at Skacke. In between times, when the object of his displeasure was out of earshot, he had laughed until he had got a cramp in his stomach.

There was a careful knock on the door and Skacke came in. He threw a timid glance at Kollberg and carefully put a piece of paper down on Martin Beck's desk.

"What's that?" said Kollberg. "Another case of feigned death?"

"A copy of a report from the Forensic laboratories," said Skacke, almost inaudibly, and retreated toward the door.

"Tell us, Benny," said Kollberg, an innocent expression on his face. "How did you come by the idea of becoming a policeman?"

Skacke stopped hesitantly and shifted his weight onto his other foot.

"That's fine," said Martin Beck, ostentatiously picking up the paper. "Thanks. You can go now."

When the door had closed, he looked at Kollberg and said:

"Haven't you been at him enough for one day?"

"Well," said Kollberg genially, "I can always continue tomorrow. What's that?"

Martin Beck glanced through the text.

"From Hjelm," he said. "He's analyzed a number of tests and objects from the fire in Sköldgatan. To ascertain any possible connection with the origin of the fire, he says. Negative results."

He sighed and put the paper down.

"That Olsen girl died yesterday," he said.

"Yes, I saw it in the papers," said Kollberg, without interest. "By the way, do you know why that nit became a policeman?"

Martin Beck said nothing.

"I know," said Kollberg. "It's down in his records. He says he wants to use the profession as a springboard in his career. He's aiming at becoming Chief of Police."

Kollberg succumbed to another attack of laughing and almost choked over his bun.

"I don't really like this fire business," said Martin Beck.

It sounded as if he were talking to himself.

"What are you sitting there mumbling about?" said Kollberg, when he had got his breath back. "Is it something one should like? Isn't it enough that four people were burned to death and that six-foot imbecile got a medal?"

Kollberg grew serious, looked attentively at Martin Beck and said:

"Everything's quite clear, isn't it? Malm turns on the gas and kills himself. What happens next he doesn't care a damned fig about, as he's self-centered and anyhow stone-dead when the bang goes. Three innocent people die too and the police lose a witness and a chance to hook in that Olofsson, or whatever he's called. And that's nothing whatsoever to do with you or me. Aren't I right?"

Martin Beck blew his nose thoroughly.

"Everything clicks," said Kollberg definitively. "And don't go and say it clicks *too* well. Or that your famous intuition . . ."

He stopped and looked critically and searchingly at Martin Beck.

"Hell, you do seem down about something, I must say."

Martin Beck shrugged his shoulders.

Kollberg nodded to himself.

They knew each other very well and had for a long time, and Kollberg knew exactly why Martin Beck was depressed. But it was a subject he was not going to take up without being asked to and so he said lightly:

"To hell with that fire. I've forgotten it already. What about coming back with me tonight? Gun's going to some class or other and we could have a drink together and have a game of chess."

"Yes, why not?" said Martin Beck.

Then at least he could escape going home for a few hours.

11

Gunvald Larsson was indeed discharged after the doctor's rounds on the morning of the fifteenth of March. The doctor told him to take it easy and put him off work for ten days, until Monday, the twenty-fifth.

Half an hour later, he stepped out into the bitter wind outside the front entrance of South Hospital, flagged down a taxi and headed straight for the police station in Kungsholmen. He didn't bother to contact any of his colleagues and went up to his office without being seen by anyone, except the man on duty in the hall. Once up there, he shut himself in and made a number of telephone calls, of which at least one would have brought a severe reprimand on his head if any of his superiors had happened to listen in on it.

As he was telephoning, he wrote down a number of facts on a piece of paper and gradually these notes grew into a list of a number of people.

Of all the policemen who in some way or another had been concerned with the fire in Sköldgatan, Gunvald Larsson was alone in coming from an upper-class environment. His father had been considered wealthy, even if there had been very little left after the winding up of the estate; he himself had grown up in the fashionable Stockholm district of Östermalm and gone to the best schools. But he had fairly soon begun to appear as a problem member of the family. His views differed and were uncomfortable, and he was also given to airing them at unsuitable as well as suitable moments. Finally his father had been unable to see any other course than to allow him to become a naval officer.

Gunvald Larsson had not liked the Navy and after a few years, had transferred to the Merchant Navy. There he soon realized that what he had learned in naval college and on board mine-sweepers and antediluvian warships did not count for much.

All his brothers and sisters had made their own way in due course and were already well established when their parents died. He was never in contact with them and largely speaking had forgotten they existed.

As he had no desire to spend the rest of his life as a seaman, he had to find himself another profession, preferably one which was not too sedentary and in which his unusual training at least to some extent would be to his advantage. So he became a policeman, much to the surprise and not inconsiderable horror of his relations in Lidingö and Upper Östermalm.

Opinions on his qualities as a policeman were greatly divided. And on top of that, nearly everyone disliked him.

He did most things his own way and his methods were usually unorthodox, to say the least of it.

As was the list that now lay before him on his desk.

Göran Malm, 42, thief, dead (suicide?)
Kenneth Roth, 27, thief, dead, buried
Kristina Modig, 14, juvenile whore, dead, buried
Madeleine Olsen, 24, redheaded whore, dead
Kent Modig, 5, child (children's home)
Clary Modig, 7 months, infant (children's home)
Agnes Söderberg, 68, senile, Rosenlund Old People's Home
Herman Söderberg, 67, senile drunk, Högalid Nursing Home
Max Karlsson, 23, gangster, 12 Timmermansgatan
Anna-Kajsa Modig, 30, whore, South Hospital (psychiatric)
Carla Berggren, ?, whore, 25 Götgatan

Gunvald Larsson read through the list and saw that it would only be worth talking to the last three. Of the others, four were dead, two were small children and wholly ignorant, and two were hopelessly senile.

So he folded up the piece of paper, put it into his pocket and left. He didn't even bother to nod to the duty officer in the hall. He sought out his car parked in the lot and drove home.

During Saturday and Sunday, he stayed indoors, strictly occupied reading a novel by Sax Rohmer.

He did not give a thought to the fire.

On Monday morning, the eighteenth of March, he got up early, took off his remaining bandages, showered, shaved and took a long time carefully choosing his

69

clothes. Then he got into his car and drove to the address in Götgatan where Carla Berggren lived.

He had to walk up two flights of stairs, then obliquely across an asphalt courtyard and then up another dirty three flights of flaking brown paint and loose bannisters, before finally arriving outside a cracked door with a metal letterbox outside and the words *Carla Berggren, Model*, written by hand on an unevenly cut piece of cardboard.

There didn't seem to be a bell, so he kicked the door lightly, opened it and stepped inside without waiting for a reply.

The apartment consisted of a single room. The torn blind was pulled halfway down over the window and it was rather dark inside. It was also very warm and the air musty and enclosed. The heat came from two old-fashioned electric elements with spiral threads. Clothes and other diverse objects were scattered around the floor and elsewhere. The only thing in the room which could not have been equally well carted directly to the garbage can was the bed. It was quite big and the bedclothes appeared comparatively clean.

Carla Berggren was alone at home. She was awake but had not got up, and was lying in bed reading a romance magazine. Just as the last time he had seen her, she was naked and looked much the same as then, apart from the fact that she had no goose flesh on her body and she was not quivering with tears and hysteria. On the contrary, she appeared very calm.

She was fine-limbed and very thin, peroxided, with small slack breasts, which presumably looked their best when she lay on her back like this, and she had mouse-colored hair between her legs. She stretched indolently, yawned and said:

"You're a bit early for me, I'm afraid, but let's get on with it."

Gunvald Larsson said nothing and she apparently misinterpreted his silence.

"The money first, of course. Put it on the table over there. I suppose you know the rate? Or do you want something extra? How about a little Swedish massage—a hand job?"

He had had to bend down to get in through the doorway, and the room was so small that he filled it almost

70

completely. It stank of sex and other body odors, ingrained tobacco smoke and cheap cosmetics. He took a step over toward the window and tried to get the blind up again, but the spring had gone and the only result was that he drew it down almost completely.

The girl on the bed followed him with her eyes. Suddenly she recognized him.

"Oh," she said. "I recognize you. It was you who saved my life, wasn't it?"

"Yes."

"Thanks a lot."

"You're welcome."

She looked thoughtful, straddled her legs a little and drew her right hand across her genitals.

"That's quite different," she said. "Naturally, it's free to you."

"Put something on," said Gunvald Larsson.

"Nearly everyone says I'm nice looking," she said coyly.

"Not me."

"And I'm good at it. Everyone says so."

"It is also against my principles to question naked ... people."

He hesitated a little over the word, as if he were not certain which category she should be counted in.

"Question? Of course, you're the fuzz."

And after a moment's hesitation:

"I haven't done anything."

"You're a prostitute."

"Oh, don't be so unfair now. There's nothing wrong with sex, is there?"

"Get dressed."

She sighed and scrabbled round in the bedclothes, found a bathrobe and pulled it on without tying up the belt.

"What's it about?" she said. "What d'you want?"

"I want to ask you a few things."

"What about, then? Me?"

"Among other things. What for instance were you up to in that house?"

"Nothing illegal," she said. "That's true."

Gunvald Larsson took out his ballpoint and a few pages extracted from his notebook.

"What's your name?"

"Carla Berggren. But really . . ."

"Really? Now don't lie."

"No," she said, with childish dignity. "I won't lie to you. Really my name is Karin Sofia Pettersson. Berggren is Mom's name. And Carla sounds better."

"Where do come from?"

"Skillingaryd. It's down in Småland."

"How long have you lived in Stockholm?"

"Over a year. Almost eighteen months."

"Have you had any regular work here?"

"We-ell, it depends what you mean. I do a bit of modeling now and again. Sometimes that's quite hard work."

"How old are you?"

"Seventeen—nearly anyhow."

"Sixteen, then?"

She nodded.

"Well, what were you doing in that apartment?"

"We were only having a little party."

"You mean you had a meal and all that?"

"No. It was a sex-party."

"Sex-party?"

"Yes, that's right. Haven't you heard of them? It can be great fun."

"Oh, yes," said Gunvald Larsson without interest, turning a page.

"How well did you know these people?"

"The guy who lived there I'd never met before. Kent, or whatever his name was."

"Kenneth Roth."

"Oh, was that his name? Anyhow, I'd never even heard of the guy before. And Madeleine I knew a little. Now they're both dead, aren't they?"

"Yes. Then what about this Max Karlsson?"

"I know him. We used to go together now and again just for fun. Just for sex. It was he who took me there."

"Is he your pimp?"

She shook her head and said with naïve solemnity:

"No, I don't need one. It's not worth it. Those guys only want money. Percentages and all that shit."

"Did you know Göran Malm?"

"The guy who killed himself and set fire to the place? The guy who lived below?"

"Exactly."

"Never heard of him. Helluva way to behave, anyhow."

"Did the others know him?"

"I guess not. Anyhow, not Max and Madeleine. Perhaps that Kent guy, or Kenneth, because he lived there, didn't he?"

"Well, what did you do?"

"Fucked."

Gunvald Larsson looked steadily at her. Then he said slowly:

"Perhaps we could have it all in a little more detail. What time did you get there? And how did it come about that you went there at all?"

"Max fetched me. Said we were going to have a good time. And we picked up Madeleine on the way."

"Did you walk there?"

"Walk! In that weather? We took a cab."

"And what time did you arrive?"

"About nine or so, I should think. Round about then."

"And what happened then?"

"That guy who lived there had two bottles of wine which we shared. Then we played a few records and all that."

"You didn't notice anything peculiar?"

She shook her head again.

"What sort of peculiar?"

"Go on," said Gunvald Larsson.

"Well, then after a while Madeleine took her clothes off. She isn't much to look at. And then I did the same. The guys too, for that matter. Then ... then we danced."

"Naked?"

"Yes, it's great."

"Oh, yes. Go on."

"We did that for quite a time. Then we sat and smoked for a bit."

"Smoked?"

"Yes. Hash. To get going. It's good."

"Who offered you the hash?"

"Max. He usually—"

"Yes? What does he usually?"

"Eghhh! I promised I'd tell you the truth, didn't I? And I haven't done anything. And anyhow, you saved my life."

"What did Max usually do?"

"He used to sell hash. To kids mostly, and all that."

Gunvald Larsson made a note.

"And then?"

"Well, then the guys tossed for us. We were in good form by then, though a bit giggly. A little high. You get like that, you know."

"Tossed a coin?"

"Yes. Max got Madeleine and they went into the other room. I and that Kenneth guy stayed in the kitchen. We meant to ... "

"Yes?"

"Oh, you must have been in on that kind of party yourself. We thought we'd do a single first and then wind up with the whole group if the guys were able to. That's the most fun, really."

"Did you put the light out then?"

"Yes. That guy and I lay on the kitchen floor. Though ..."

"Though what?"

"Well, something funny happened. I passed out. And I was waked up by Madeleine creeping in and shaking me and saying that Max was annoyed I didn't come. And at that point I was lying sprawled out on top of that guy."

"Was the door between the kitchen and the room shut?"

"Yes, and that Kenneth guy was asleep too. Madeleine began to shake him. I lit my lighter and looked at the time and then I saw that I'd been in the kitchen with him for over an hour."

Gunvald Larsson nodded.

"Well, I felt awfully listless. But I got up all the same and went into the room and there was nothing wrong with Max. He grabbed at me and slung me down and said ..."

"Well, what did he say?"

"Come on and get going now, he said. That redheaded bitch wasn't much to have. And then ..."

"Yes?"

"Then I don't remember anything else until there was a bang like a gun and then smoke and flames all over the place. And then you came ... Christ, it was awful."

"And you didn't notice anything strange?"

"Just that time when I fell asleep. That doesn't usually happen. I've been with lots of real experts and they all say I'm damned good. And nice to look at."

Gunvald Larsson nodded and put away his pieces of paper. He looked at the girl for a long time. Then he said:

"I think you're rather ugly. You've got flabby breasts and bags under your eyes and you look sick and wretched. In a few years' time you'll be a complete wreck and you'll look so damned awful, no one'll want to touch you with a bargepole. Goodbye."

He stopped on the first flight of stairs and went back up to the apartment. The girl had taken off the bathrobe and was standing feeling under her armpit with her fingers. She giggled and said:

"I've got stubble under my arms while in the hospital. Have you changed your mind?"

"I think you ought to buy a ticket to Småland and go home and get yourself an honest job," he said.

"There aren't any jobs," she said.

He slammed the door behind him with such force that it almost jumped off its hinges.

Gunvald Larsson stood still in Götgatan for a minute or so. What had he found out? That the gas in Malm's apartment had seeped up into the kitchen of the apartment above, presumably along the waterpipes and the drains. That the concentration was sufficient that the people up there had fallen asleep, but not sufficient to be set alight when Karin Sofia Pettersson lit her cigarette lighter.

What did that mean? Nothing, on the whole, anyhow nothing that brought him any joy.

He felt sticky and unhealthy. His confrontation with that sixteen-year-old girl in her grimy room had given him a feeling of purely physical discomfort. He went straight to the Sture Baths and spent three thought-free hours in the gentlemen's Turkish baths.

That Monday afternoon, Martin Beck made a telephone call which he did not wish anyone else to hear. He waited until Kollberg and Skacke were out of the way, then dialed the Forensic labs and asked to speak to a man called Hjelm, who was considered to be one of the most skillful criminal technologists in the world.

"You saw Malm's body both before and after the autopsy, didn't you?" he said.

"Yes, I certainly did," said Hjelm sourly.

"Was there anything at all that you consider unusual?"

"Not exactly. If anything, it would be that the body was so well burned, so to speak. From all sides, if you see what I mean. Even on his back, although he was lying on his back."

Hjelm paused and then added reflectively: "Of course, the mattress was burning too."

"Yes, that's right," said Martin Beck.

"I don't understand you guys," complained Hjelm. "Isn't that case closed? But all the same . . ."

At that moment Kollberg opened the door and Martin Beck hurriedly put an end to the conversation.

12

At lunchtime on Tuesday the nineteenth, Gunvald Larsson was just about to give up altogether. He knew that some of his activities during the last few days had been anything but according to the regulations, and hitherto he had not found anything that might justify his actions. In actual fact, he had not even succeeded in proving that any connection whatsoever existed between Göran Malm and the other people in the house when the fire started, and he knew even less than before about where the igniting spark had come from.

His morning visit to South Hospital had not produced anything more than simple confirmation of various possible presumptions. Kristina Modig had slept in one of the small attics because there was a shortage of space in her mother's apartment and because she did not want to be crowded in with her noisy small brother and sister. The girl's habits were presumably not what they ought to have been, but actually what business was that of the police? As a minor, she had at one time been a charge of the state, and also nowadays there was an increasing tendency among the authorities to look the other way when it came to young girls going astray. Their escapades were too numerous, the social-welfare workers too few and ways of correction either nonexistent or out of date. The result was that in many cases the youngsters did as they liked, which gave the country a bad reputation and left parents and teachers in a state of despair and impotence. And anyhow, that did not, as has already been mentioned, concern the police in any way.

That Anna-Kajsa Modig was in great need of psychiatric care was obvious even to a relatively insensitive person such as Gunvald Larsson. She was distrait and difficult to communicate with, shaken by shudders, and she kept bursting into tears. He found out that there had been a kerosene stove in the attic, a fact he had already known. Their conversation produced nothing, but all the same he remained until the doctor grew tired of him and drove him out.

At the apartment in Timmermansgatan where Max Karlsson was said to live, there was no sign of life, although Larsson energetically kicked on the door. The answer was quite probably simply that there was no one at home.

Gunvald Larsson went home to Bollmora, tied a checkered apron around his waist, went out into the kitchen where he cooked a tasty meal of eggs, bacon and fried potatoes. Then he chose a brand of tea that suited his mood. By the time he had finished and had washed the dishes, it was already past three in the afternoon.

He stood for a moment by the window, staring out at the high blocks of apartments in this respectable but paralyzingly dull suburb. Then he went down to his car and drove back to Timmermansgatan.

Max Karlsson lived on the second floor in a building that was old but well maintained. Gunvald Larsson left his car three blocks away, less out of caution than because of the chronic lack of parking space. He walked along the pavement with long quick strides and was less than ten yards away from the entrance when he observed a person coming in the opposite direction; a girl of about thirteen or fourteen, like thousands of others, with long straggly hair, stitched black jeans and a jacket. She was carrying a worn leather bag in one hand and had presumably come straight from school, such an extremely usual type of girl and clothing that he would probably never have noticed her if she had not behaved as she did. There was a kind of nonchalance in her movements, as if she were trying hard to appear candid and natural, and yet she could not help looking around with a blend of anxiety and guilty excitement. As she met his eyes, she hesitated a fraction and held back, so that he continued to walk straight on, past her and past the entrance. The schoolgirl tossed her head and swung in through the entrance door.

Gunvald Larsson stopped abruptly, turned and followed her. Although he was a large and heavy man, he moved quickly and silently, and when the girl knocked on Karlsson's door, he was already halfway up the stairs. She knocked lightly four times, clearly some kind of simple signal, and he made an effort to remember the rhythm, which was made much easier for him by her repeating it almost at once, after an interval of perhaps five or six seconds. Immediately after the second knocks, the door was opened; he heard a safety-chain being unhooked and the door being opened and then at once closed again. He went down onto the porch and stood absolutely still with his back against the wall, waiting.

Two or three minutes later, the door up there opened and light steps could be heard on the stairs. It had clearly been a rapid deal, for when the girl came out onto the porch, she was still fumbling with the catch on the outer pocket of her bag. Gunvald Larsson stretched out his left hand and grasped her wrist. She stopped abruptly and stared at him, but without any attempt to shout for help or tear herself away and run. She did not even appear to be especially frightened, but more resigned, as if she had been prepared for something like this to happen sooner or later. Still without saying anything, he opened the bag and took out a matchbox. It contained about ten white tablets. He let go the girl's wrist and nodded at her to be off. She gave him a surprised gray look and half ran out through the door.

Gunvald Larsson was in no hurry. He looked at the tablets for a moment, then put them into his pocket and walked slowly up the stairs. He waited for thirty seconds outside the door, listening. Nothing could be heard from inside the apartment. He raised his hand and with the tips of his fingers gave two swift series of knocks, with an interval of about five seconds between them.

Max Karlsson opened the door. He looked considerably tidier than when they had last met, but Gunvald Larsson remembered his face and there was no doubt about their recognition being mutual.

"Good afternoon," said Gunvald Larsson, putting his foot in the door.

"Oh, so it's you?" said Max Karlsson.

"Just thought I'd find out how you were."

"Very well, thanks."

The man was in a tricky situation. He knew his visitor was a policeman and that he had used the prearranged signal. The safety-chain was on, and if he attempted to shut the door and really had something to hide, then he would automatically have revealed himself.

"Thought I'd ask you a few things," said Gunvald Larsson.

His situation was not all that simple either. He had no right whatsoever to enter the apartment and officially could not even question the man, if the man himself did not agree to it.

"Well," said Max Karlsson, vaguely. He made no move to unhook the chain, but it was clear that he did not know what attitude to take.

Gunvald Larsson solved the problem by putting his right shoulder against the door, suddenly and with all his weight behind the blow. There was a creaking sound in the fastening of the chain as the screws were ripped away from the dry woodwork. The man inside retreated hastily so as to avoid being hit by the door. Gunvald Larsson walked in, closed the door behind him and turned the key. He looked at the ruined chain and said:

"Rotten work."

"Are you crazy?"

"You should use longer screws."

"What the hell is all this? How dare you break in like this?"

"I didn't mean to," said Gunvald Larsson. "It wasn't my fault that it broke anyhow. I said you should have used longer screws, didn't I?"

"What do you want?"

"Just a little chat."

Gunvald Larsson looked around to make sure the man was alone. The apartment was not large, but looked pleasant and comfortable. Max Karlsson himself was quite respectable, and also large, broad-shouldered and at least 170 pounds in his stockings. Sure to be able to look after himself, thought Gunvald Larsson.

"Chat?" said the man, clenching his fists. "What about?"

"About what you were doing in that apartment before it caught fire."

The man seemed to relax a little.

"Oh, that," he said.

"Yes, that. Exactly."

"We were just having a little party. A few sandwiches and some beer, and playing some records."

"Just a family party, eh?"

"Yes, that chick Madeleine was my girl and . . ."

He stopped and tried to look grief-stricken.

"And what?" said Gunvald Larsson quietly.

"And Kenneth went around with that girl Carla."

"So it wasn't the other way around?"

"The other way around? What d'you mean?"

"That schoolgirl who was up here five minutes ago, who does she go around with?"

"Which schoolgirl? No one's been here . . ."

And Gunvald Larsson hit him, swiftly and hard, catching him unawares.

Max Karlsson staggered back two steps, but did not fall. Instead, he said:

"What the hell are you up to, you goddam cop?"

Gunvald Larsson hit him again. The man clutched at the edge of the table, but could not keep his balance. He caught hold of the tablecloth and pulled that down with him. A decorative carafe of thick cut-glass fell to the floor. He got up with a thin stream of blood running out of one corner of his mouth and his right hand clasping the heavy piece of glass.

"No, now you damned . . ." he said.

He ran the back of his left hand across his face, looked at the blood and raised the weapon.

Gunvald Larsson hit him for the third time. Karlsson reeled backward against a chair and tumbled to the floor with it. As he stood there on all fours, Gunvald Larsson kicked him hard on the right wrist. The glass carafe shot away across the floor and hit the wall with a dull thump.

Max Karlsson rose slowly onto one knee, holding his hand over one eye. The look in the other eye was frightened and uneasy. Gunvald Larsson looked calmly at him and said:

80

"Now, where's your stock?"

"What stock?"

Gunvald Larsson clenched his fist.

"No, no, for Christ's sake," the man said hurriedly. "Stop now. I'll . . ."

"Where?"

"In the kitchen."

"Where in the kitchen?"

"Under the bottom plate in the stove."

"That's better," said Gunvald Larsson.

He looked at his clenched right fist. It was very large and had reddish patches on the places where the coarse fair hairs had been singed off. Max Karlsson looked at it too.

"And how was it now, with Roth and those two whores?" said Gunvald Larsson.

"We fu—"

"I'm not interested in your sexual filthiness. I want to know who set the house on fire?"

"Set the house on fire . . . no, for Christ's sake, I don't know anything about that. And Kenneth was killed . . ."

"What was Roth up to? Drugs?"

"How should I know . . . ?"

"Tell the truth," said Gunvald Larsson warningly.

"No, no. Stop now. Take me down to the station instead, for Christ's sake."

"Oh, you'd like that, now, wouldn't you?" said Gunvald Larsson, taking a step nearer.

"Was Roth a pusher too?"

"No . . . booze . . ."

"Liquor?"

"Yes."

"Stolen?"

"Yes."

"Smuggling?"

"Yes."

"Where did he keep his stock then?"

"In . . ."

"Yes, just carry on now."

"In the attic of the house he lived in."

"But you don't deal in liquor?"

Karlsson shook his head.

"Just whores and drugs?"

81

"Yes."

"And Malm, then? What did he do?"

"I didn't know Malm."

"Oh, yes."

"Not very well, anyhow."

"But you did a bit of business together, you and Roth and Malm?"

Karlsson licked his lips. He was still holding his hand over his right eye; the left one glinted with a bizarre mixture of hatred and fear.

"In a way," he said finally.

"And Roth and Malm knew each other?"

"Yes."

"So Roth was a bootlegger?"

"Yes."

"And you sold drugs. Until about ten minutes ago. Now you've ceased operating. What did Malm do?"

"Something with cars, I think."

"Ah-hah," said Gunvald Larsson. "So you were three small dealers, each in his own branch. What had you in common?"

"Nothing."

"I mean who was the boss at the top?"

"No one. I don't understand what you're talking about."

The fist came out for the fourth time, with tremendous force. It hit the man on his right shoulder and threw him helplessly backward against the wall.

"The name," roared Gunvald Larsson. "The name! And quickly too, like hell."

The reply came in a hoarse whisper.

"Olofsson. Bertil Olofsson."

Gunvald Larsson looked at the man called Max Karlsson for a long time, the man whose life he had saved ten days earlier. Finally he said philosophically:

"Tell the truth, it'll always win, summer, winter, autumn, spring; the truth goes out in all weathers, is always clad in summer clothes."

The man stared witlessly at him through his undamaged eye.

"Well, now," said Gunvald Larsson. "Up you get and go ahead out into the kitchen and show me where the stuff is."

The hiding place had been cunningly devised and would quite easily have been overlooked in a superficial search. The bottom part of the stove had been cleared and there was a lot of stuff there, both hash and amphetamines, all neatly done up in packets. On the other hand, it was not a matter of sensational quantities. Karlsson was a typical small-timer, the one who finally delivered the narcotics to schoolchildren in their lunch periods in exchange for their pocket-money and what they could steal from their parents, or from breaking into phone booths and vending machines. How many middlemen the goods had been through before they reached him, he certainly would have no idea, and between him and the root of the evil lay an enormous complex of political miscalculations and failed social philosophy.

Gunvald Larsson went out into the hall and rang the police.

"Send a couple of those guys who hunt out drug pushers," he said laconically.

The men who came for Karlsson belonged to a special department which dealt with narcotics. They were large and rosy-cheeked and brightly dressed in colored sweaters and woolly caps. One of them saluted as he came in and Gunvald said acidly:

"Fine disguise. Perhaps you ought to have brought a fishing rod with you, though. And don't uniform trousers get spoiled when you crumple them into your socks like that? And also, one doesn't in fact salute when wearing an Icelandic sweater."

Both the narcotics men reddened even more and glanced from the scattered furniture to their suspect's black eye.

"There was a little trouble," said Gunvald Larsson casually.

He looked round and added:

"You can tell the person who takes on this case from me that he's called Max Karlsson and he won't say anything."

Then he shrugged his shoulders and left.

He was right. The man said nothing, not even that his name was Max Karlsson. He was that type.

Gunvald Larsson had found out that there had been three small-time gangsters in the house in Sköldgatan and that two of them were dead and the third on his way to prison. He had not found out where the much-discussed spark had come from and his chances of doing so appeared to be even remoter than before.

On the other hand, it occurred to him that he was actually off sick. He went home, undressed and showered. Then he pulled out the telephone plug, lay on his bed and opened the novel by Sax Rohmer.

13

The blow that produced a veritable constellation of stars was delivered before lunch on the following day, that is, Wednesday, the twentieth of March, and it was Kollberg who quite undeservedly received it.

He was sitting at his desk in the South police station out in Västberga, trying to solve the chess problem in *Svenska Dagbladet*. It was not going too well, because he kept thinking about what he was going to have for lunch and as a result found it difficult to concentrate. An hour earlier, he had called his wife and told her that he was thinking of coming home for lunch. This was cunningly worked out insofar as he had given her plenty of time to make preparations and thus he might be able to reckon on something extra specially good.

Martin Beck had called up in the morning and mumbled something about a meeting at headquarters and that he would be late, which had inspired Kollberg to send Skacke out on an assignment that might possibly strengthen his leg muscles but was otherwise quite useless.

He glanced at his watch and felt at peace with the world and his expectations for the future.

And at that moment the telephone rang.

He lifted the receiver and said:

"Yes, Kollberg."

"Mm. Uhuh. Hjelm here. Hello!"

Kollberg could not remember asking the Forensic Institute about anything special lately and he said unsuspectingly:

"Hello! Anything I can do for you?"

"In that case it would be the first time in the history of criminology," said the man sourly.

Hjelm was a querulous and easily irritated person, but at the same time a famous criminal-technologist, and experience had shown that it was unwise to rub him the wrong way. So Kollberg usually avoided speaking to him more than absolutely necessary, and neither did he say anything this time.

"Sometimes I begin to doubt your sanity," complained Hjelm.

"In what way?" asked Kollberg courteously.

"Ten days ago, Melander sends several hundred objects from a fire to us, piles of shitty rubbish ranging from old tins to a stone with Gunvald Larsson's fingerprints on it."

"Oh, yes," said Kollberg.

"Oh, yes. Well, you can say that, but you don't have to sit here grubbing around in the mess all day long. It's very much easier to put bits of frozen dog-shit into a plastic bag and write 'unknown object' on the label than it is to try to find out what it is. Don't you agree?"

"I know you've got a lot to do," said Kollberg, ingratiatingly.

"A lot to do? Is that meant to be some kind of joke? Do you know how many analyses we do every year?"

Kollberg had not the slightest idea and refrained from guessing.

"Fifty thousand. And do you know how many staff we have here?"

There was a moment's silence.

"Well, then," said Hjelm. "When we've worked on that stuff for six days, Rönn calls up and says the case has been closed and we can chuck the whole lot into the garbage can."

Kollberg looked irritably at the time.

"That's right," he said. "Quite correct."

"Oh, yes? I think it's as correct as hell, because before we'd even begun to clear up, Gunvald Larsson rings up and says the case isn't closed at all and that we must go on and there's a terrific hurry and it's important."

"He had no authority to do that," said Kollberg hastily. "He's had a bang on the nut and is even nuttier than usual."

"Uhuh. And on Monday I met Hammar by chance and

he says exactly what you've just said, that the case is closed and everything tied up."

"Yes?"

"And quarter of an hour later, Beck of all people calls up and wonders whether we can't find something 'unusual' about that blasted fire."

"Martin?"

"Yes. Exactly. So now all these people have been on to us, Melander and Rönn, and Larsson and Hammar and Beck. One after another and every one of them said different things and we don't know what's what at all."

"Yes?"

"And now, today, I try to get hold of someone responsible for all this. And what do I get as an answer? Larsson is off sick and is at home. I call up his home and get no reply. Then I try to get hold of Hammar and he's on leave. When I ask for Melander, someone says he went to the john an hour ago and hasn't been seen since. Rönn has gone for the day and Beck's at a meeting and Skacke has gone to look for Rönn. Finally I get hold of Ek and he's just back from his holiday and hasn't the faintest idea what I'm talking about and tells me to call up Hammar, who's on leave, or Beck, who's at a meeting, or Rönn, who's gone for the day, or Skacke, who's out looking for Rönn. You're the only person I can talk to at all."

Unfortunately, thought Kollberg. Aloud, he said: "What do you want, then?"

"Well, this man Malm was lying on his back on a mattress and as I pointed out to Beck, he was remarkably badly burned on his back as well. Both Beck and I came to the conclusion that this was due to the fact that the mattress had burned too. That sounds logical, doesn't it?"

"Of course. But listen, this case is in fact closed."

"I rather doubt that," said Hjelm, nastily. "We've found a few things in the mattress which shouldn't have been there."

"What kind of things?"

"A small spring, for instance, and an aluminum capsule and the remains of certain chemicals."

"And what does that mean?"

"That it was arson," said Hjelm.

14

Lennart Kollberg was not a person one would normally describe as tongue-tied, but this time he sat as if turned to stone for a whole minute as he stared out through the window at the repulsive, noisy suburban and industrial area which surrounded the South police station. Finally, he said, feebly and incredulously:

"What? What d'you mean?"

"Didn't I make myself quite clear?" said Hjelm smugly. "Or do I perhaps express myself indistinctly? It was deliberate. In other words, arson."

"Arson?"

"Yes. Not much doubt on that point any longer. Someone had placed a detonator with a delayed fuse in the mattress. A small chemical incendiary bomb, if you like. A time bomb."

"A time bomb?"

"Exactly. Cute little thing. Simple and easy to handle, probably no bigger than a matchbox. Of course, there's not much left of it."

Kollberg said nothing.

"Without an extremely thorough examination, you would be unlikely to find a trace of it," Hjelm pointed out. "You really do have to know what you're looking for."

"And you knew that? Just by chance, I suppose?"

"In our profession, we don't usually rely on chance. It so happened that I took note of certain details and then drew certain conclusions."

Kollberg had now collected himself sufficiently to begin to get annoyed. He drew down his bushy eyebrows.

"Just stop sitting there chewing over your own excellent qualities. If you've got something to say, then just say it, for Christ's sake."

"I've already done that," said Hjelm, loftily. "If you want it in words of one syllable all over again, then someone had placed a chemical time bomb in Malm's mattress. A chemical compound with a detonator, which

87

was connected to a small apparatus with a spring, roughly like a very simple clock. You'll be getting further details when we've had time to analyze the remains."

"Are you certain about this?"

"Am I certain? Out here we don't usually guess at things. Anyhow, it seems somewhat peculiar that no one else thought about the fact that the clothes and skin of the man's back were quite charred, although the body was found in the fencing position. Or that the mattress was as good as wholly destroyed while the bed itself was still in quite good shape, under the circumstances."

"An incendiary in the mattress," said Kollberg doubtfully. "A time bomb as big as a matchbox? There are still ten days to go before April the first."

Hjelm muttered something incomprehensible. Anyhow, it was not polite.

"I've never heard anything like it," said Kollberg.

"Well, I have. Here in Sweden, this method is new, as far as I know, but I know of several cases from the Continent, most of all from France. I've even seen this kind of apparatus. In Paris. At La Sûreté."

Skacke came into the room without knocking. He stopped suddenly and gaped at Kollberg's bewildered face.

"It wouldn't do any harm if you gentlemen went on a study trip or two now and again," said Hjelm poisonously.

"And how long is the time factor on this damned thing?"

"The ones I saw in Paris could be set for up to eight hours. And you can get them to detonate practically on the minute."

"But surely you can hear it? Ticking?"

"No more than a wristwatch."

"And what happens when it detonates?"

"Then a high-temperature chemical fire is rapidly ignited. It spreads over a limited area within a period of two seconds and cannot be extinguished by ordinary means. A person lying asleep would have next to no chance of escaping, if any. And in nine cases out of ten, the police think it's from smoking in bed, or make some other guess ... "

Hjelm made a dramatic pause before completing the sentence.

". . . if the criminal-technologist investigating the case isn't extremely knowledgeable and observant."

"No," said Kollberg suddenly. "This is absolutely ridiculous. There must be some limit to coincidences. Are you trying to tell me that that guy Malm first went home and blocked up all the cracks and ventilators and turned on the gas and then lay down on a bed in which someone else had already placed a time bomb? And that he took his own life and was dead when he was murdered? And that the bomb ignited the gas so that the house exploded and three other people were burned to death right in front of the nose of the stupidest detective in the history of criminology? Who was standing outside gaping? How do you explain that?"

"That's really nothing to do with me," said Hjelm with unusual warmth. "I'm just telling you the facts. Explanations I leave completely to you. That's what the police are for, aren't they?"

"Goodbye," said Kollberg, flinging down the receiver.

"What's all that about?" said Skacke. "Is someone dead? Rönn, by the way, isn't—"

"Shut up," said Kollberg. "And knock before you come charging into a superior's room. Don't forget what happened to Stenström."

He got up and went over to the door. He put on his hat and coat. Then he pointed at Skacke with his pudgy forefinger and said:

"I've a number of very important assignments for you. Ring headquarters and tell Martin he must break up that meeting at once. Find Rönn and Hammar and get hold of Melander even if you have to break down the john door. Tell them that they must call up Hjelm immediately, the superintendent at the Forensic Institute. Tell Ek and Strömgren the same thing, and any other stupid fool you can find in the division. When you've done all that, then you can go and sit in your own office and call up Hjelm yourself and ask him what it is all about."

"Are you going out?" asked Skacke.

"Official business," said Kollberg, looking at his watch. "I'll see you at Kungsholmsgatan in two hours' time."

He was almost nabbed for speeding right in Västberga Allé.

At his apartment in Palandergatan, his wife came out of the kitchen in a swirling cloud of aromatic fumes.

"Christ, you look peculiar," she said, lightheartedly. "Food's not ready. We've got a quarter of an hour."

"No," said Kollberg, glancing at the bedroom door. "Not there. The mattress might explode."

15

By afternoon of that day, several efforts had produced results, in that Hammar was found and managed to collect himself and his somewhat astonished team together. The team consisted of Martin Beck, Fredrik Melander, Lennart Kollberg and Einar Rönn.

Hammar looked grimmer than ever. Spring had arrived, with sun and warmth, and at breakfast he had talked to his wife about retiring and spending his leave on a trip to their cottage in the country. He had been secure at the time in his belief that the fire did not concern him and he had almost forgotten it. The detestable Hjelm had suddenly upset his plans.

"Is Larsson still off sick?" asked Hammar.

"Yes," said Kollberg. "He's resting on his laurels."

"He's coming back on Monday," said Rönn, blowing his nose.

Hammar leaned back in his chair, ran his fingers through his hair and scratched the back of his head.

"Looks as if we have to concentrate on this Bertil Oloffson," he said. "Malm was just small fry and a pitiful object, sick, alcoholic and lazy and God knows what else. It is hard to imagine that anyone would take the trouble to get rid of such a person. The only thing that is clear about Malm is that he must have known something about Olofsson, something incriminating. And that's more than we are able to say that we know. So let's take a closer look at Olofsson."

"Yes," said Kollberg, who was tired of clichés.

"What do we know about Olofsson?" said Hammar inquisitorily.

"That he's missing," said Rönn pessimistically.

"He was sentenced to a year in prison a few years ago," said Martin Beck. "For theft, I think. We'll have to go through the proceedings."

Melander took his pipe out of his mouth and said:

"Eighteen months for theft and forging documents. 1962. He served his sentence in Kumla."

The others looked at him with resigned astonishment.

"We know about your memory, but we didn't know you had all the sentences in your head too," said Kollberg.

"Actually, I took a look at Olofsson's records the other day," said Melander imperturbably. "I thought it'd be interesting to know who he is."

"You didn't by any chance find out where he is, did you?"

"No."

Silence reigned in the room. Then Kollberg said:

"Well? Who is he?"

Melander sucked at his pipe and appeared to think about the matter.

"A rather common type, I should say. The sentence Martin mentioned was by no means the first. But it was the first time he was given an unconditional prison sentence. Before that he had been found guilty of receiving, illegal possession of drugs, theft of vehicles, motoring offenses and a number of other minor items. He was on probation until two years ago."

"And presumably already sought after when Malm was caught in Olofsson's car," said Kollberg. "For car theft, or what was it?"

"Yes, exactly," said Martin Beck. "I've found all that out. It was the police in Gustavsberg who discovered that Olofsson had several stolen cars at his place on Värmdö. He had a cottage there, which he'd inherited from his father. The cottage is very remote, deep in the forest, and to get there you have to drive for more than half a mile along a narrow forest road. By sheer chance, a radio car from Gustavsberg happened to go there. Anyhow, there was no one there, but in the yard behind the house there were three sedans. Inside the garage, they found another car which had been recently sprayed. They also found paint, sprayers, polishing materials, number plates, registration certificates and a number of other things in the garage. As soon as it was confirmed that the four cars were stolen, two men were sent to Olofsson's home in Ärsta to get him. He wasn't there. And he's still missing."

Martin Beck went over to the cupboard containing the carafe and poured out a glass of water and drank it.

"When did this happen?" asked Hammar.

"Twelfth of February," said Martin Beck. "More than a month ago."

Kollberg took out his pocket diary and leafed through it.

"A Monday," he said. "Were any efforts made to get hold of Olofsson before then?"

Martin Beck shook his head.

"Not outside the routine ones. At first they were just expecting him back sooner or later. Then when Malm was caught, he said that Olofsson had gone abroad, so they went on waiting, keeping his apartment and the cottage under observation all the time."

"Do you think Olofsson may have found out that the boys in Gustavsberg had discovered what he was up to, and had time to get away before the police came?" asked Rönn.

Kollberg yawned.

"You mean that he deliberately kept out of the way?" said Martin Beck. "I doubt it. There wasn't a soul anywhere near the cottage who could have warned him that the police had been there snooping around."

"Does anyone know when he was last in his apartment?" asked Melander. "Have the neighbors been questioned, for instance?"

"Don't think so," said Martin Beck. "This business of a search for Olofsson has been carried out in a very routine manner."

"In other words, apathetically," said Hammar.

Then he struck the top of the desk with the palms of his hands and rose to his feet. In a loud voice he said:

"Get going, then, gentlemen. Ask the neighbors and everyone you can get hold of. Everyone who had anything to do with Olofsson. And read the court records and personal files and everything else there is to read on this blasted rogue, so you know who you're looking for. And above all, find him! Now! Immediately! If he was the person who planted that thing in Malm's mattress, then

92

naturally he'll keep out of the way now, even if he didn't do so before. If you need more men, just say so."

"What men?" said Kollberg. "Where from?"

"Well," said Hammar, shrugging his shoulders, "you've got that lad Skacke, of course."

Kollberg had already got up and was on his way out of the door when he heard Skacke's name mentioned. He stopped and opened his mouth to say something, but Martin Beck pushed him out into the corridor and shut the door behind him.

"Helluva lot of chatter about nothing," said Kollberg. "If you went by Hammar's behavior, then perhaps Skacke's got great chances of becoming Chief of Police."

He shook himself and added:

"Thank God I'm old enough not to have to experience *that,* anyhow."

They devoted the remainder of the afternoon to collecting additional information on Bertil Olofsson.

Martin Beck spoke to, among others, the larceny division, where they were keen to lay hands on Olofsson, but owing to staff shortages had stopped keeping watch on his apartment and the cottage on Värmdö.

From his personal files, it appeared that among other things Bertil Olofsson had been born thirty-six years earlier, had been to school six years, lacked any further education and had had a large number of short-lived jobs of varying natures, but that recently he had largely been unemployed. His father had died when Bertil Olofsson was eight and his mother had married again two years later and still lived with the stepfather. His only sibling was a half-brother ten years younger than he, who was a dentist in Göteborg. His own marriage had been childless and generally an unsuccessful one, now behind him, and since his prison sentence he had lived spasmodically with a woman five years older than himself.

The psychologists described him as emotionally unstable and asocial. He was also inhibited. His probation officer said he had had poor contact with Olofsson, because of the man's hostile attitude and unwillingness to cooperate.

Before they parted for the day, Martin Beck dealt out the most imminent assignments. Einar Rönn was to go to Segeltorp to talk to Olofsson's mother and stepfather, while Melander was to try to find some reliable information on his activities through contacts he had in the underworld. Martin Beck himself was to get the necessary warrants and, together with Kollberg, search the apartment and the cottage.

Until further notice, Benny Skacke was left outside the hunt for Olofsson.

16

It was not yet eight o'clock on Thursday morning when Kollberg came to pick up Martin Beck. The latter was still not dressed, but was sitting in the kitchen in his dressing gown, talking to his daughter, Ingrid, who had a free morning and for once had time to eat a decent breakfast before going to school. He himself was just having a cup of tea, but the girl was vigorously dunking her cheese-and-crispbread sandwich into her cocoa as she chatted about the Vietnam protest meeting she had been to the evening before. When the doorbell rang, Martin Beck pulled the knot around his waist tighter and put down his cigarette, although he suspected Ingrid would sneak a puff as soon as he was out of sight. Then he went and opened the door.

"Aren't you dressed yet?" said Kollberg reproachfully.

"Didn't we say eight o'clock?" said Martin Beck.

He went ahead into the kitchen.

"It's two minutes to," said Kollberg. "Hi, Ingrid."

"Good morning," mumbled Ingrid, guiltily waving away the cloud of smoke above her head.

Kollberg sat down on Martin Beck's chair and surveyed the breakfast table. He himself had actually just consumed a hefty breakfast, but nevertheless he felt quite capable of trying another. Martin Beck had got out another cup and poured out tea for his visitor, while Ingrid pushed the butter dish, cheese and breadbasket over to his side of the table.

"I'll be with you in a moment," said Martin Beck, and went into his room.

As he was dressing, he heard through the half-open kitchen door Ingrid questioning Kollberg about his seven-month-old daughter, Bodil, and Kollberg extolling her virtues with ill-concealed paternal pride. When Martin Beck came into the kitchen a moment later, shaved and dressed, Kollberg said:

"I've just got hold of another sitter."

"Yes, I've promised I'll sit with Bodil next time someone's needed. I can, can't I? Babies are such fun."

"A year ago you were saying they were the most disgusting things in the world," said Martin Beck.

"Oh, that was then. I was awfully childish then."

Martin Beck winked at Kollberg and said respectfully:

"Of course, yes. I'm sorry. You're a mature woman now, aren't you?"

"Don't be silly," said Ingrid. "I'm never going to be a mature woman. I'm just going to be a chick and then I'm going to be an old lady."

She poked her father in the midriff and disappeared into her room. When Martin Beck and Kollberg came out into the hall to put on their overcoats, loud pop-music was pouring out through her closed door.

"The Beatles," said Martin Beck. "It's a miracle her ears don't drop off."

"The Rolling Stones," said Kollberg.

Martin Beck looked at him in surprise.

"How can you tell the difference?"

"Oh, there's a great difference," said Kollberg, starting down the stairs.

At this time of the morning, the traffic into town was already heavy, but Kollberg, who was considered by everyone else except himself to be a nervous and not very good driver, was nevertheless good at finding his way around Stockholm and drove down sidestreets and roads quite unknown to Martin Beck, through residential districts and areas with tall office and apartment buildings. He parked the car outside a relatively newly built building on Sandfjärdsgatan in Årsta.

"I bet the rents are quite something around here," said Kollberg, as they went up in the self-service elevator. "One wouldn't think anyone like Bertil Olofsson would rise to this."

It took Martin Beck less than thirty seconds to open the door, which was considered a long time, as he had already got the key from the real estate agent. The apartment turned out to consist of one room, a hall, kitchen and bathroom, and according to the rent bill lying on the doormat among the advertisements and other rubbish, the rent for the past quarter was 1,296 kroner. 51 öre. Apart from this, there was nothing of interest in the pile of advertising pamphlets, brochures and free samples of various kinds, which had been put through the letter slot and had had almost a month to collect. At the bottom of the heap lay a stenciled sheet from a nearby grocery store. SPECIAL OFFER was the headline, and then followed a list of various delicacies, giving the prices before and after reductions. The price of a can of Baltic herring had, for instance, tumbled from 2 kronor 63 öre to 2 kronor 49 öre. Martin Beck folded up the piece of paper and stuffed it into his pocket.

In the main room, there was a dining table, three chairs, a bed, a bedside table, two armchairs, a low table, a television set and a chest of drawers. All the furniture looked as if it had been bought at the same time and recently. The room was not very clean. A creased bedspread lay over the unmade bed. On the table was an empty but unwashed ashtray. The library seemed to consist of an apparently unread paperback copy of *Raff and Rififi* by Jerry Cotton. There were no pictures, but a number of magazine photographs of cars and women in various stages of nudity were fastened to the wall with Scotch tape.

In the kitchen there were some glasses, plates and cups lying upside-down on the drainboard, which was spotted with dishwater long since dried. The refrigerator was on and contained half a pound of margarine, two small beers, a withered lemon and a stone-hard piece of cheese. In the cupboards, there were a few household supplies, a box of crackers, a bag of granulated sugar and an empty can of coffee. The cleaning cupboard was empty, but under the sink there was a dustpan and brush and also a paper bag containing garbage. One of the drawers was full of empty matchboxes.

Martin Beck went out into the hall and opened the door into the bathroom. There was an unpleasant smell from the toilet, which had probably never been cleaned. Lines of grime around the tub and basin also indicated that they had not been subjected to much cleaning fervor either. In the bathroom cabinet there was a worn toothbrush, a razor, a tube of toothpaste squeezed flat, a broken comb, grease, dust and tufts of hair. The towel on the hook by the basin was stiff with grime.

Martin Beck had had enough and went to examine the wardrobe.

On the floor were two pairs of shoes, uncleaned, with a thick layer of dust both inside and out, and a canvas bag of stinking dirty linen. There was also a rod of wire hangers. On these hung two grimy shirts, three even grimier sweaters, two pairs of Dacron trousers, a tweed jacket, a pale gray summer suit and a dark blue poplin coat.

Martin Beck was just about to feel through the pockets when Kollberg called him from the kitchen.

Kollberg had tipped the contents of the garbage bag onto the drainboard and he was holding up a thin crumpled plastic bag.

"Look at this," he said.

In one corner of the bag were a few greenish grains. Kollberg took a pinch of them and rubbed them between his thumb and forefinger.

"Hash," he said.

Martin Beck nodded.

"That explains why he collected empty matchboxes," he said. "If that bag was full, it would have been enough to fill at least thirty."

The remaining examination of the apartment yielded poor results. A few souvenirs indicated that Bertil Olofsson had spent his holidays in the Canary Isles in Poland. Four old bills in the pockets of his tweed jacket were dated in December and stemmed from the Ambassador Restaurant. In the drawer of the bedside table were two contraceptives and an amateur photograph of a plump dark woman in a bikini on a beach. On the back of the photograph someone had written *"Berra with love, Kay"* with a ballpoint.

There were no other personal possessions in the apartment and most of all, nothing which gave any indication of where the man was at present.

Martin Beck rang the doorbell of the neighboring apartment. A woman opened the door. They asked a few questions.

"Well, you know what it's like in this kind of building,"

she said. "You don't think about who lives in the other apartments. I think I've seen him a few times, but I don't think he's lived here all that long."

"Can you remember when you last saw him?" asked Kollberg.

The woman shook her head.

"I've no idea," she said. "But it's certainly a long time ago. At Christmas, or about then. But I don't really know."

In the other two apartments on the same floor there was no one at home. At least, no one answered the bell. There did not seem to be a superintendent; a notice in the entrance told tenants to contact a mechanic at a completely different address about the apartments.

When they came out through the front entrance, Kollberg went and sat in the car while Martin Beck crossed over the street to the grocery store on the other side. He spoke to the manager and showed him the leaflet advertising special offers.

"I can't tell you exactly when we sent that out," the man said. "We usually distribute lists like that on Fridays. Wait a moment."

He vanished into the inner regions of the store and returned a moment later.

"Friday, the ninth of February," he said.

Martin Beck nodded and went back to Kollberg.

"He hasn't been home since the ninth of February anyhow," said Martin Beck.

Kollberg shrugged his shoulders listlessly.

They drove along Sockenvägen and Nynäsvägen, through Hammarby industrial area and came out onto the Värmdö road. When they got to Gustavsberg, they went into the police station and talked to one of the two patrolmen who had discovered the stolen cars in Olofsson's yard. He told them the way to the cottage.

It took them a quarter of an hour to get there.

The cottage lay well protected from observation. The drive up to it was uneven and twisting, scarcely more than a forest path. The grounds around the cottage had once been well kept, with lawns, rock gardens and sand paths, but only barely visible traces of them remained now. The snow had almost completely gone from the graveled area near the house, but in the woods, which lay very close to the cottage, there were still grayish drifts. Just at the edge of the woods at the farthest part of the garden was a fairly recently built garage. It was empty and the three cars, which judging by the tire marks had been lined up on the gravel, had also gone.

"Stupid to move the cars," said Kollberg. "If he comes back, he'll know at once the police have been here."

Martin Beck studied the door of the cottage. It was locked with both a safety lock and a large brass padlock. The only person who could give them the keys was Olofsson, so it was clearly a matter of manual labor. They got screwdrivers and several other gadgets out of the glove compartment and did a few minutes' manual labor, and then all they had to do was to open the door.

The cottage contained a large room, furnished in rustic style, with two beds built into the wall, a kitchen and a washroom. The air inside was raw and damp and it smelled musty with mold and kerosene. In the large room there was an open fireplace and in the kitchen a wood-burning stove, but otherwise the heating arrangements were confined to a kerosene stove in one of the sleeping cabins. Sand and dried lumps of mud covered the floors, and the furniture in the main room was dirty and shabby. In the kitchen, the table, benches and shelves were covered with rubbish, empty bottles, greasy plates, cups containing coffee dregs, and dirty glasses. One of the bunks was made up with dirty sheets and a torn grubby quilt.

There were no human beings in the house.

In the small hall there was a door and behind this a cupboard with shelves laden with stolen goods, probably articles taken from stolen cars. There were transistor radios, cameras, binoculars, flashlights, tools, a couple of fishing rods, a hunting rifle and a portable typewriter. Martin Beck got up onto a stool and looked on the top shelf. There lay an old croquet set, a faded Swedish flag and a framed photograph. He took the photograph with him into the main room and showed it to Kollberg.

It was of a fair-haired young woman and a small boy in short trousers and a short-sleeved shirt. The woman was pretty and both she and the boy were laughing at the camera. The woman's dress and hair style indicated the late thirties and in the background was the cottage in which Martin Beck and Kollberg were now standing.

"One or two years before the father died, I should think," said Martin Beck. "The place looked a bit different then."

"Nice-looking mother he's got," said Kollberg. "Wonder how things have gone for Rönn."

Einar Rönn had wandered round Segeltorp in his car for quite a while before finding the house where Bertil Olofsson's mother lived. Her surname was Lundberg now and Rönn had found out that her husband was head of a department in a large store.

The woman who opened the door was quite white-haired, and yet did not look older than fifty-five. She was thin and sunburned, although the spring had hardly started. The fine wrinkles around her lovely gray eyes shone white against her tan when she raised her eyebrows inquiringly.

"Yes?" she said. "Can I help you?"

Rönn transferred his hat to his other hand and got out his identification card.

"It's Mrs. Lundberg, is it?" he said.

She nodded and a trace of anxiety came into her eyes as she waited for him to go on.

"It's about your son," said Rönn. "Bertil Olofsson. I'd like to ask you a few questions, if I may."

She frowned.

"What's he been up to now?" she said.

"Nothing, I hope," said Rönn. "May I come in for a moment?"

The woman hesitantly removed her hand from the door handle.

"Ye-es," she said slowly. "Please come in."

Rönn hung up his coat, placed his hat on the hall table and followed her into the living room, which was pleasant and well furnished without exaggerated elegance. The lady of the house pointed to an armchair by the open fire and herself sat down on the sofa.

"Oh, well," she said laconically. "Please go ahead. I'm fairly hardened when it comes to Bertil, so you might as well tell me the truth at once. What has he done?"

"We're looking for him because we hope he will be able to help us clear up a case," said Rönn. "I really only want to ask you if you know where he is, Mrs. Lundberg."

"Isn't he at home then?" she asked. "In Årsta?"

"No, he doesn't seem to have been there for quite a while."

"At the cottage then? We've got . . . he has a cottage on Värmdö. Bertil's father, my first husband, built it and now it's Bertil's. Perhaps he's there?"

Rönn shook his head.

"Did he say nothing to you about his going away somewhere?"

Bertil Olofsson's mother threw out her hands.

"No. But we so seldom talk to each other nowadays. I never have the slightest idea what he's up to or where he is. He hasn't been here, for instance, for over a year, and then he only came to try to borrow some money."

"He hasn't phoned you lately then?"

"No. Of course, we've just been to Spain for three weeks, but even so, I don't think he would have called. We've nothing to do with each other any longer."

She sighed.

"My husband and I gave up hope for Bertil a long time ago. Now it sounds as if he's no better."

Rönn sat silent for a moment, looking at the woman. She had bitter lines around her mouth now.

"Do you know anyone who might possibly know where he is?" he said. "A steady girl, or a friend, or someone like that?"

She laughed, hard and briefly, and falsely.

"I can tell you one thing," she said. "He was actually a very nice boy once. But he got into bad company and was easily led and he opposed me and my husband and his brother, well, practically everyone. Then he went to a reformatory and that didn't make things any better. There he just learned to hate society even more. He also learned to become a real professional there and how to use drugs."

She looked fiercely at Rönn.

"But I suppose it's an accepted fact now that our reform schools and institutions act as a sort of introduction to drug-taking and crime. What you call treatment isn't worth a cent."

By and large, Rönn agreed with her, and did not really know what to say.

"Well," he said finally. "Perhaps that's what it looks like."

Then he pulled himself together and said:

"I didn't mean to come here and upset you. May I just ask you one more question?"

She nodded.

"What's the relationship between your two sons? Do they meet or keep contact in any other way?"

"Not any longer," she said. "Gert is a qualified dentist now, and he's got his own practice in Göteborg. But when he was still at dentistry college here, he did actually manage to persuade Bertil to go to him and get his teeth done. Gert is such a nice kind boy. They were really good friends for a while. But then something happened, I don't really know what, and they stopped meeting. So I don't think it's much use asking Gert, because he knows nothing about Bertil nowadays. That's certain."

"Don't you know what it was that caused them to stop meeting?" asked Rönn.

"No," she said, turning away. "Not at all. Something happened. Something's always happening to Bertil. Isn't that right?"

She looked straight at Rönn, who cleared his throat uneasily.

Perhaps the time to end the conversation had come?

Rönn got to his feet and held out his hand.

"Thank you very much for your help, Mrs. Lundberg," he said.

She shook his hand but said nothing. He took out his card and put it down on the table.

"If you hear anything from him, perhaps you'd be kind enough to call me?"

She remained silent, but went with him out of the room and opened the door.

"Goodbye, then," said Rönn.

When he was halfway to the gate, he turned around and saw her standing upright and immobile in the doorway, watching him. She looked considerably older now than when he had arrived.

17

The picture of Bertil Olofsson had clarified somewhat, but not really very much. It was known that he dealt in stolen cars. He either resprayed them or changed the number before selling them. It was also presumed that he sold drugs. He was probably not a big trader, but in all likelihood belonged to the category of pushers who sold the stuff to pay for their own needs.

None of these discoveries were particularly sensational. As Olofsson had been known to the police for a number of years, it was known at least to some extent what he had been up to. What Malm might have eventually revealed must have been of a much more serious nature, as Olofsson had felt it necessary to take great risks in order to silence him.

If in fact it had been Olofsson who had made that ingenious little apparatus in Malm's mattress. Despite everything, there was only a guess to support the suspicion, but at headquarters at this stage there was no one who doubted that the guess was corret.

Fredrik Melander had bad luck at first during his inquiries in the underworld. First it turned out that one of his most reliable contacts, a one-time safe-breaker who had gone straight for several years, had had a relapse and was already serving the eighth month of a three-year sentence in Härlanda prison. Then he discovered that the beer hall on the south side frequented by the clientele which might have known Malm and Olofsson, and where he had also been well in with the owner, no longer existed, as the building it had been in had been demolished. The owner had moved away from Stockholm and it was said that she had opened a cigar store in Kumla. After these setbacks, Melander had gone to a third-rate café, on the south side, too, which among its regulars could count a couple of old thieves who in their best moments might hand over valuable information in exchange for a drink or two. But even there his luck was against him. The place had changed name and a notice above the entrance announced DANCING TONIGHT. In the windows were large color photographs of the orchestra, a collection of dark-haired men with strange instruments in their hands, which in turn were almost hidden by the men's frilly shirtsleeves. In the display case by the door, where, previously, modest little handwritten menus had appeared offering customers cabbage and meatballs and pea soup, there as now a colorful menu in Spanish.

Melander went in, stood just inside the door and looked around the place. The ceiling had been lowered, the lights were dimmer and the tables more numerous, now covered with checked table cloths. Posters showing bullfights and flamenco dancers had been put up on the walls. It was Friday night and about half the tables were taken up by youthful, noisy customers. No one took the slightest notice of him and after a while he saw a waitress whom he recognized. She was dressed as if she were at a fancy-dress ball and could not decide whether she meant to be a peasant girl from Dalarna or Carmen.

Melander waved her over and asked her if she knew where their old customers had gone to. She did know and mentioned a place a little farther up the same street. Melander thanked her and left.

Here his luck was better. Sitting on a bench along the far wall, he saw a well-known figure gloomily sipping a drink. He was one of the people Melander had hoped to get hold of. This man had once been a skillful forger, but increasing age and alcoholism had forced him to abandon this intermittently profitable occupation. He had also had behind him a brief and not very successful career as a burglar. Nowadays he could not hardly manage pilfering an odd pair of stockings from Woolworth's without getting caught. He was called Curly because of his curly reddish hair, which long before it became the fashion he had worn long and wavy, although this unusual style made it easy to identify him and had several times helped to catch him.

Melander sat down opposite Curly, who immediately brightened up at the prospect of an offer of a drink.

"Well, Curly, how're things with you?" asked Melander.

Curly swirled around the last remaining drops in his glass and gulped them down.

"Not so good," he said. "Hard up for bread and no pad. Been thinking of getting a job."

Melander knew that Curly had never done an honest day's work in his life and he took the news with great calm.

"Oh, so you've nowhere to live?" he said.

"We-ell. I was at Högalid for a bit last winter, but that's a hell of a place."

A waitress appeared in the kitchen doorway and Curly said swiftly:

"And I've a hell of a thirst on too."

Melander waved to the waitress.

"If you're paying, perhaps I can go on to grander things," said Curly, ordering a large gin and tonic.

Melander asked for the menu. When the waitress had gone, he said:

"What do you usually drink then?"

"Plain old akvavit and sugar. Not exactly nectar, but a guy's got to consider his financial situation."

Melander nodded in assent. That was something he was wholly in agreement with. But this time the State was paying, even if somewhat deviously, so he ordered pork and mashed turnips for them both, despite Curly's protests. When the food was put on the table, Curly had already put away his drink and Melander generously ordered the same again. As he was afraid that Curly would shortly be so drunk it would be impossible to communicate with him at all, he hurried to reveal the true purpose of his visit.

Curly savored the name and the drink. Then he said:

"Bertil Olofsson. What does he look like?"

Melander had never actually met him personally, but he had seen Olofsson's photograph and had his description in his head. Curly thoughtfully ran his hand over his famous hair.

"Ho-ho," he said. "Oh, yes, I know. Pusher, eh? Cars and a bit of this and that, eh? I don't know the guy personally, but I know who he is. What d'you want to know?"

Melander pushed his plate away and began to busy himself with his pipe.

"Everything you know about him," he said. "For instance, do you know where he is?"

Curly shook his head.

"No, I haven't seen him for quite a time. But then we

don't exactly move in the same circles, you see. He hangs out at places I never go to, see? For instance, there's some sort of club a few blocks away from here, where I think he used to go. Mostly kids there. That guy Olofsson would be older than most of them."

"What else does he do besides drugs and cars?"

"I dunno," said Curly. "Only that, I think. But I've heard he works for some guy, but don't know who. Olofsson's never been a big shot, but a year or so back he suddenly seemed to come into favor like. I think he works for someone who's got big things going, see? That's the talk, you know, but no one knows anything definite like."

Curly had begun to slur a bit. Melander asked him if he knew Malm.

"Only seen him once or twice at Uven," said Curly. "I heard he was in that place what burned down. He was only some kind of small-time guy. Nothing to bother with, him, see. Anyhow, he's dead, poor guy."

Before Melander left, after a moment's hesitation, he thrust two 10-kronor notes into Curly's hand and said:

"Give us a call if you hear anything else. You might make some discreet inquiries, eh?"

When he turned around at the door, he saw Curly beckoning to the waitress.

Melander hunted out the club Curly had mentioned. When he saw its young customers crowding round the entrance, he realized he would melt into his surroundings about as effectively as an ostrich in a flock of hens, so he went on. Homeward.

As soon as he got home, he called Martin Beck and asked whether they might risk assigning Skacke the job of going to the club.

Benny Skacke was delighted. As soon as Martin Beck had put down the receiver, Skacke called up his girl and told her that owing to an important assignment, he would not be able to meet her that evening. He explained in somewhat veiled language that it was a question of catching a dangerous murderer. But she did not seem especially impressed. In fact, she was rather sour.

He devoted most of the day to carrying out the program that he had set himself to follow every Friday. First he practiced for half an hour on the horizontal bar, then he went to Åkeshov Baths, had a steambath and swam a thousand yards, and when he got home he sat down at his desk and studied law for two hours.

Late in the afternoon he began to wonder how he should be dressed in order to look as little like a policeman as possible. He would have preferred to look like a playboy. Normally he dressed formally and could not imagine himself going to work without a tie on, for instance. As Skacke could hardly be described as a frequenter of bars and very rarely indeed went to either a restaurant or a nightclub, he was not absolutely certain what people usually wore in such places. However, he did have a faint idea that the rather ordinary ready-made suits that hung in his wardrobe would not be what fashion demanded of youthful playboys. Finally he went out to his parents' home in Kungsholm and borrowed a suit from his younger brother. His mother had cooked beefburgers, so he took the opportunity of having dinner there too. At the table, as an example of his dangerous life as a detective, he told some totally untrue stories to his astonished and proud parents, rounding off the whole with something he had heard was supposed to have happened to Gunvald Larsson.

When he got back to Abrahamsberg, he at once put the suit on. It felt peculiar, but he was pleased when he saw himself in the mirror. He was convinced that no one in the whole of the police force possessed such a creation.

The jacket was long and sharply nipped in at the waist, with slanting pockets and a wide collar which went high up at the back of the neck. The trousers were very tight and were buttoned just below his navel, and the legs, which clung to him over his thighs like tights, flared out conically below the knee and flapped unpleasantly around his shins as he walked. The suit was of brilliant blue corduroy and with it went a bright orange turtlenecked shirt.

Benny Skacke considered himself disguised into unrecognizability when soon after ten o'clock he made his entry into the nightclub. It was located in the basement and before he was shuffled down the stairs, he was relieved of a 35-kronor membership fee.

The club consisted of two large rooms and one smaller

one. The air down there was thick with tobacco smoke and the smell of human sweat.

In one of the larger rooms people were dancing to a frenzied pop group, while others sat drinking beer and carrying on deafening conversations. In the smaller room, relative silence reigned. It seemed to be reserved for those who preferred sitting at a table, eating a little, drinking wine and holding hands in the romantic light of flickering candles. The people there were presumably silent because of the candles, thought Skacke, as naturally they were on the point of death owing to a lack of oxygen.

He pushed his way through to the bar and after a while managed to acquire a stein of beer, and with it in his hand, he circulated around, studying the clientele. A number of the girls did not look a day older than fourteen, and he saw at least five gentlemen who were certainly over fifty, but generally speaking the average age appeared to be between twenty-five and thirty.

Skacke decided to listen to what people were saying before he himself fell into conversation with anyone. He moved discreetly nearer to four men in their thirties who were standing close together in one corner. From their expressions, the subject of the conversation was a serious one; they were frowning, sipping their beer thoughtfully, listening attentively to whoever was speaking and now and again interrupting each other with impatient gestures. Skacke could hear nothing of what they were saying until he was right beside them.

"I'm not convinced that generally speaking she's in possession of any libido at all," said one of them. "So I would suggest Rita."

"She just does a solo job," said another. "So I think Bebban's better."

The other two muttered in agreement.

"Okay," said the first man. "We'll take Bebban, so then we've three anyhow. Come on then, let's go and find her."

The four gentlemen vanished in among the dancers. Skacke remained where he was and wondered what a libido was. He would have to look it up when he got home.

The crowd around the bar had thinned out and Skacke managed to force his way up to the counter. When the barman came to him, he ordered a beer and said in passing:

"Seen Berra Olofsson anywhere?"

The man wiped his hands on his striped apron and shook his head.

"No, not for several weeks," he said.

"Are any of his buddies here?"

"I don't know. Yes, I saw Olle a moment ago."

"Where is he now?"

The barman let his eyes run over the crowd. He nodded toward a point diagonally behind Skacke.

"There he is."

Skacke turned round and saw at least fifteen people who might be Olle.

"What does he look like?"

The man behind the bar raised his eyebrows in surprise.

"I thought you knew him," he said. "He's standing over there. The one with sideburns and a black turtleneck."

Skacke took his beer, put the money down on the counter and turned around. He at once saw the man called Olle, who was standing with his hands in his pockets, talking to a little blonde with a voluminous hair-style and large breasts. Skacke went across and gave the man a light slap on the shoulder.

"Hi, Olle!" he said.

"Hi," said the man hesitantly.

Skacke nodded to the blonde, who gave him a gracious look back.

"How's life treating you?" said the man with the sideburns.

"Fine," said Skacke. "Listen, I'm looking for Berra. Berra Olofsson. Have you seen him around lately?"

Olle took his hands out of his pockets and poked his forefinger into Skacke's chest.

"No, I haven't. I've been looking for that guy all over the place. But he's not at home. Don't know where the hell he is."

"When did you see him last?" said Skacke.

"Hell of a long time ago. Wait a moment. Beginning of February, I guess, early in the month. He had to go to Paris for a week or two, he said. I haven't seen him since then. What d'you want him for, anyway?"

The blonde had moved over to other company a few

feet away. Now and again she glanced in Skacke's direction.

"Oh, just wanted to talk with him about something," said Skacke vaguely.

Olle took hold of his arm and leaned forward.

"If it's about a dame, you can talk with me," he said. "I've taken several over from Berra, actually."

"Well, someone has to see to the business when he's away," said Skacke.

Olle grinned.

"Well?" he said.

Skacke shook his head.

"No," he said. "Not dames. Other things."

"Aha. I see. No, well, I'm afraid I can't help there. I've hardly got enough for myself."

The blonde came over and pulled at Olle's arm.

"I'm coming, chick," said Olle.

Skacke was not exactly a brilliant dancer, but all the same he went up to a lady who looked as if she belonged to either Olofsson's or Olle's stable. She looked at him with a bored expression, followed him onto the dance floor and mechanically began to move her body. She was not easy to converse with, but he found out that she didn't know Olofsson.

After four laborious dances with different partners of varying verbosity, Skacke got a bite.

The fifth girl was almost as tall as he was, had prominent light blue eyes, a large backside and small pointed breasts.

"Berra?" she said. "Of course I know Berra."

She stood as if nailed to the floor through her feet as she swung her hips, pushed out her breasts and clicked her fingers. Skacke only really needed to stand in front of her.

"But I don't work for him any longer," she added. "I work solo."

"D'you know where he is?" said Skacke.

"He's in Poland, I heard someone say the other day."

She ground her hips round and round. Skacke clicked his fingers a little so as not to appear too inactive.

"Are you sure? In Poland?"

"Yes. Someone said so, I don't remember who."

"Since when?"

She shrugged.

110

"Don't know. He's been away a while, but he'll appear again, no doubt. What do you want? Horse?"

The conversation had to be carried on at a roar for them to be able to hear one another over the music.

"Perhaps I can fix you up, in that case," she yelled. "But not until tomorrow."

Skacke met three more girls who knew Bertil Olofsson, but they did not know exactly where he was either. No one had seen him during recent weeks.

At three o'clock the lights began to wink on and off and guests were encouraged to leave. Skacke had to walk for a while before getting hold of a taxi. His head felt thick from the beer and the bad air and he longed for home and bed.

In his pocket he had the telephone numbers of two girls who had offered to pose for him, of another who was only interested in general and of the girl who wanted to sell him drugs. Otherwise the evening's ultimate outcome had not been much. Tomorrow he would have to report to Martin Beck that all he had found out was that Bertil Olofsson had disappeared.

But there were two facts in the credit column.

He knew roughly when Bertil Olofsson had disappeared.

And that one about Poland.

Always something, thought Benny Skacke.

18

When Gunvald Larsson, fresh from his bath, stepped into the police station in Kungsholmsgatan and went up to the Homicide Squad's offices, he had no idea how the Malm affair had developed. It was Monday, the twenty-fifth of March, and the first day after his sick leave.

He had not answered his telephone after his confrontation with Max Karlsson on the previous Tuesday and the newspapers had not said a word about the fire since the item on Madeleine Olsen's death. He would in fact get his medal sooner or later, but both his heroic deed and the tragedy were now dead news and the name Gunvald Larsson already fading into some obscure corner of the public memory. The world was evil and flooded with front-page news. Suicide is not approved news in the Swedish press, partly for aesthetic reasons, partly because there are so compromisingly many of them, and a fire with three victims is not a lasting tidbit. Neither was there any cause for great ovations for the police; so long as they could not stop this wretched drug-trafficking, or deal with the innumerable demonstrations, or guarantee elementary freedom of movement in the streets. And so on.

So Gunvald Larsson stared with undisguised astonishment at the illustrious gathering which was just pouring out from a meeting with Hammar. Melander and Ek, Rönn and Strömgren were all there, not to mention Martin Beck and Kollberg, two people to whom he spoke extremely unwillingly and then only when absolutely necessary. Even Skacke was rushing about the corridor, with artificial solemnity trying to live up to the heights at whose feet he was temporarily tarrying.

"What the hell's going on?" said Gunvald Larsson.

"Well, Hammar's trying to decide whether we should set up our headquarters here or in Västberga," said Rönn gloomily.

"Who are we looking for?"

"Guy called Olofsson. Bertil Olofsson."

"Olofsson?"

"You'd better read this," said Melander, tapping the bowl of his pipe on a pile of typescript.

Gunvald Larsson read it.

He frowned heavily with his bushy eyebrows and his expression grew more and more puzzled. Finally he put down the document and said incredulously:

"What does all this mean? Some kind of joke?"

"Unfortunately not," said Melander.

"Arson is one thing, but incendiary bombs in mattresses . . . do you mean to say someone's taken all this seriously?"

Rönn nodded dismally.

"Are there such things, anyhow?

"Well, Hjelm says there are. They're supposed to have been discovered in Algeria."

"In Algeria?"

"They're very popular in some places in South America," said Melander.

"But what about this blasted guy Olofsson then? Where's he?"

"Missing," said Rönn laconically.

"Missing?"

"He's said to be abroad, but no one knows. Interpol can't find him either."

Gunvald Larsson pondered deeply as he poked a paper-knife between his large front teeth. Melander cleared his throat and went out. Martin Beck and Kollberg came in.

"Olofsson," said Gunvald, more or less to himself. "The same guy who delivered drugs to Max Karlsson and smuggled liquor to Roth. And who was behind Malm's car racket."

"And whose name was on the name plate on Malm's car when he was nabbed on Södertäljevägen," said Martin Back. "It was to get at him that the guys in the larceny department were so keen not to lose sight of Malm. They were waiting for Olofsson to appear and thought that Malm would testify against him to save his own skin."

"So Olofsson's the key man in the whole affair. His name keeps popping up time and time again."

"D'you think we've not noticed that?" said Kollberg, with profound and intense distaste.

"Then all there is to do is to go out and get him and then that's that," said Gunvald Larsson triumphantly. "Naturally, it must have been he who set the house on fire."

"The guy has vanished without trace," said Kollberg. "Haven't you grasped that?"

"Why don't we put a public notice in the papers?"

"So as not to frighten him away," said Martin Beck.

"You can't very well frighten away someone who's already missing, can you?"

Kollberg gave Gunvald Larsson an exhausted look and shrugged his shoulders.

"Just how dumb can a man get?" he said.

"So long as Olofsson thinks that we think that Malm killed himself and that the gas exploded accidentally, he feels safe," said Martin Beck, patiently.

"Why is he keeping out of the way then?"

"Well, that's a good question," said Rönn.

"I've got another question," said Kollberg, gazing up at the ceiling. "We talked to Jacobsson in the Narcotics

Squad last Friday and he said that Max Karlsson looked as if someone had put him through a mincer when he was brought here on Tuesday. I wonder who that person might be?"

"Karlsson admitted that ilt was Olofsson who supplied him, Roth and Malm," said Gunvald Larsson.

"He doesn't say that now."

"No, but that's what he told me."

"When? When you questioned him?"

"Exactly," said Gunvald Larsson, unmoved.

Martin Beck took out a Florida, pinched the filtertip and said:

"I've told you before and I'm telling you again, Gunvald. Sooner or later they'll get you."

The telephone rang and Rönn answered it.

Gunvald Larsson yawned indifferently.

"Oh, yes. D'you think so?"

"Not just think so," said Martin Beck seriously. "I'm convinced of it."

"Under no circumstances," said Rönn into the telephone receiver. "Disappeared? But that's impossible. Nothing can disappear just like that. Well, of course I realize he's upset ... what ... give him my love and tell him it doesn't help to start crying, just because something's disappeared. A man's disappeared here, for instance. Supposing I just sat down and started crying. If something or someone's disappeared, then one ... what?"

The others looked inquiringly at him.

"Yes, exactly, one goes on looking for it until one finds it," said Rönn, replacing the receiver emphatically.

"What's disappeared?" asked Kollberg.

"Well, my wife—"

"What?" said Gunvald Larsson. "Has Unda disappeared?"

"No," said Rönn. "I gave our boy a fire engine for his birthday the other day. It cost 32 kroner 50 öre. And now he's lost it. At home in the apartment. And now he's crying and wants to have another one. Disappearing, eh? It's crazy. In my own apartment. It was this big."

He held up two fingers.

"Well, that is remarkable," said Kollberg.

Rönn was still sitting with his fingers poking upward.

"Remarkable. Yes, you might well say that. A whole

fire engine, which has quite simply disappeared. That big. And 32 kronor 50 öre."

There was silence in the room. Gunvald Larsson stared a Rönn, frowning. At long last he said to himself:

"The fire engine that disappeared . . ."

Rönn gaped uncomprehendingly at him.

"Has anyone spoken to Zachrisson," asked Gunvald Larsson suddenly. "That fool in Maria?"

"Yes," said Martin Beck. "He doesn't know anything. Malm was sitting alone at a beer place in Hornsgatan until it shut at eight o'clock. Then he went home. Zachrisson followed him and stood there freezing for three hours. He saw three people go into the house and of those three one is now dead and another under arrest. Then you came."

"That wasn't exactly what I was thinking about," said Gunvald Larsson.

He got up and went out.

"What's up with him?" Rönn asked.

"Nothing, I suppose," said Kollberg absently.

He was standing wondering how it had come about that Gunvald Larsson had referred to Rönn's wife by her Christian name. He himself had not even known that Rönn had a wife. Presumably owing to his general lack of observation.

Gunvald Larsson was wondering how anyone could ever find a missing murderer when one could not even get hold of a policeman.

It was five o'clock in the evening and he had been looking for Zachrisson for nearly six hours. This occupation had taken him back and forth across the city and had become more and more like some kind of wild goose chase. At Maria police station, they had said that Zachrisson had just left for the day. No one answered his telephone and at long last someone mentioned that he had probably gone swimming. Where? Probably at the Åkeshov Baths, which lie to the west, halfway to Vällingby. Zachrisson was not at the Åkeshov Baths, but on the other hand a couple of other policemen were and they helpfully pointed out that they had never heard of a colleague of that name, and that he was probably at the Eriksdal Baths, where the police force also had a training time.

Again Gunvald Larsson crossed the city, which was gray and cold and windy and full of shivering human beings. The attendant in the men's part of Eriksdal Baths was singularly unfriendly, refusing to let him into the pool if he did not undress. Some naked people coming out of the steambath maintained that they were policemen and actually knew Zachrisson and said they had not seen him for several days. And thus it had gone on.

Now he was standing on the first floor of an old but well-maintained apartment building in Torsgatan, glaring angrily at a snuff-colored door. Above the letterbox was a piece of white cardboard stating the name *Zachrisson,* very neatly written with a ballpoint and embellished with some kind of peculiar vine, obviously drawn with great care and with a green ballpoint.

He had rung the bell and banged and also kicked the door a little, but with no more result than that a neighboring old woman had stuck her head around her door and glared reproachfully at him. Gunvald Larsson had glared back with such ferocity that the old woman had at once retreated. Then she had rattled safety-chains and bolts behind the locked door and she would probably soon be dragging furniture up to barricade it.

Gunvald Larsson scratched his chin and wondered what to do. Write a note and stick it through the letterbox? Or perhaps scribble a message directly on that abominable piece of cardboard?

The street door opened and a woman of about thirty-five came in. She was carrying two paperbags full of groceries and as she walked toward the elevator, she glanced anxiously at Gunvald Larsson.

"Hello there!"

"Yes?" she said in alarm.

"I'm looking for a policeman who lives here."

"Oh. Oh, yes. Zachrisson?"

"That's right."

"The detective?"

"What?"

"Detective Zachrisson. The one who rescued all those people out of that burning house?"

Gunvald Larsson stared at her. Finally he said:

"Yes, that seems to be the person I'm looking for."

"We're very proud of him," said the woman.

"Oh, yes."

"He's our janitor here," she informed him. "Very good at it, he is, too."

"Uhuh."

"But strict. Keeps the kids in order. Sometimes he puts his cap on to frighten them."

"Cap?"

"Yes, he's got a police cap in the boiler room."

"In the boiler room?"

"Yes, of course. Did you look down there for him, by the way? He's usually working down there. If you knock on the door, perhaps he'll open up."

She took a step toward the elevator, but then stopped and giggled at Gunvald Larsson.

"Hope you're not up to some mischief," she said. "Zachrisson's not a man to play around with."

Gunvald Larsson stood transfixed to the spot until the creaking elevator had vanished out of sight. Then he strode quickly across to the basement door, down the spiral stone stairs and stopped at a closed fire door. He grasped the handle with both hands but could not budge it.

He banged with his fists. Nothing happened. He turned around and kicked five times with his heel. The thick iron plates thundered.

Suddenly something did happen.

From the other side of the protective door, an authoritative voice said: "Scram!"

Gunvald Larsson was far too shaken by the experience of the last few minutes to be able to reply immediately.

"You may not play here," said the voice, muffled and threatening. "I've told you that, once and for all."

"Open up!" roared Gunvald Larsson. "Get this door open before I knock the whole damned building down."

Ten seconds' silence. Then the huge iron hinges began to squeak and the door slid open, slowly and noisily. Zachrisson peeped out, a terrified and dumfounded expression on his face.

"Oh," he said. "Oh, dear. Excuse me . . . I didn't know . . ."

Gunvald Larsson pushed him to one side and stepped into the boiler room. Once there, he stopped and stared around in astonishment.

117

The boiler room was spotlessly clean. On the floor was a brightly colored rug made of plastic strips and opposite the oil-fired boilers stood a white-painted coffee table with wrought iron legs and a circular top. There were two cane chairs as well, with checkered cushions in blue and orange, a large flowery cloth and a hand-painted red vase containing four red and two yellow plastic tulips. There was also a green porcelain ashtray, a bottle of lemonade, a glass and an open magazine. On the wall hung two objects, a police cap and a framed colored print of His Majesty the King. The magazine was some kind of crime paper of the type that contained half striptease girls and half unrecognizably altered and dramatized versions of classic crimes. It was lying open and it was obvious that Zachrisson had either been reading an article entitled "Mad Doctor Dismembered Two Naked Women into 60 pieces" or had been interrupted in his study of a full-page colored picture of a bright pink lady with huge breasts and well-used shaven genitals, which she was invitingly opening with two fingers toward the viewer.

Zachrisson himself was wearing an undershirt, felt slippers and dark blue uniform trousers.

It was very warm in the room.

Gunvald Larsson said nothing. He contented himself with thoroughly inspecting the various decorative details. Zachrisson followed his gaze and nervously shifted his feet. Finally he seemed to decide it would be best if he adopted a lighter tone, and said with forced cheerfulness:

"Well, when you have to work in a place, then you might as well make it look nice, mightn't you?"

"Is that the thing you use for frightening the kids?" said Gunvald Larsson, pointing at the uniform cap.

Zachrisson turned scarlet in the face.

"I don't see—" he began, but Gunvald Larsson interrupted him immediately.

"I have not, however, come here to discuss the bringing up of children or interior decorating."

"Oh," said Zachrisson, humbly.

"I just want to know one thing. When you got to the fire in Sköldgatan, before you began rescuing all those people, you dithered on about something about the fire department ought to have been there already. What the hell did you mean by that?"

"Well, I . . . I mean . . . when I said . . . it wasn't me who . . ."

"Don't stand there mumbling all that shit. Answer me instead."

"Well, I saw the fire when I got to Rosenlundsgatan, so I ran back to the nearest telephone booth. And Central Alarm said they'd already been called and that the fire truck was already there."

"Well, was it there then?"

"No, but . . ."

Zachrisson fell silent.

"But what?"

"The man who replied at Central Alarm did in fact say that. We've sent a hook-and-ladder truck, he said. It's already there."

"How could that be? Had the darned truck disappeared on the way?"

"No, I don't know," said Zachrisson in confusion.

"You ran back again, didn't you?"

"Yes, when you . . . when you . . ."

"What did the guys at Central Alarm say then?"

"I don't know. That time I ran to an alarm box."

"But the first time you called from a phone booth?"

"Yes, I was nearer to it then. I ran there and called and then Central Alarm said—"

"—that a hook-and-ladder truck was already there. Yes, yes, I've heard that already. But what did Central Alarm say the second time?"

"I . . . I don't remember."

"You don't remember?"

"I was probably rather excited," said Zachrisson lamely.

"The police are called to fires too, aren't they?"

"Of course . . . I think so, anyway . . . I mean . . ."

"Where was the police car that should have come, then? Had that disappeared too?"

The man in the undershirt and uniform trousers shook his head resignedly.

"Don't know," he said dismally.

Gunvald Larsson looked straight at him and raised his voice.

"How can you be so unimaginably stupid that you've not told anyone about this?"

"What? What should I have told them?"

"That the fire department had already been alerted when you called them! And that the fire engine had disappeared! Who, for instance, was it that sounded the alarm the first time? You've been questioned about this, haven't you? And you knew I was off sick, didn't you? Am I wrong?"

"No, but I don't understand—"

"Christ Almighty, I can see that. You don't remember what they said at Central Alarm the second time. Do you remember what you said yourself then?"

"There's a fire, there's a fire ... or something like that. I ... I was a bit shaken up. And then I'd been running."

" 'There's a fire, there's a fire'? You didn't by any chance mention where the fire was?"

"Yes, of course I did. I think I shouted, at least almost shouted: There's a fire in Sköldgatan. Yes, and then the fire department came."

"And didn't they say that the fire engine was already here? When you called, I mean."

"No."

Zachrisson thought for a moment.

"It wasn't there then, either, was it?" he said sheepishly.

"But the first time, then? When you called from the phone booth? Did you shout the same thing then? There's a fire in Sköldgatan?"

"No, when I called from the phone booth I wasn't so upset. Then I left the right address."

"The right address?"

"Yes, 37 Ringvägen."

"But the house was in Sköldgatan."

"Yes, but the correct address is 37 Ringvägen. Presumably so that it's easier for the postman."

"Easier?"

Gunvald Larsson frowned.

"Are you certain about all this?"

"Yes. When we started in Maria, we had to learn all the streets and addresses in the Second District."

"So you said 37 Ringvägen when you called from the booth, but Sköldgatan when you sounded the alarm the second time?"

"Yes, I think so. Everyone knows that 37 Ringvägen is in Sköldgatan."

"I didn't know."

"I mean everyone who knows the Second District."

Gunvald Larsson was stumped by this for a moment. Then he said:

"There's something fishy here."

"Fishy?"

Gunvald Larsson went across to the table and looked at the open magazine. Zachrisson sneaked past him and tried to snatch it away, but the other man put his large hairy hand on it and said:

"That's wrong. It should be sixty-eight."

"What?"

"That doctor in England, Dr. Ruxton. He sawed up his wife and the maid into sixty-eight pieces. And they weren't naked. Goodbye."

Gunvald Larsson left that singular boiler room in Torsgatan and drove home. The moment he put his key into the lock of his apartment in Bollmora, he completely forgot his usual habits and did not begin to think again until he was again sitting in his office, the next morning, that is.

It was mystifying. He could not get things right and finally he was driven to taking the matter up with Rönn.

"It's darned peculiar," he said. "I don't understand."

"What?"

"Well, this business of the fire engine that disappeared."

"Yes, that's almost the oddest thing I've ever come across," said Rönn.

"Oh, so you've been thinking about it too, then?"

"Yes, I have indeed. Ever since our boy said it had gone. And he's not been out either, as he's got a cold and has to stay indoors. It's simply disappeared somewhere inside the apartment."

"Are you really such a fool that you think I'm standing here talking about a toy you've lost?"

"What are you talking about then?"

Gunvald Larsson explained what he was talking about. Rönn scratched his nose and said:

"Have you checked with the fire department?"

"Yes, I called them just now. The person I spoke to sounded half-witted."

"Perhaps he thought you were half-witted?"

"Huh!" said Gunvald Larsson.

He slammed the door behind him as he left.

Next morning, Wednesday, the twenty-seventh, a summary was made of the results of the search and it was established that there were none. Olofsson was just as missing as he had been when the notification of his disappearance had been sent out a week earlier. Quite a lot had been found out about him, for instance that he was a drug addict and a professional criminal, but that had been known before. Inquiries were being made after him all over the country and also through Interpol; all over the world, it could be said, if one were given to exaggeration. Photographs, fingerprints and descriptions had been sent out by the thousand. A number of worthless tips had come in, but not many, as the Great General Public, thank heavens, had not yet been informed via the press, radio or television. Soundings in the underworld had produced very little. The work done on the inside had been useless. No one had seen Olofsson since the end of January or the beginning of February. He was said to be abroad. But no one had seen him abroad either.

"We must find him," said Hammar, with great emphasis. "Now. At once."

That was roughly all he had to say.

"Instructions of that kind aren't very constructive," said Kollberg.

He said it cautiously, after the meeting, as he was sitting on Melander's desk, apathetically dangling his legs.

Melander leaned back in his chair, his shoulders supported against the back of the chair, his legs crossed and outstretched. He was holding his pipe between his teeth and his eyes were half-closed.

"What are you up to?" said Kollberg.

"He's thinking," said Martin Beck.

"Yes, I can see that, for Christ's sake, but what's he thinking about?"

"About one of the cardinal faults of the police," said Melander.

"Oh, yes, which one?"

"Lack of imagination."

"And that from you?"

"Yes, I suffer from it myself," said Melander calmly. "And the question is whether this case isn't a perfect example of lack of imagination. Or perhaps narrow-mindedness in search activities."

"There's nothing wrong with my imagination," said Kollberg.

"Wait a moment," said Martin Beck. "Can you explain a little further?"

He was standing in his favorite place, just inside the door, his elbow propped up against the filing cabinet.

"At first we were satisfied with the theory that the gas exploded accidentally," said Melander. "Then we at last get clear evidence that someone tried to kill Malm with an ingenious incendiary arrangement, and then we've already got the tracks clearly marked out. We must find Olofsson. Implied: Olofsson is the man who did it. And then we follow that track as if we were a pack of bloodhounds with blinkers on. Who knows if we're not rushing straight into a cul-de-sac?"

"Rush is the right word," Kollberg said dejectedly.

"This is an error which is repeated over and over again and which has ruined hundreds of important investigations. The police get hold of what they think are definite facts. These point in a certain definite direction. And the whole search is directed in that particular direction. All other views are stifled or thrown overboard. Just because what lies nearest to hand is usually right, one acts as if this were always so. The world is seething with criminals who have got away with it because of this doctrinaire way of thinking by the police. Supposing someone finds Olofsson now, at this very moment. He's perhaps sitting outside a restaurant in Paris, or on a hotel balcony in Spain or Morocco. Perhaps he can prove that he's been sitting there for two months. Where do we stand then?"

"Do you mean that we should simply say to hell with Olofsson?" asked Kollberg.

"Not at all. Malm was dangerous to him and he knew that the moment Malm was nabbed. So he's the one who's nearest to hand. There is every reason in the world to try to find him. But we forget the possibility that he may prove to be quite useless for our case, the fire. If it then turns out that he peddled drugs and put false numbers on a few cars, then we're no further on at all. On the contrary, that's a matter which quite simply has nothing to do with us at all."

"It'll be darned peculiar if Olofsson's not mixed up in this at all."

"Quite correct. But peculiar things happen occasionally. That Malm killed himself at the same time as someone tried to murder him, is, for example, a very peculiar coincidence. It foxed me, too, on the site of the crime. Another peculiarity, which clearly no one has thought about, is the following: it will soon be three weeks since the fire and no one has either seen or heard from Olofsson during that time, which has caused certain people to draw certain conclusions, but it is still no less a fact that neither, as far as we know, had anyone had any contact with Olofsson for a whole month *before* the fire."

Martin Beck straightened up and said thoughtfully:

"No, that's true."

"That argument undoubtedly has certain implications," said Kollberg.

They thought about the implications.

A little farther down the same corridor, Rönn slunk into Gunvald Larsson's room and said:

"You know, I thought about something last night."

"What?"

"Well, about twenty years ago I was working for a couple of months down in Skåne. In Lund. I've forgotten why."

He paused thoughtfully and then said with some profundity:

"It was awful."

"What was?"

"Skåne."

"Aha. And that was what you had thought about?"

"Just pigs and cows and fields and students. And hot. I almost dropped dead. But there was one thing. We had a big fire while I was there. A factory burned down in the middle of the night. Later on, it turned out that it was some nightwatchman who had set it on fire by mistake. He sounded the alarm himself, but was so confused that he called the fire department in Malmö. He came from there, you see. So while the fire was burning in Lund, the firemen stood around in Malmö gaping, with extension ladders, fire pumps, jumping nets and the lot."

"Do you mean that Zachrisson's so dumb that he stood

124

there in the middle of the south side and called up Nacka fire department?"

"Something along those lines, yes."

"Well, he didn't, anyhow," said Gunvald Larsson. "I've called up every single police district within beating distance of the city. And none of them had any fire alarms that night."

"If I were you, I'd call up the firehouses too."

"If you were me, you'd be darned tired of fires by now. And also, there's a better chance of getting a sane answer from the police. Only fractionally better, of course."

Rönn went over toward the door.

"Einar?"

"Yes."

"What did they want jumping nets for? At a factory on fire in the middle of the night?"

Rönn thought about it.

"Don't know," he said at last. "Perhaps I've got too lively an imagination."

"D'you think so?"

Gunvald Larsson shrugged his shoulders and went on picking his teeth with a letter opener.

But all the same, the next morning he began calling up all the firehouses in the areas around Stockholm. The solution came surprisingly quickly.

"Okay-doke," said an exaggeratedly chummy member of the fire station staff at Solna-Sundbyberg. "Of course I can check."

And ten seconds later.

"Yes, we had a false alarm to 37 Ringvägen in Sundbyberg that evening. It came at 23:10 hours to be exact. Telephone alarm. Anything else?"

"The police didn't say anything about that," said Gunvald Larsson. "The police must've been there, mustn't they?"

"A radio car went of course. Funny otherwise."

"Did that call come through Stockholm Central Alarm or directly through to you?"

"Direct, I expect. But I can't tell you that for certain. There's only one report. Anonymous telephone alarm. False."

"And what do you do when that kind of call comes in?"

"We go out, of course."

"Yes, I realize that, but do you send the information on to anyone?"

"Yes, to the fuzz out here."

"To whom did you say?"

"The fuzz. And we also inform Central Alarm. You see, if it's a big fire, which is visible, I mean, then there's a hell of a lot of calling hither and thither. We might get twenty-five calls here while a hundred other people are calling the emergency number or sounding off fire alarms and what have you. That's why we report when we go out. Otherwise there'd be a hell of a mess all round."

"I see," said Gunvald Larsson coldly. "Do you know who received the call?"

"Of course. A chick called Mårtensson. Doris Mårtensson."

"Where can I get hold of her?"

"Nowhere, old man. She went off on vacation yesterday. To Greece."

"To Greece?" said Gunvald Larsson with profound distaste.

"Yes, anything wrong with that?"

"Just about as much wrong as anything could be."

"Oh, shit. I wouldn't have expected the fuzz to sit there spouting communist propaganda. I was at the Acropolis, or whatever it's called, myself last autumn. It was fine. Damned orderly, I thought. And the police, what style they've got! You boys have a lot to learn from them."

"Shut your big mouth, idiot," said Gunvald Larsson, flinging down the receiver.

There was one important matter he had not had time to mention, but he could not stand it any longer. Instead, he went into Rönn's office and said:

"Would you do me a favor and call up the fire department in Solna-Sundbyberg and ask when a person called Doris Mårtensson is coming back from her vacation?"

"Well, I suppose I could. What's up with you, anyhow? You look as if you were just about to have an attack of something."

Gunvald Larsson did not reply. He marched back to his desk and immediately dialed the number of the police station in Råsundavägen in Solna. Just as well to get that done too, while he was up to it.

"Yesterday I called you and asked about a very important matter. It was whether there had been any fire alarm at about eleven on the seventh of March," he said, by way of an introduction. The man in Solna replied:

"Yes, and I was the person who took your call and said that there was no report of any such thing."

"Now, however, I happen to know that there was a false alarm that night, to be more exact, to 37 Ringvägen in Sundbyberg, and that the police were informed in the ordinary way. So a police radio car should have been at the place."

"Funny. There's no report about that."

"Then check it, for Christ's sake, with the guys who were on duty then. Who were they, anyhow?"

"On patrol? I should be able to look that up. Wait a moment."

Gunvald Larsson waited, impatiently drumming his fingertips on his desk.

"Here we are. Car Number Eight, Eriksson and Kvastmo, with a cadet called Lindskog. Car Number Three, Kristiansson and Kvant . . ."

"That's quite enough," said Gunvald Larsson. "Where are those two crass morons now?"

"Kristiansson and Kvant? They're on duty, on patrol."

"Then send them straight here, for Christ's sake. Immediately!"

"But—"

"No buts. I want to see both those morons standing like statues in my office here in Kungsholmsgatan within fifteen minutes."

He replaced the receiver just as Rönn put his head around the door and said:

"Doris Mårtensson is coming back in three weeks' time. She starts work again on the twenty-second of April. Dreadfully bad-tempered, by the way, the guy who answered. He didn't exactly belong to your fan club."

"No, it's getting smaller and smaller," said Gunvald Larsson.

"Yes, I expect it is," Rönn said gently.

Sixteen minutes later, Kristiansson and Kvant were standing in Gunvald Larsson's office. Both were from Skåne, blue-eyed, broad-shouldered and nearly 6 feet. Both of them had also had painful experiences of previous encounters with the gentleman now sitting behind the desk. The moment Gunvald Larsson's eyes fell on them, they stiffened and actually did look very much like a couple of concrete statues representing two radio policemen in leather tunics with shoulder straps and polished buttons. They were also equipped with pistols and billy clubs. A finer point in the grouping was that Kristiansson was holding his cap rigidly clamped under his left arm, while Kvant's was still on his head.

"Christ, it's him!" whispered Kristiansson. "That lousy . . ."

Kvant said nothing. His forbidding expression showed that he was not going to allow himself to be intimidated.

"Aha," said Gunvald Larsson. "Here you are, standing here, you miserable blockheaded morons."

"What is it you want to . . . ?" began Kvant, and then he stopped suddenly as the man behind the desk rose to his feet.

"It's a matter of a small technical detail," said Gunvald Larsson, in a friendly voice. "At ten past eleven on the night of the seventh of March, you were called to 37 Ringvägen in Sundbyberg to check up on a fire alarm. Do you remember that?"

"No," said Kvant, impudently. "I don't remember that."

"Don't stand there lying to me," roared Gunvald Larsson. "Were you at that address or weren't you? Answer me!"

"Yes, perhaps," said Kristiansson. "We were ... I mean, I think I remember it. But . . ."

"But what?"

"But it was nothing," said Kristiansson.

"Don't say any more, Kalle, you're just making a fool of yourself," Kvant said warningly.

He himself added in a loud voice:

"I don't remember it."

"If either of you tells me one more lie," said Gunvald Larsson, the volume of his voice now ten times as great, "then I'll personally kick you back into the lost-property office in Skanör-Falsterbo, or wherever the hell you come from. You can lie in court, or anywhere else you like, but not here! And take your cap off, for Christ's sake!"

Kvant removed his cap, clamped it tightly under his left arm, glanced at Kristiansson and said ambiguously:

"It was your fault, Kalle. If you hadn't been so damned lazy . . ."

"But it was you who didn't want us to go there at all," said Kristiansson. "You said we'd heard nothing and you wanted to drive back and clock in. There was something wrong with the radio, you said."

"That's quite another matter," said Kvant, shrugging. "No one can help it if there's something wrong with the radio. That's a circumstance outside the control of an ordinary policeman."

Gunvald Larsson sat down again.

"Out with it now," he said, laconically. "Quickly and simply."

"I was driving," said Kristiansson. "We received a radio message—"

"Very indistinctly," Kvant interjected.

Gunvald Larsson gave him a withering look and said:

"No report-prose, thank you. And a lie doesn't get any nearer the truth by half-repeating it."

"Well," said Kristiansson, anxiously, "we drove there, to that address, 37 Ringvägen in Sundyberg, and there was a fire engine there, but there was no fire, so it was nothing."

"Except a false alarm, which you quite simply didn't report, for Christ's sake. Out of sheer idleness and stupidity. Is that right?"

"Yes," mumbled Kristiansson.

"We were exhausted," said Kvant, with a glimpse of hope.

"By what?"

"Lengthy and demanding duty."

"Christ, kiss my ass," said Gunvald Larsson. "How many arrests had you made during your patrol?"

"None," said Kristiansson.

Perhaps not so brilliant, but truthful, thought Gunvald Larsson.

"It was foul weather," said Kvant. "Poor visibility."

"We were just about to go off duty," said Kristiansson, appealingly. "Our tour was over."

"Siv was very ill," said Kvant. "That's my wife," he added informatively.

"And there was nothing there," repeated Kristiansson.

"No. Exactly," said Gunvald Larsson mildly. "There

was nothing. Nothing but the key evidence of a threefold murder."

Then he roared:

"Out! Get out! Scram!"

Kristiansson and Kvant tumbled out of the room. Their appearance was now not particularly sculptural.

"Jesus!" said Kristiansson, wiping the sweat from his brow.

"So," Kvant said, "that's the last time I'm going to tell you, Kalle. You should see nothing, and you should hear nothing, but if you happen to see or hear anything, then for Christ's sake, you must report it."

"Jesus," said Kristiansson, unimaginatively.

Twenty-four hours later, Gunvald Larsson had thoroughly, stage by stage, thought out everything and even succeeded in formulating it all into comprehensible sentences down on paper. As follows:

At 23:10 hours on 7th March, 1968, the house in Sköldgatan caught fire. The official name of the building is 37 Ringvägen. At 23:10 hours of the same day and year, a hitherto unidentified person called the exchange at the fire station in Solna-Sundbyberg to say that fire had broken out at 37 Ringvägen. As there is a street called Ringvägen in Sundbyberg, the firemen went to this. At the same time routine messages on the presumed fire went to the police and Central Alarm for Stockholm Region, to avoid duplication. About 23:15 hours Patrolman Zachrisson called from a telephone booth in Rosenlundsgatan to Central Alarm and reported a fire at 37 Ringvägen, without further identification of district. As the duty officer at Central Alarm had just received the message from Solna-Sundbyberg, he thought it was about the same fire and told Patrolman Zachrisson that a fire engine had gone out and should be already at the site of the fire. (It was, but at Ringvägen in Sundbyberg.) At 23:21 Patrolman Zachrisson again called Central Alarm, this time from an alarm box. As this time, according to his own statement, he expressed himself: "There's a fire! There's a fire in Sköldgatan!" there was no possible misunderstanding. As a result the firemen went to 37 Ringvägen in Stockholm, in other words, to the house in Sköldgatan.

It was not Patrolman Zachrisson who called the fire department in Solna-Sundbyberg.

Conclusions: The fire was deliberate and caused by a

130

chemical incendiary with a timed detonator. This may, if Patrolman Zachrisson's testimony is to be believed, have been placed in Malm's apartment at 21:00 hours at the latest. In that case, the timing mechanism was set for three hours. During this time the perpetrator had time to move freely in any direction. The only person who with any certainty could have known that the fire was to break out at 23:10 hours is the person who planned (or instigated, if instigation exists) the fire. Thus it is probable that it was this person who called the fire department in Sundbyberg.

Question No. 1: Why did this person call the wrong fire station? Possible answer: Because he happened to find himself in Solna or Sundbyberg and because his knowledge of Stockholm and its surroundings were poor.

Question No. 2: Why did this person call the fire station at all? Possible answer: Because he wished to murder Malm and had no desire to kill or injure the other ten people in the building. In my opinion this aspect is significant, insofar as it emphasizes even more the careful planning and the professional character of the crime.

Gunvald read through what he had written. He thought for a few minutes and then crossed out the last letter in *messages* and *the police and*. He did this with a ballpoint pen and so thoroughly that a laboratory examination would have been necessary if the original words were to be deciphered.

"Gunvald is on the track of something," Martin Beck said.

"Oh, is he?" said Kollberg skeptically. "A bit of railway track, I suppose?"

"No. This is something constructive. The first real clue."

Kollberg read through the report.

"Bravo, Larsson!" he said. "This is tops. Especially the brevity of the sentences. 'Or instigated, if instigation exists.' That's brilliant."

"D'you think so?" said Gunvald Larsson amiably.

"Joking apart," said Kollberg, "all we've got to do now is to find this darned guy Olofsson and then link him with the telephone call. But how're we going to do that?"

"Simple," said Gunvald Larsson. "A girl answered the telephone. I expect she can identify his voice. Telephone operators are usually good at that sort of thing. Unfortu-

131

nately she's on holiday and can't be got at. But she'll be back in three weeks."

"And before that we simply must get hold of Olofsson," said Kollberg.

"Yes," Rönn said.

That was all that was said on the afternoon of Friday the twenty-ninth of March.

The days went by. A new month began. Another week passed. Soon almost two. And still no trace of the man called Bertil Olofsson.

19

Malmö is Sweden's third largest city and is very different indeed from Stockholm. It has less than a third of the number of inhabitants and sprawls over a flat plain, while Stockholm is built on a system of elevated islands. Malmö also lies 360 miles farther south and is the country's port to the Continent. The rhythm of life is calmer there, the atmosphere less aggressive, and even the police are said to be more friendly and attuned to society, just as the climate is milder. It often rains, but seldom gets really cold, and long before the ice begins to thaw around Stockholm, the waves in Öresund are rippling against flat sandy shores and limestone plateaus.

Spring usually comes early, in comparison with the rest of the country, and the months of February, March and April often come as a surprise with their sun and clear views and occasional dead calm.

Saturday, the sixth of April of this year was a day like that.

The Easter school holidays had started and many people had gone away, if no more than for a weekend to look at their summer cottages and visit friends and acquaintances in the country. The leaves were not yet out, but their time was not far off and yellow spring flowers were already blooming along the roadsides.

In Industrihammen, which lies in the northeast part of the city, this particular Saturday afternoon was exceptionally still, in itself a natural phenomenon, as the area not only lies quite a long way outside the city center, but also could hardly be described as attractive either to walkers or to people taking trips in their cars; long silent docks with drooping cranes and immobile freight cars, heaps of timber and piles of rusty iron girders, the isolated bark of some lonely watchdog inside an enclosed factory site and a few moored Danish sand-excavators, the crews of which had gone back home for Easter. Outside one of the locked warehouses stood 200 bright blue tractors which had just come by ship from England and which would soon be delivered to purchasers in the surrounding farm districts.

Apart from the dog, the slight sounds from the oil refinery a few hundred yards farther away was all that could be heard. There was a smell of crude oil too, sufficient to irritate people with sensitive noses.

Over the whole area there were only two visible human beings, a couple of small boys lying on their stomachs, fishing. They were lying close together, their legs apart, their heads hanging over the edge of the wharf. These two young men had much in common. Both were six and a half years old, both were dark-haired, brown-eyed and looked sunburned, although technically speaking it was still winter.

They had walked here from their wretched homes at the east end of the city, sheath knives in their belts and fishing lines rolled up in their pockets. Then they had run about for an hour or so among the 200 tractors and sat on at least fifty of them. They had also found a couple of empty bottles which they had thrown into the water and then hurled stones at them, without hitting them, and an old abandoned fork-truck, ready for the scrap heap, from the engine of which they had succeeded in unscrewing a few interesting and, in their eyes, valuable parts. And now they were lying on the wharf, fishing, which was really why they had come.

These youngsters were not Swedish, which to some extent explained their behavior. No native of the country, even at their age, would ever think of fishing here, simply because their chances of catching anything were about as great as finding a live herring in a can of anchovies. Here there was nothing but muddy old eels foraging about in the slime of the harbor-bed. And they are not caught on a hook.

The boys were named Omer and Miodrag and they were Yugoslavs. Their fathers were dockworkers and their mothers worked in a textile factory. Neither of them had lived here long enough to master the language. Miodrag could say, "one, two, three," but that was all. Their prospects of learning much more were not very great, as they spent their days in a day nursery in which 70 per cent of the children were foreigners, and their parents were going to return home as soon as they had earned sufficient money to make them feel wealthy.

They lay quite still and stared down into the water, and both were thinking that soon a giant fish would bite, perhaps such a big strong one that they would be pulled into the water and drowned in the harbor basin. At that very moment, something happened which happens only very seldom and then only under special climatic and hydrological conditions. At a quarter past three on this still, sunny afternoon, a belt of fresh pure water which had come drifting in on the currents from outside the strait, slowly moved through the dirty harbor basin. Suddenly Omer and Miodrag discovered they could see their fishing lines under the water too, and then they saw the leads and even the worm they had as bait. The water slowly grew clearer and clearer until they could see the bottom and an old chamber pot and a rusty iron girder. And then they saw, perhaps ten yards out from the dock, something which filled them with utter astonishment, immediately setting their imaginations in a whirl.

The object was a car. They saw it quite clearly. It appeared to be blue and it was standing with its rear end facing the wharf, the doors closed and the wheels sunk in the mud, just as if someone had parked it there, in a market square in a secret city on the bottom of the sea. As far as they could see, it was quite whole and not in the least buckled or damaged.

And then the water began to thicken again, the vehicle down there vanishing before their eyes, and only a minute or two later neither the car, nor the chamber pot, nor either fishing line was visible, only the dirty gray-green surface of the water with its mother-of-pearl sheen of gasoline and gray sticky lumps of escaped oil.

They looked around for someone to whom they could show their discovery, or at least tell, for there was no longer anything to show. But Industrihammen was empty and deserted on this lovely Saturday in April and even the lonely watchdog had stopped barking.

Omer and Miodrag rolled up their fishing lines and stuffed them into their pockets, already bulging with old plugs and bits of copper piping and rusty nuts and bolts. Then they ran off, as far as they could manage, but when they were forced to stop for breath, they were still in the eastern harbor area, for it is very large and, when all is said and done, the boys were very small.

Another ten minutes went by before they came out on Vätkustvägen, where there were people, and even then they did not know what to do, for the people were in their cars, rushing along the road, cold and impersonal and purposeful, and no one could be bothered with two small boys standing waving on the pavement, especially as they had dark faces and were the usual "foreign rabble."

The twenty-fifth car did not drive past, however, but stopped. A black-and-white Volkswagen with a radio aerial on the roof and the word POLICE in block letters on the side.

In this car sat two uniformed policemen named Eloffson and Borglund. They were feeling peaceable and kindly and neither of them understood a word of what the boys were saying. Elofsson thought he could make out that they were pointing toward the harbor basin and that one of them said something about "auto." Then he offered them each a piece of candy, rolled the window up again, smiled and waved goodbye.

As Elofsson and Borglund were fairly conscientious policemen and also had nothing special to do, they drove in a wide circle through the eastern dock area. When they had got out to the farthest point and swung to the left along the parapet, they stopped the car and Borglund got out. He even got up onto the parapet and stood there for a few minutes. All he could see was the strange artificial marshland which the sand-excavators had created by their activities. He also heard a dog bark and a hissing noise from the oil refinery.

Twenty-four hours later, another policeman was standing on the edge of the dock in Industrihammen: He was a police inspector and his name was Månsson. He did not see a car. He saw nothing but filthy water and an empty beer can and a limp contraceptive.

The rumor which had brought him there had come a long way around and had become considerably distorted. Two Yugoslavian boys were said to have seen a police car drive into the water and disappear here on Järnkajen. The boys were not yet of school age and did not speak Swedish. They had also pointed out quite different places on the wharf, and, naturally, there were no police cars missing.

Månsson was thoughtfully chewing a toothpick and listening absently to a dog barking somewhere in the vicinity. He was in his fifties, a large, heavily built man with a slow manner and a peaceable nature. He was thorough and walked slowly up and down the whole length of the wharf without finding anything special or unusual.

Månsson took the chewed toothpick out of his mouth and threw it into the water. It bobbed peacefully between the contraceptive and the beer can. He shrugged his shoulders and walked back toward his car.

He thought: Tomorrow I'll get hold of a frogman.

20

When the frogman surfaced for the thirty-first time, he had found the car.

"Uhuh," said Månsson.

He rolled the toothpick back and forth between his lips as he thought about what should be done.

Until this very moment, twenty-three minutes past two on the afternoon of the eighth of April, 1968, he had been as good as utterly certain that the car existed only in the imaginations of those two small boys.

Now the situation had changed.

"How is it placed?"

"Damned difficult to see anything down there," said the frogman, "but as far as I could make out it's standing with its rear toward the wharf, about fifteen yards out. Slightly at an angle, as if it had come along the parapet and had not had time to turn."

Månsson nodded.

"There aren't any warning notices," said the frogman.

He was not a policeman, and he was also young and inexperienced.

Månsson himself had taken part in the hauling out of the water of at least ten cars over the last twenty years. In each case, they had been empty and reported as stolen. No one had ever been taken to court, but there was reason to believe that the owners themselves had chosen this way of not only disposing of worn-out vehicles, but also of collecting the insurance money.

"Anything else to tell?"

"Well, as I said, you can't see anything. It's quite small and also full of mud and muck."

The frogman paused.

"It's certainly been there a long time," he said.

"Oh well then, we'd better get it up," said Månsson. "Is there any point in your going down again? Before we get hold of a winch, I mean?"

"Not really. I can't do much until we start getting the hooks on."

"Go and get something inside you, then," said Månsson.

The beautiful weather seemed to have literally blown away. The sky was gray and it looked like rain, with low driving clouds, the wind blowing in from the northwest, cold and angry and blustery. The docks were back to normal, outside the parapet the sand-excavators and dredgers rattling and hooting, a little tug shuffling about in the harbor entrance, a diesel locomotive shunting a few freight cars, preceded by a man with a red flag, and three cargo boats, which had arrived the same morning, being unloaded. Some paid informer in the police force or the fire department had warned the press and ten or so reporters and photographers had already been standing freezing for hours on the wharf, or were sulkily huddled in their cars. The reporters and the frogman in their turn had attracted a number of the usual inquisitive people who were now tramping back and forth in the wind, their collars turned up and their hands thrust deeply into their pockets.

Månsson had not bothered to rope off the area or in

any other way limit people's freedom of movement. Now and again, one of the reporters came up to him and said: "Well?" Or something in that line. This happened again now. A man stepped out of one of the parked cars and indeed said:

"Well?"

"Well," said Månsson slowly. "There's a car down there. We'll probably be getting it up in half an hour or so."

He looked at the journalist, a man he had known for several years, winked and said:

"You can tell the others, can't you? For we can't stop it getting out, can we?"

"It's empty, of course?" said the newspaper man.

"Well," said Månsson, changing toothpicks. "As far as I know."

"Insurance thing, as usual?"

"We'll have to get it up and look first," said Månsson, yawning. "And that won't be for at least another half an hour, that's certain. So you might as well scram and get something to eat."

"See you," said the journalist.

"Mmm," said Månsson, and went over to his car.

He pushed his felt hat onto the back of his head and began fiddling with the radio. As he gave his instructions, he noticed a number of the pressmen had in fact taken his advice and driven away.

Elofsson and Borglund were also there. They were sitting 25 yards away in their Volkswagen, aching for coffee. A few minutes later, Elofsson came stumping over with his hands behind his back and said:

"What shall we say to people who ask what we're up to?"

"Tell them we're getting an old car out of the water," said Månsson. "In half an hour's time. You can go off and have some coffee in the meantime."

"Thanks," said Elofsson.

The little police car vanished at record speed. Both the policemen in front looked grave and determined, as if they were on an important and urgent mission. As soon as they were out of hearing, they would probably switch on their siren and flashing light, thought Månsson, chuckling to himself.

Almost an hour elapsed before everything was ready to haul the car out. Elofsson and Borglund, and the journalists had returned, and a number of dockers, seamen and people who worked for firms in the harbor area had joined the spectators. Altogether there were about 150 people around.

"Well," said Månsson, "let's get going, shall we?"

The operation was swift and undramatic. The chains creaked as they tightened and then the muddy water began to swirl around in a bubbling whirlpool and a metal roof came up to the surface.

"Mind the winch, there," said Månsson.

And then the car came up, dripping with mud and dirty water. It was hanging a little crookedly in the hooks and Månsson studied it appraisingly as the photographers took as many pictures as possible. The car was small and old and more or less worthless. A Ford, an Anglia or a popular model, anyhow a type rarely seen now, but which had once been found in great numbers on the roads.

The car appeared to be blue, but it was not easy to be more definite, as its surface was covered with a layer of grayish-green slime. The side windows were broken, or rolled down, and the whole car was full of mud and rubbish.

"Let's get it down, then," said Månsson.

People began to push around him and he said calmly:

"Would you mind moving, please? So that we have room to put the wreck down."

The people moved away immediately, Månsson with them. The little car landed on the quay with a dismal rattle, mainly from the fenders and the front bumper, which had broken off at one end.

The vehicle did indeed look dismal, and it was difficult to imagine that it had once rolled out of its factory in Dagenham, new and shiny, and that its first owner had once long ago sat at the wheel with his heart beating with excitement and swelling with pride.

Elofsson was the first to go up to the car and look inside. The people watching him from behind saw him gradually stiffen and then quickly straighten up.

Månsson followed him with slow steps, bent down, and peered through the open window of the right-hand door.

Among the tipped-up seats with their rusty springs and

blackened frames sat a muddy corpse. One of the most horrible he had ever seen. With empty eye-sockets and the lower jaw torn away.

He straightened up and turned around.

Elofsson had mechanically begun to push the nearest bystanders back.

"Don't push people," said Månsson.

Then he looked straight at the people nearest to him, one by one, and said in a loud calm voice:

"There's a dead man in the car. And he looks horrible."

Not a single person pushed forward to look.

21

Månsson did not think much of the police doctrine of keeping the general public out of their activities or of not allowing himself to be photographed "so long as this does not for some reason occur on the orders of the Chief of Police, or when it cannot be avoided," as police regulations demanded. On the other hand, he found it easy to be natural even in unnatural situations, and as he had great respect for other people, people also respected him.

Although neither he nor anyone else had given a thought to the matter, he had in fact done a very good job on the dock in Industrihammen that Monday afternoon.

If he had been in charge of the disturbances which had taken place during that long hot summer and which were generally regarded with great anxiety, then probably most of them would not have occurred. Instead, they were handled by people who thought that Rhodesia was somewhere near Tasmania and that it is illegal to burn the American flag, but positively praiseworthy to blow your nose on the Vietnamese. These people thought that water cannons, rubber billy clubs and slobbering German shepherd dogs were superior aids when it came to creating contact with human beings, and the results were according to those beliefs.

But Månsson had other things to think about, namely, a drowned corpse.

Corpses found in the water are never very pleasant, and

this particular one was the least pleasant he had ever come across.

Even the pathologist doing the autopsy said:

"Phew! What a nasty bit of work."

Then he set to work while Månsson, in line of duty, stood watching in a corner. He was looking extremely thoughtful and the doctor, who was young and somewhat green, now and again glanced inquiringly at him.

Månsson was certain that he was going to have trouble with the man from the car. He had suspected that something was seriously awry the moment the vehicle had risen out of the water. The solution that usually lay nearest to hand was this time out of the question from the start. It could not be an insurance swindle. Who would take the trouble to push a battered twenty-year-old wreck of a car into the harbor? And why?

The logical answer to those questions was frighteningly simple and so he did not move a muscle when the pathologist said:

"This friend of ours was dead before he went into the water."

After a while, Månsson said:

"How long might he have been there?"

"Hard to say," said the doctor.

He looked at the horrible swollen remains on the autopsy table and said:

"Are there eels down there?"

"Expect so."

"We-ell. Couple of months. At least two, perhaps four."

He poked about a bit with his probe and said:

"It's happened quite quickly. Not just the usual decomposition process. Presumably there are a lot of chemicals and other muck in the water."

Just before he left at the end of the day, Månsson asked one more question.

"That business about eels, isn't that just an old wives' tale?"

"The eel is a mysterious creature," said the doctor.

"Thanks," said Månsson.

The autopsy was completed the following day and made a very lugubrious story.

The criminal investigation took considerably longer, but the conclusion was generally no less depressing.

Not because nothing was found. In fact almost too much was found.

On Monday, the twenty-second of April, Månsson knew a great deal, the following, for instance:

The car was a Ford Prefect, 1951 model. It was blue and had been carelessly resprayed some time ago. It had false number plates, and the registration certificate, tax receipt and name plate were all missing. Its last two legal owners had been contacted through the registry of motor vehicles. A market gardener in Oxie had bought it second-hand but in relatively good condition as long ago as 1956 and then used it for eight years, after which he had sold it to one of his employees for 100 kronor. This man had used the car for three months. He said that it worked but looked so damned awful he had left it standing in a parking lot behind the indoor market in Drottningtorget. After a few weeks he had reported it as missing. He presumed that the police or the highway authorities had towed it away.

Neither the police nor the highway authorities had any reports on it. So it must have been stolen. No one had seen it since.

Of the vehicle's last passenger, there was also quite a lot to say. A man in his early forties, 5 feet 9 inches, with ash-colored hair. He had not died by drowning, but from an injury to the back of his head. The implement used had left a hole in the skull. No bone splinters ran out from the edge of the injury which pointed to the fact that the weapon which had caused the fracture was ball-shaped.

Quite simply, the man had been killed outright.

The weapon used was inside the car. A round stone, pushed down into a gentleman's nylon crepe sock. The stone was about 4 inches in diameter and of a natural formation. A small granite rock, in fact. The sock was 10 inches from top to toe and had been made in France. It was also of good quality, of a well-known brand and had probably never been used for its original purpose.

The dead man's fingerprints were unobtainable. The outer skin of his fingers had loosened and the pupillary pattern only barely visible in the remaining skin.

There was not a single object in the car that gave any

indication of the dead man's identity. Nor in his clothing, which was considered to be of second-rate quality and foreign manufacture; where from was uncertain. Neither was there anything which would help lead the inquiries about the murderer in any definite direction.

People who knew something about a resprayed 1951 blue Prefect, not registered since 1964, had been asked to come forward. No one had done so. Quite naturally, actually, when one considered that the whole country was rapidly being converted into a vast graveyard for scrap cars, in which battered old retainers rested shrouded in the poisonous fumes of their successors.

Månsson put the reports away, left his office and eventually the police station too. With his head down, he walked diagonally across Davidshallstorg toward the liquor store.

He was thinking about his drowned corpse.

Månsson was both a married man and a bachelor. He and his wife had begun to get on each other's nerves ten years earlier, when their daughter had married a South American engineer and moved to Ecuador. He had got himself a bachelor apartment in Regementsgatan, near Fridhemstorget, and lived mostly there. But every Friday evening, he went home to his wife and stayed there until Monday morning. This was a wise procedure, thought Månsson. All irritation vanished and during the second half of the week, both of them nowadays looked forward with pleasure to their weekend marital existence.

Månsson liked sitting in his sagging old armchair, taking a drink or two before going to bed. On this Monday evening, too. Monday evening was another of the week's pinnacles. Not only was he tired of his old lady and knew that he would not have to see her until Friday, although he would be looking forward to seeing her by Thursday, but also he had not even had as much as a mild beer with his food during the last three days. Liquor was no longer available in his wife's home.

He mixed his third Gripenberger and thought about his drowned corpse.

A Gripenberger consists of about one jigger of gin, a bottle of grape soda and crushed ice. A Finnish-Swedish cavalry officer, who was called Gripenberg, had taught him how to mix it in Villmanstrand, just after the war, when grape juice was still an exclusive drink, and he had stuck to it ever since.

Månsson had been involved in many murder cases, but there was nothing within his experience that seemed to fit in with the dead man in the car. It was obvious that it was a question of deliberate murder. And also the murderer had used a weapon, as effective as it was simple, which was almost impossible to trace and not in the least sensational. Round stones could be found everywhere and the fact that someone was the owner of a French black sock was not likely to arouse anyone's attention.

The man in the car had been killed with a single blow. Then the murderer had packed the body into an old scrap car and pushed it into the water.

As time went on, they would probably find the victim's identity, but he had an uncomfortable feeling that this would not particularly worry the murderer.

The case appeared to be unpleasantly difficult to solve. Månsson had a feeling that it would be a long time before it was cleared up. If ever.

22

Doris Mårtensson arrived back home on the evening of Saturday the twentieth of April.

It was now eight o'clock on Monday morning and she was standing in front of her large mirror in her bedroom, admiring her suntan and thinking how envious her friends at work would be. She had an ugly love-bite on her right thigh and two on her left breast. As she fastened her bra, she thought that perhaps it would be necessary to keep things on for the coming week to avoid awkward questions and involved explanations.

The doorbell rang. She pulled her dress over her head, thrust her feet into her slippers and went to open the door. The doorway was filled by a gigantic blond man in a tweed suit and a short open sports coat.

He stared at her with his china-blue eyes and said:

"What was Greece like?"

"Wonderful."

144

"Don't you know that the military junta there allows ten of thousands of people to rot away in political prisons and that people are tortured to death every day? That they hang women from the ceiling on iron hooks and burn off their nipples with electric steel cutters?"

"You don't think about things like that when the sun's out and everyone's dancing and happy."

"Happy?"

She looked appraisingly at him and thought that her suntan must look fine against her white dress. This is a real man, she could see that at once. Big and strong and blunt. Perhaps a little brutal too; nice.

"Who are you?" she said, with interest.

"Police. My name's Larsson. At ten past eleven on the evening of the seventh of March this year, you received a false alarm over the telephone. Do you remember it?"

"Oh, yes. We very seldom get false alarms. Ringvägen in Sundbyberg."

"Good. What did the person say?"

"There's a house on fire at 37 Ringvägen. Ground floor."

"Was it a man or a woman?"

"A guy."

"Did he say anything else?"

"No, just that."

"Are you certain about the actual words?"

"Yes, as good as."

He took a few loose bits of paper and a ballpoint pen out of his pocket and noted something down.

"Did you notice anything else?"

"Oh, yes. Lots of things."

The man seemed surprised, frowned and stared greedily straight at her with his blue eyes. There was something about Swedish men after all. Pity about those marks. But perhaps he was one of the unprejudiced ones.

"Oh, yes, indeed. What were they?"

"First of all, he was calling from a public telephone. I heard it clicking in the coin-box before the call was put through. He was probably calling from a call-box in Sundbyberg."

"Why do you think that?"

"Well, you see, because the old kind of notices are still in some of the booths there, with a line direct to us.

Otherwise they're trying to get everyone to ring the emergency number now. To Central Alarm in Greater Stockholm, you see."

The man nodded and wrote on his bit of paper.

"But I repeated the address and then I said: 'Here in town? In Sundbyberg, I mean?' Then I was going to ask him what his name was and all that."

"But you didn't?"

"No. He just said 'Yes' and put down the receiver. It sounded as if he was in a hurry. But people who call and say there's a fire are usually upset and nervous."

"So he interrupted you?"

"Yes. I don't think I even got the word Sundbyberg out."

"No?"

"Well, I said it. But he interrupted me in the middle and said 'Yes' and put back the receiver. So I don't expect he even heard it."

"Did you know there was a fire at the same address in Stockholm at the same time?"

"No. There was a big fire in Stockholm at that time. I got a message about it from Central Alarm about ten or twelve minutes later. But that was in Sköldgatan."

She looked piercingly at him and said:

"Say, aren't you the guy who saved all those people out of that burning house?"

He did not reply and after a pause, she said:

"Yes, it *was* you. I recognize you from the pictures. But I didn't imagine you were so big."

"You've obviously got a good memory."

"As soon as I found out that it was a false alarm, I tried to remember that conversation. The police usually want to know about it afterward. The police out here, I mean. But this time they didn't inquire."

The man scowled. It suited him. She thrust her right hip forward a little and at the same time bent her knee so that the heel came up from the floor. She had good legs, and now they were sunburned as well.

"What else do you remember? About the man?"

"He wasn't Swedish."

"A foreigner?"

He frowned even more heavily and stared sharply at

146

her. Blast that she'd put on her slippers. She had good feet, she knew that. And feet can be good.

"Yes," she said. "He had an accent, quite a strong one."

"What accent was it?"

"He wasn't a German or a Finn," she said. "And naturally not a Norwegian or a Dane."

"How do you know that?"

"I recognize Finns and I was ... engaged to a German boy for a while."

"Would you say he spoke bad Swedish?"

"No, not at all. I understood what he said, and he talked fluently and very quickly."

She frowned and thought back. She must look quite interesting now.

"He wasn't a Spaniard either. And not an Englishman."

"American?" suggested the man.

"Certainly not."

"How can you be so certain?"

"I know a lot of foreigners here in Stockholm," she said. "And I go south for my holidays at least twice a year. Anyhow, Englishmen and Americans never learn to speak Swedish. Perhaps he was a Frenchman. Possibly Italian. Perhaps a Frenchman, as I said."

"But that's a guess, isn't it?"

"We-ell, he said *howze*, for instance."

"Howze?"

"Yes, or rather *owze*, for house. I hardly heard the *h*."

He looked at his notes and said:

"Shall we take it word for word. First he said: 'There's a fire in the house at 37 Ringvägen'?"

"No, he said: 'There's a fire *at* the house at 37 Ringvägen, ground floor.' And he said *owze* and *zeven*. It sounded like a French accent to me ..."

"Were you engaged to a French boy too?"

"Well, I know a few. . . . I've several French friends."

"How did he say 'yes'?"

"With an open *e*, like someone from Skåne."

"We'll be getting in touch with you again," he said. "You're the greatest."

"Wouldn't you like to—?"

"At remembering things, I mean. Goodbye."

"Is it even possible that Olofsson speaks Swedish with a

147

strong accent and says *owze* instead of *house* and *zeven* instead of *seven?*" asked Gunvald Larsson, when they were all together at the police station in Kungsholmsgatan the next day.

The others stared inquiringly at him.

"And *ground floor* instead of *first floor?*"

No one replied and Gunvald Larsson also sat in silence for a moment. Then he turned to Martin Beck and said:

"That Shacky guy you've got out there in Västberga . . ."

"Skacke."

"Yes, him. Is he usable?"

"It depends."

"Would he be capable of going around Sundbyberg looking in all the telephone booths?"

"Can't you get the police out there to do it themselves?"

"Not on your life. No, send that kid out there. He can take a map and mark in all the public telephone booths where there are still the old-type notices with the Sundbyberg fire department alarm number on them."

"Could you explain a bit more?"

Gunvald Larsson explained.

Martin Beck thoughtfully held his chin.

"Mysterious," said Rönn.

"What's mysterious?" asked Hammar, who had just come thundering into the room, Kollberg at his heels.

"Everything," said Rönn gloomily.

"Gunvald, you've been reported for dereliction of duty," said Hammar, waving a paper at him.

"Who by?"

"A Sub-Inspector Ullholm in Solna. He says he has been informed that you've been spreading bolshie propaganda among the firemen out there. When on duty."

"Oh, Ullholm," said Gunvald Larsson. "It's not the first time."

"Was the charge the same then?"

"No, I'd damaged the reputation of the force by saying a dirty word in the guard room in Klara."

"He's reported me too," said Rönn. "Last autumn, after the bus murder. Because I didn't give my name and rank when I was trying to question a dying old man at Karolinska Hospital. Although he could see for himself that the

148

guy wasn't conscious for more than thirty seconds before he died."

"Well, how're things going?" asked Hammar challengingly, sweeping a look round the room.

No one replied and a few seconds later Hammar went out again, back to his endless deliberations with prosecutors, police staff officers and other senior staff, who also incessantly asked him how things were going. He had much to endure.

Martin Beck looked gloomy and thoughtful. He had also caught his first cold of the spring and blew his nose about every fifth minute. At long last he said:

"If Olofsson was the person who telephoned, then he might well have disguised his voice. Anyhow, it seems more than likely that he would do that, doesn't it?"

Kollberg shook his head and said:

"But would Olofsson, a native of Stockholm, go and ring for the fire department in Sundbyberg?"

"No. Exactly," said Gunvald Larsson.

That was approximately what happened on Tuesday, the twenty-third of April.

Wednesday and Thursday were singularly uneventful, but when they met again on Friday, Gunvald Larsson said:

"How're things going for Tacky?"

"Skacke," said Martin Beck sneezing.

"He's very quiet," said Kollberg.

"I ought to have done it myself, of course," said Gunvald Larsson sourly. "A job of that kind shouldn't take longer than an afternoon."

"He had one or two other things to do, so he couldn't get going with it properly until yesterday," said Martin Beck apologetically.

"What other things?"

"Well, actually, we have got other things besides telephone booths in Sundbyberg to think about."

The search for Olofsson was making no progress and there was no means of intensifying it. Everything that could be sent out had been sent out, from descriptions and photographs to fingerprints and dental cards.

For Martin Beck, the holiday weekend proved extremely trying. He was feeling a gnawing anxiety about the case, which was clearly about to become totally entangled, and apart from his rapidly developing virus infection, he received yet another blow of an even more private nature. Ingrid, his daughter, informed him that she was thinking of moving away from home. There was nothing unnatural or surprising about this. She would soon be seventeen and she was grown-up in most respects. She was also sensible and mature. Naturally she had a right to live her own life and do as she thought best. It was true that for a long time he had seen this moment approaching, but what he had not been able to foresee was his own reaction. His mouth went dry and he felt slightly dizzy. He sneezed helplessly, but said nothing, for he knew her well and knew that she had not taken this decision without weighing the situation thoroughly and at length.

As if to add to his burdens, his wife said coldly and practically:

"We'd better go through what Ingrid is to take away with her from here. And you needn't worry about her. That girl will manage. I ought to know, as I brought her up."

To add insult to injury, that was largely true.

Their boy, who was thirteen, took the announcement even more laconically. He just shrugged his shoulders and said:

"Good. Then I can have your room. The electrical outlets are in a better place in there."

Sometime on Sunday afternoon, Martin Beck happened to find himself alone with Ingrid in the kitchen. They were sitting opposite each other at the plastic-covered table at which they had so often drunk cocoa together on so many mornings for so many years. Suddenly she stretched out her hand and placed it over his. They sat in silence for a few seconds. Then she swallowed and said:

"I know I shouldn't really say this, but I'm going to all the same. Why don't you do the same? Move out?"

He looked at her in surprise.

She did not look away.

"Yes, but . . ." he said hesitantly, and then he stopped. He simply did not know what to say.

But he already knew that he would think a great deal about this brief conversation for a long time.

On Monday, the twenty-ninth, two events occurred practically simultaneously.

One of them was not particularly remarkable. Skacke came into the office and put a report down in front of Martin Beck. It was well written and as detailed as one could wish. So far as he could make out, there were six telephone booths in Sundbyberg in which the old notices still remained. Also, two more possible ones, in other words those in which the notices might still have been up on the seventh of March, but had been taken away since then. In Solna, there were no telephone booths with such notices. No one had asked Skacke to find this out, but he had obviously done so all the same.

Martin Beck was sitting hunched up at his desk, poking at the papers with his right forefinger. Skacke stood 6 feet away from him, strongly resembling a dog sitting up and begging for a sugar-lump.

Perhaps he ought to say something in praise before Kollberg came in and started being sarcastic, thought Martin Beck indecisively.

At that moment the problem was solved by the telephone ringing.

"Yes. Beck."

"There's some inspector who wants to speak to you. I didn't really catch what his name was."

"Just put him through . . . yes, Beck here."

"Hi. It's Per Månsson in Malmö."

"Hi. How are you?"

"Not so bad. Always feel a bit off on Mondays. And then we've had all that hullabaloo over that tennis match. Against Rhodesia, you know."

Månsson paused for a long while, then said:

"You're looking for someone called Bertil Olofsson, aren't you?"

"Yes."

"I've found him."

"Down there?"

"Here in Malmö, yes. Dead. We found him three weeks ago, but I didn't know who he was until today."

"Are you certain?"

"Yes, ninety per cent certain, anyhow. The dental card for his upper jaw fits. And it's quite special too."

"All the rest, then? Fingerprints, other teeth and—"

"We haven't found his lower jaw. And couldn't check on fingerprints. He'd been in the water for a long time, I'm afraid."

Martin Beck straightened up.

"How long?"

"At least two months, the doc says."

"And when did you get him out?"

"Monday the eighth. He was sitting in a car at the bottom of the harbor. A couple of little kids . . ."

"That means he must've been dead on the seventh of March?" interrupted Martin Beck.

"Seventh of March? Oh, yes. For at least a month, perhaps longer. When was he last seen up there where you are?"

"Third of February. He was to go abroad then."

"Was he now? Good. That helps me fix a date. Then he must have been finished off between the fourth and the eighth of February, roughly."

Martin Beck sat in silence. It was, however, only too easy to see what this meant. Olofsson had been dead a month when the house in Sköldgatan had burned down. Melander had been right. They had been on the wrong track.

Månsson did not say anything either.

"What's it like?" asked Martin Beck.

"Peculiar. Damned peculiar. He was killed with a stone stuffed into a sock and given an old car wreck as a coffin. There wasn't a thing in the car or among his clothes. Except the weapon and two-thirds of Olofsson, I mean."

"I'll be coming down as soon as I can," said Martin Beck. "Or Kollberg. Then you'll have to come up here, I suppose."

"Must I?" said Månsson, with a sigh.

To him, the Venice of the North was more or less equivalent to the Gates of Hell.

"Well, this is a complicated story," said Martin Beck. "Worse than you can imagine."

"Oh, I'll bet," said Månsson, with mild irony. "Then I'll be seeing you."

Martin Beck put down the receiver, looked absently at Skacke and said:

"That's a good job you've done there."

23

It was Walpurgis Eve and spring had come at last, at least to southern Sweden. The morning plane from Bromma landed on time, that is, at five to nine, at Bulltofta in Malmö and spewed out a handful of businessmen plus a pale and sweaty Chief Inspector. Martin Beck had a cold and a headache and did not like flying, and the liquid the Scandinavian Airlines System called coffee had not added to his sense of well-being. Månsson was standing at the gate, large, solid and round-shouldered, his hands in his overcoat pockets and the first toothpick of the day in his mouth.

"Hi," he said. "You look all in."

"I am," said Martin Beck. "Is there a toilet around here?"

Walpurgis Eve is an important day in Sweden, a day when people put on their spring clothes and get drunk and dance and are happy and eat food and look forward to the summer. In Skåne, the roadsides are in bloom, and the leaves are coming out. And out on the plain, the cattle are grazing the spring grass, and the other crops are already sown. Students put on their white caps and trade union leaders get out their red flags from their moth-bags and try to remember the text of *Sons of Labor.* It will soon be May Day and time to pretend to be socialist for a short while again, and during the symbolic demonstration march even the police stand to attention when the brass bands play the *Internationale.* For the only tasks the police have are the redirection of traffic and ensuring that no one spits on the American flag, or that no one who really wants to say anything has got in among the demonstrators.

The last day of April is a day of preparation; preparations for spring, for love and for political cults. It is a happy day, especially if it happens to be fine.

Martin Beck and Månsson spent this happy day looking at what was left of Bertil Olofsson and wandering once or twice around the old car that was standing dismally in the police station lot. They also looked at the stone and the black sock, the cast of the teeth in Olofsson's upper jaw, and they spent a long time leafing through the autopsy report. They did not say much, but then there was nothing special to say. On one occasion Månsson asked a question.

"Is there anything that connects Olofsson with Malmö? Except that he was killed here?"

Martin Beck shook his head. Then he said:

"It looks as if Olofsson mainly dealt in stolen cars. Some drugs, of course. But mostly cars, which he resprayed and gave false numbers. Then they were given false registration certificates and taken out of the country, presumably to be sold abroad. It seems likely that he at least passed through the city quite often. Possibly he may even have stayed here now and again. And it would be strange if he hadn't had a few acquaintances here."

Månsson nodded.

"Obviously a pretty poor specimen," he said, more or less to himself. "Physically in bad shape too. That's why the doc misjudged his age. Miserable sort of wretch."

"That's true of Malm too," said Martin Beck. "But it doesn't make things any better, does it?"

"No, of course not," said Månsson.

Several hours later, they were sitting in Mansson's office looking out at the asphalted yard, with its parked black-and-white cars and occasional policemen charging around.

"Well," said Månsson. "Our starting point isn't quite so bad as it seems."

Martin Beck looked at him with a certain surprise.

"We know he was in Stockholm on the third of February and the doctor swears he must have been dead at the latest on the seventh. The actual time has shrunk to three or four days. I'll probably find someone who has met him. Whatever that entails."

"How can you be so certain of that?"

"This city isn't that big and the circles Olofsson moved in are even smaller. I have certain contacts. That they've not been much help to me hitherto is because they didn't know who I was looking for. And I'm thinking of letting the press have this story."

"We can't have anything published. And anyhow, that's the public prosecutor's business."

"That's not the way I do things."

"But you're not going to involve us?"

"What happens in Stockholm doesn't interest me in the slightest," said Månsson with feeling. "And all that about the prosecutor is just a matter of form. Down here, at least."

Martin Beck flew back home that evening. He got into Stockholm at about ten, and two hours later was lying in his sofa-bed in the living room in Bagarmossen, the light already out.

But he was not asleep.

His wife, on the other hand, was, and her light, even snores could be clearly heard through the closed bedroom door. The children were out. Ingrid was painting posters for the youth demonstration the next day and Rolf was probably at some parentless party, with beer and phonograph music.

He felt lonely. Missing something. For instance, the desire to get up and go into the bedroom and tear off his wife's nightgown. He thought that he at least ought to feel a desire to do that to someone else, someone else's wife, for instance. In which case, whose?

He was still awake when Ingrid came in at two o'clock. Presumably his wife had told her not to be back any later. Rolf, on the other hand, did not have to keep any special time, although he was four years younger than his sister and only half as intelligent and had not even a hundredth of his sister's instinct for self-preservation and ability to look after herself. He was a boy, of course.

Ingrid padded into the living room, bent down and kissed him lightly on the forehead. She smelled of sweat and paint.

Ridiculous, he thought.

Another hour elapsed before he fell asleep.

Martin Beck arrived at the police station in Kungsholm on the morning of the second of May and stepped

155

straight into a conversation between Kollberg and Melander.

"Ridiculous," said Kollberg, thumping his fist on the desk so that everything except Melander jumped.

"Yes, it's peculiar," said Melander gravely.

Kollberg was in his shirtsleeves and had loosened his tie and unbuttoned his collar. He leaned over the desk and said:

"Peculiar! Perhaps we're the peculiar ones. Some-one puts a time bomb in Malm's mattress. We think it's Olofsson. But Olofsson's already been dead a month, because someone's cracked open his skull and crammed his body into an old scrap car and driven the whole kit and caboodle into the sea. And now here we sit like birds in the wilderness."

He fell silent, to get his breath back. Melander said nothing. Both nodded at Martin Beck, but in passing, as if he had not been there at all.

"If we presume that there's a connection between the attempted murder of Malm and the murder of Olofsson . . ."

"Then it's just a guess, despite everything," said Melander. "We've no evidence whatsoever to show that any such connection exists. Though it seems un-likely that the two events should be wholly independent of each other."

"Perfectly correct. Such coincidences are highly un-likely. So there is reason to assume that the third component in this story has a natural connection with both of the other two."

"You mean the suicide. That Malm killed himself."

"Of course."

"Yes," said Melander. "He may have done it because he knew the game was up."

"Exactly. And because he thought it was pleasant to turn on the gas taps in comparison with what he was in for otherwise."

"He was scared, in fact."

"And he'd darned good reason to be so, too."

"The conclusion then would be that he did not count on being allowed to stay alive," said Melander. "That he was scared of being killed. But in that case, by whom?"

Kollberg thought. Then he made a sudden leap forward in his thoughts and said:

"Perhaps Malm killed Olofsson?"

Melander took half an apple out of his desk drawer, cut a bit off it with a letter opener and put the piece into his tobacco-pouch.

"Doesn't sound very likely," he said, without looking up. "I find it hard to imagine that a wretch like Malm would be capable of committing a crime of that caliber. Morally, he perhaps had no scruples, but this would entail his managing the technical details too."

"Excellent, Fredrik. There's nothing wrong with your logic. Well, what conclusions do we draw from all that?"

Melander said nothing.

"What are the glaringly logical consequences?" Kollberg asked stubbornly.

"That both Olofsson and Malm were gotten rid of," said Melander, with a certain reluctance.

"By whom?"

"We don't know."

"No, that's true indeed. But one thing we can damned well work out."

"Yes," said Melander. "You're probably right."

"Professional job," said Martin Beck to himself.

"Precisely," said Kollberg. "A pro. Only pros use things like stones inside socks and that darned bomb."

"Agreed," said Melander.

"And because of that we're sitting here scratching our heads, eyes popping, as if we'd seen a miracle. Because we've never dealt with anyone else but amateurs. And we've been doing that for so long that we're more or less amateurs ourselves, too."

"Ninety-eight per cent of all crimes are amateur ones. Even in the United States."

"That's no excuse."

"No," said Melander. "But it's an explanation."

"Wait a moment," said Martin Beck. "That fits in with other points too. Ever since Gunvald wrote his memorandum or whatever we should call it, I've been wondering about something."

"Yes," said Kollberg. "Why did the person who put that incendiary in Malm's bed then go and call the fire department?"

Thirty seconds later he answered his own question.

"Because he was a professional. A professional criminal. It was his job to finish off Malm, and he wasn't the slightest bit interested in seeing ten people getting knocked off too."

"Hm," said Melander. "There's some sense in that argument. I've read that professionals are often less bloodthirsty than amateurs."

"I've read the same thing," said Kollberg. "Yesterday. If we look at the other side of the coin and take a typical amateur like our one-time honored colleague Hedin, the cop who killed nine people in Skåne seventeen years ago, then he was not burdened with any such considerations. He set fire to an entire old people's home just because he thought his fiancée was the end."

"But he was insane," said Martin Beck.

"All amateurs who kill people are mentally sick, if only at the actual moment when the crime is committed. But pros are not the same."

"But there aren't any professional murderers in Sweden now," said Melander thoughtfully.

Kollberg gave him a searching look and said:

"What is there to say that this guy is Swedish?"

"If he's a foreigner, then that fits in with what Gunvald has produced," said Martin Beck.

"First and foremost, it fits in with our guesses," said Kollberg. "And while we're at it, we might as well go on guessing. Do you think, for instance, that whoever mined Malm's bed and cracked open Olofsson's skull is in Sweden at this moment? Do you think he even stayed here until the next day?"

"No," said Melander. "Why should he do that?"

"Of course, there's no evidence that we're talking about the same murderer," said Kollberg thoughtfully.

"Yes," said Melander. "One small point."

"Yes," said Martin Beck. "There is one thing which makes that assumption likely. Both to be able to carry out the murder in Malmö and cause the fire in Sköldgatan demanded a certain local knowledge."

"Hm," said Kollberg, pushing out his lips. "Someone who had been here in Sweden before."

"Someone who speaks the language passably," said Melander.

"Someone who knows quite a bit about Stockholm and Malmö.'"

That was Kollberg.

"But who at the same time knows sufficiently little to make the mistake of giving the alarm to the fire station in Sundbyberg instead of Stockholm."

That was Martin Beck.

"Whoever, by the way, thought up the idea of calling the house in Sköldgatan 37 Ringvägen?" Kollberg asked suddenly. "I mean apart from the highway department people and occasional policemen. Among the administrative staff, I mean."

"Someone who has had the address written down for him instead of having it pointed out for him on a map," said Melander, lighting his pipe.

"A person with a limited knowledge of the city streets," said Martin Beck.

"A foreigner," said Kollberg. "A foreign pro. In both cases, he uses a weapon never before used in Sweden. Hjelm maintains that that detonator mechanism was invented in France and in its time was common in Algeria. If a Swedish gangster suddenly wanted to kill Olofsson, he'd do it with a piece of pipe or a bicycle chain."

"The trick with the stone inside a sock was used during the war," said Martin Beck. "By spies and agents and such like. People who were sent over to liquidate collaborators and others considered to be displeasing. By people who didn't dare take the risk of being searched and found with a knife or a gun."

"There were cases like that in Norway," said Melander.

Kollberg scratched his fair head.

"Yes, that's all very well," he said. "But there must be some motive."

"Most certainly," said Martin Beck. "The connection between Malm and Olofsson is in fact strengthened. Why are people got rid of by professional killers?"

"Because they're uncomfortable," said Melander.

159

"One can guess at the relationship between Olofsson and Malm. They were presumably the car thieves. Anyhow they dealt with the stolen cars."

"A stolen car is often not worth much to the thief," said Martin Beck. "He sells it very cheaply, at whatever price he can get."

"And Olofsson and Malm resprayed the cars and found false number plates and papers. Then they drove them across the border. To some country where they either sold them themselves or simply handed them over to someone else."

"The latter sounds the most likely, doesn't it?" said Kollberg.

He shook his head irritably and continued:

"Together with someone else, or several other people, they were managing the Swedish end of a large enterprise which was concerned with a lot of other things. But they made some kind of blunder and the firm decided to get rid of them."

"Yes, something in that line," said Melander.

Kollberg shook himself gloomily and said:

"And what do you think people here are going to say when we put forward that sort of theory? Who the hell would believe anything like that?"

No one replied to his question and, perhaps thirty seconds later, he pulled a telephone toward him, dialed a number, waited, and said:

"Einar? I'm in Melander's room. Could you come in for a moment?"

Less than thirty seconds later, Rönn appeared in the doorway. Kollberg looked solemnly at him and said:

"We've come to the conclusion that Malm and Olofsson worked for an international crime syndicate, some kind of Mafia. We also think that this gang got tired of them and sent a hired assassin from abroad to finish them off."

Rönn stared from one man to the next. At long last, he said:

"Who thought up all that nonsense? That sort of thing only happens in films and books. Or are you pulling my leg?"

Kollberg shrugged his shoulders eloquently.

160

24

Benny Skacke had marked the eight telephone booths on the city map of Sundbyberg with black crosses. Then with the help of a pair of compasses he had drawn a circle around every cross. Although some of the booths lay inside central Sundbyberg and several of the circles overlapped one another, the encircled sections covered an area of more than a half-mile square. Gunvald Larsson had not much hope of any results or any form of success when he had sent Skacke out to try within this thickly populated area of the city to find any trace of the man who had called up the fire station on the seventh of March. That the man had called from one of the eight booths was no more than a guess, and even if this showed itself to be correct, the problem of finding a person about whom nothing was known beyond that he spoke Swedish with a foreign accent, still remained.

Skacke, however, took on his assignment with great enthusiasm and after receiving some reluctant assistance from the police in Solna-Sundbyberg for the first weeks, was now alone on the job. His work consisted of visiting tenants in every building within the encircled areas, and even for a young man with well-trained leg muscles, this was somewhat fatiguing. But Skacke was obstinate, and although Gunvald Larsson and Martin Beck had long since given up hope of any results and no longer even bothered to ask him how things were going, he went on knocking at doors in Sundbyberg whenever he had a moment to spare. He literally fell into bed at night and for the last few weeks had neglected his training program and his law studies. He had also neglected Monica, which was worse.

Skacke had met Monica eight months earlier, when they were both taking part in a swimming meet. Since then they had met more and more often and although they had never actually spoken about marriage directly, it was understood that they would move in together as soon as they could find a passable apartment. Skacke lodged with a landlady, and Monica, who was twenty and training to be a physiotherapist, still lived at her parents' home.

When Monica phoned him on the evening of the sixteenth of May and for the seventh time that week in vain asked to see him, she was, to say the least, somewhat annoyed.

"Do you have to do all the jobs in that darned police force," she said crossly. "Or aren't there any other policemen except you?"

It was the first time that that question had been put to Benny Skacke, but presumably would not be the last. Most of his superiors, not least Martin Beck, often heard their wives asking the same question and they had long since ceased attempting to reply. But Benny Skacke did not know that. Consequently, he said:

"Of course there are. I'm determined to find this guy who called from a phone booth in Sundbyberg, but unfortunately I can't do that and nothing else. But tomorrow anyhow, I'll be knocking on doors all day and I'd thought I'd start early, so I've simply got to get to bed early tonight."

He heard Monica draw in her breath to say something, and added swiftly:

"Don't be angry with me, darling. Of course, I *want* to see you, but I must stick at my work if I'm to get anywhere."

Monica was not placated and finally slammed down the receiver after threatening to go out with a physical training instructor called Rulle. Skacke knew this in his opinion nauseous creature only too well. He was not only considered unusually good-looking, but also had shown himself to be superior to Skacke in most branches of sport, including swimming. Football was in fact the only sport at which Skacke could say with any certainty that he excelled, and he often dreamed of the day when he would be able to entice the gentleman in question out onto the football field, however it could be arranged. He grew so agitated at the thought of Monica with that smug slob that he had to drink two glasses of milk to calm himself down before calling her up again.

Just as he put his hand on the receiver, the telephone rang again. It was Monica, wonder of wonders, full of regrets and begging his forgiveness, and after they had talked for more than an hour, they decided to meet in Sundbyberg the following day and have a late lunch there after Monica had finished at school.

On Friday morning, Skacke went directly to his beloved Sundbyberg to continue his Operation Doorknocking. Every day, he had crossed out on his map the areas he had covered and had also made a list of the apartments where no one had been at home when he had rung. The Office for Aliens had given him another list, covering the non-Scandinavian citizens registered under addresses in Sundbyberg. He had set off before seven o'clock in order to get to some of the addresses on the list of those not yet interviewed, before people had . gone to work.

By nine o'clock, he had reduced the number of names on the list by half, but that was the only result he had succeeded in achieving.

Benny Skacke walked through Sundbyberg toward the residential quarter he had chosen to visit that day. He went into a park which sloped up toward a group of tall buildings on the top of a hillside. The park did not appear artificial, but was more like a piece of untouched countryside, which with rare generosity had been allowed to remain when the area had been planned. The grass on either side of the path was fresh and green and farther on between the pine trees on a forested slope, gray blocks of granite and moss-covered stones protruded from the pine-needle-strewn ground. The path on which he was walking was neither asphalted nor sanded, but had been trampled there by human feet, winding its way through birch trees and oaks. Sunlight sifted down through the light foliage and threw shimmering spots of gold onto the dry hard earth of the path and the worn roots of the trees. Skacke slowed his pace and suddenly noticed the smell of pine needles and sun-warmed soil, but only for a brief moment. The next time he drew air in through his nostrils, he could smell nothing but gasoline fumes and the rancid odor of frying-oil from a grill down on the street.

Skacke was thinking about Monica. They were to meet at three o'clock and he was looking forward to seeing her. It had seldom happened that a whole week had gone by between their meetings.

In the first building, there was someone at home in all the apartments except two. No one knew any foreigner who might have lived there at the beginning of March or had ever heard of any alarm call to the fire department. In the next building, there were two foreigners, but one was a Finn and spoke somewhat incomprehensible Swedish and not with the accent Doris Mårtensson had described. The other was an Italian, who had been safely at home in Milan on the seventh of March. Without being asked to, he had got out his passport and shown the date-stamps. Had either of these people acquaintances who were foreigners? Yes, they had lots of friends who were foreigners, and so what?

Yes, one might well ask.

By the time Skacke had cleared the buildings farther up the slope, it was nearly twelve o'clock and he was hungry. He went into a café on the ground floor of one of the high blocks and ordered cocoa and an open-faced cheese sandwich. The place was empty except for Skacke and the waitress. After she had served him, she returned to her counter and stared in a bored way out of the window. Outside was a large square of the type usually found between high buildings in most suburbs on the outskirts of Stockholm, and which is seldom called a square but a shopping center, preferably a piazza, presumably a pathetic attempt by the city planners to give these dismal stone deserts some kind of Mediterranean flavor.

The door opened and a man stepped cautiously inside. He was wearing a blue velvet skullcap on his head and was carrying an empty nylon string bag. He walked slowly across the floor and gave Skacke a crafty look beneath his frowning eyebrows. When he caught sight of the waitress, his brown eyes began to glitter and spreading out his arms he said in lilting Finnish-Swedish:

"Ah, my God, Miss, I've such a terrible hangover

164

today. What's that excellent new soft drink I usually buy?"

"Tom Collins," said the girl.

"Yes, I must have eight cans at once, my dear. But they must be cold. Cold as a Tibetan mountain waterfall."

He handed the bag over to her and she vanished into the back quarters. The man in the skullcap rummaged in his wallet with a troubled expression. Skacke heard a refrigerator door shut and the waitress came back with the net bag full of cans of soft drink.

"I suppose I can't have credit?" asked the man.

"Yes, that'll be all right," said the girl. "You live here, sir, so . . .

"Yes, that'll be quite all right," she repeated, as if bewitched.

The man put his wallet away and took the bag.

"Well, that's excellent then. So perhaps it's not such a terrible day after all."

He moved toward the door. Then he turned round and said:

"You're an angel, Miss. I'll bring the money on Monday. Goodbye."

Skacke pushed his cup away and took the map out of his inside pocket. It was beginning to look rather well-used now and he had had to tape it together at the folds. He crossed out the area around the square. Then he looked at the time and reckoned he would be able to do the buildings down on the other side of the slope before meeting Monica. Then he would have covered a large connected position of the town, as he had already done the older buildings along the main street down the slope. The buildings on the slope were modern but not so tall as those on the hill.

By twenty past two, Skacke had worked his way through all the buildings except the corner one at the bottom of the slope. At that corner was one of the telephone booths in which the notice giving the local fire station number still remained.

In the entrance of this building, a man was standing drinking beer. He thrust the bottle under Skacke's nose and said something which at first was incomprehensible. Then he realized that the man was a Norwegian and saying that he was celebrating the seventeenth of May. Skacke showed the man his identity card and informed him in a stern and authoritative voice that it was forbidden to consume intoxicating liquors on the street. The man looked at Skacke in alarm and Skacke said:

"As you're not Swedish, I shall allow mercy to go before justice this time. Give me the bottle and scram."

The man gave him the half-empty bottle and Skacke poured the remainder of the beer down the drain in the gutter. Then he walked across the road and dropped the bottle into the wastepaper basket. When he turned around, he saw the Norwegian disappearing around the corner with a vacant glance at him over his shoulder.

Skacke took the elevator to the top floor and rang the bells of the three doors there in turn. No one came and he wrote the three names down on his list for another visit. Then he went down to the next floor.

The first door was opened by a lady with henna-colored hair, and glasses with green plastic frames. Her hair was gray at the roots and she looked about sixty. Skacke repeated his piece twice before she understood what he wanted.

"Oh, yes," she said, "I rent one of my rooms. That is, I used to before. A foreigner, did you say? At the beginning of March? Let me see. Yes, I think it was the beginning of March when that Frenchman lived here. Or was he an Arab? I don't really remember."

You could have knocked Skacke down with a feather by this time.

"Arab?" he repeated. "What language did he speak, then?"

"Swedish, though not all that well, of course. But enough so that one could understand him."

"Can you remember exactly when he lived here?"

Skacke had not looked at the name plate on the door before ringing and now he leaned to one side pretending to blow his nose as he glanced at the plate above the letterbox. He just had time to see the name *Borg* before the woman opened the door wide and said:

"Won't you come in?"

He stepped into the hall and closed the door behind him. The red-haired lady went ahead of him into the apartment. She pointed to a blue plush-covered sofa over by the window and Skacke sat down. The woman went over to a desk, opened one of the drawers and took out a cash-book with a reddish-brown cover.

"I can soon tell you when it was," she said, leafing through the book. "I always put the rent down here and that man was the last to take the room, so it shouldn't be difficult ... here it is. On the fourth of March, he paid in advance for a week. But strangely enough, he moved out earlier, after four days. The eighth, that is. He didn't ask for any money back for the remaining three days."

She took the book with her and sat down at the table in front of the sofa.

"It was funny, I thought. Why do you want him? What has he done?"

"We're looking for a person who can perhaps help us with an investigation," said Skacke. "What was his name?"

"Alfonse Lasalle."

She pronounced the *e* in both Alfonse and Lasalle, from which Skacke deduced that she was not very conversant with the French language. Neither was he, for that matter.

"How did it happen that you rented your room to him in particular?" asked Skacke.

"How did it happen? Well, I rented one of my rooms, as I told you. That was before my husband was taken ill and had to be home in the daytime. He didn't want strangers in the house then, so I told the agency to take us off the register until further notice."

"So you received tenants through an agency? What was it called?"

"Svea Agency. It's in Sveavägen. They've been getting tenants for us since 1962, when we first got the apartment here."

Skacke took out his notebook and pen. The woman looked on inquisitively as he wrote.

"What did he look like?" he asked, holding his pen poised in readiness.

The woman tilted her head and looked up at the ceiling.

"Well, how can I put it," she said. "He looked Mediterranean. Dark and rather small. Thick black hair, which grew down his forehead and at his temples. A little taller than me; I'm five foot five. Rather big nose, a little hooked, and quite straight black eyebrows. Quite powerful, but not fat."

"How old do you think he was?"

"Well, thirty-five or so, I should think, perhaps forty. Difficult to say."

"Anything else that you remember about his appearance? Or anything special otherwise?"

She thought for a moment and then shook her head.

"I don't think so. He wasn't here very long, you see. He was polite and seemed well brought-up. Neatly dressed."

"How did he speak?"

"He had an accent like a foreigner, you know. It sounded rather funny."

"Can you describe his accent a bit more? Do you remember anything special that he said?"

"We—ell, I don't know. He said *Mizziz* instead of *Missis* and *café* when he meant *coffee*. It's difficult to remember after such a long time and I can't imitate accents very well."

Skake wondered what he ought to ask next. He bit his pen and looked at the red-haired woman.

"What did he do here? Was he a tourist or was he working? What times did he keep?"

"That's hard to say," said Mrs. Borg. "He didn't have much luggage, just one case. And he went out sometime in the morning and mostly didn't come back until late in the evening. Of course, he had his own key, so I didn't always know when he came in. He was very quiet and discreet."

"Do you usually allow your tenants to use the telephone? Did he make any calls?"

"Not really, allow them to use it, I mean, but if someone had to make a call then of course he could do so. But this Lasalle never did, as far as I know."

"Might he have used the phone without your noticing. Late at night, for instance?"

"Not late at night, anyhow. I've jacks in the hall and in our bedroom and I always move the telephone in there at night."

"Do you remember when he came home on the seventh of March? The last night he was here?"

The woman took off her unbecoming glasses, looked at them, rubbed them on her skirt and then put them on again.

"The last evening," she said, "I don't think I heard him come in then. I usually go to bed at half-past ten or thereabouts, but I'm not absolutely certain about that night."

"Perhaps you'd like to think about it, Mrs. Borg, and I can get in touch with you again and ask you if you remember anything else," said Skacke.

"Yes, certainly," she said. "I'll do that."

He put the telephone number down in his black notebook.

"Mrs. Borg, you said earlier that Lasalle was your last tenant," he said.

"Yes, that's right. Only a few days after he moved out, Josef was taken ill. That's my husband. I had to phone and cancel someone I'd promised the room to."

"May I look at the room?"

"Certainly."

She got up and showed him the way. The door to the room was in the hall, opposite the outer door. The room was about 15 feet square and high, and contained a bed, a bedside table and a large old-fashioned wardrobe with oval mirrors in the doors.

"The toilet is just next door," said the woman. "My husband and I have our bathroom adjoining our bedroom."

Skacke nodded and looked around. The room was as impersonal as a third-rate hotel room. On the table by the armchair was a checked linen cloth, and on the desk an inky blotter. Two prints and a wreath of artificial flowers hung on the walls. The rug, bedspread and curtains were thin and faded after much laundering.

Skacke went across to the window, which faced the

street. He could see the telephone booth on the corner and the wastepaper basket into which he had thrown the Norwegian's beer bottle. Farther down the street, the clock outside a watchmaker's showed ten past three. He looked at his own watch. It was ten past three.

Benny Skacke took a hasty farewell of Mrs. Borg and raced down the stairs, two at a time. In the entrance, he remembered something, rushed into the elevator and went up to the fifth floor again. The woman looked at him in surprise, evidently not expecting him back quite so soon.

"Have you cleaned the room, Mrs. Borg," he asked breathlessly.

"Cleaned? Of course, I've—"

"Dusted and polished? Furniture and all?"

"We-ell I usually clean up just before a guest comes to live in it. There's no point in doing it all that thorough before that. The room may stand empty for several days, weeks sometimes, so I usually strip the bed, empty the ashtray and air the room after someone moves out. What do you mean? Why do you ask?"

"Please don't touch anything. We must come back and see if there are any clues. Fingerprints and all that."

She promised not to go into the room again. Skacke said goodbye and raced headlong down the stairs again.

He ran to his delayed meeting with Monica, wondering at the same time if he had got a bite at last.

When he arrived at the restaurant where Monica had been waiting for twenty-five minutes, in his thoughts he had already been promoted and was yet one more step on toward becoming Chief of Police.

But in Kungsholmsgatan, Gunvald Larsson said:

"What was he wearing?"

And ten seconds later:

"What kind of overcoat did he have? Suit? Shoes? Socks? Shirt? Tie? Did he use hair oil? What were his teeth like? Did he smoke? In that case what and how much? What did his bedclothes look like when he'd slept in them? Did he sleep in pajamas or a night-shirt? Did she give him coffee in the morning? For instance."

And after another thirty seconds:

"Why didn't that fool of a woman send in a registration card as usual when she had a foreigner living with her? Did she look at his passport? Did you frighten the old bitch properly?"

Skacke gave him a shattered look and turned around to go.

"Stop a minute, Racky."

"Yes."

"Get one of those fingerprint boys there immediately."

Skacke went.

"Fool!" said Gunvald Larsson to the closed door.

They found several fingerprints in the room in Sundbyberg. When they had eliminated all those that were Mrs. Borg's and Skacke's, three were left, one of which was a thumbprint preserved in thick greasy hair oil.

On Tuesday, the twenty-first of May, they sent out copies of the fingerprints to Interpol. What else could they do?

25

On Monday after Ascension Day, Martin Beck called up Malmö and asked how things were going.

Hammar was standing 6 feet away from him and had just said:

"Call up Malmö and ask how things are going."

He regretted asking the moment he heard Månsson's voice, for suddenly he remembered the innumerable times over the years when he himself had been the recipient of the same idiotic question. From people in more senior Positions. From the press. From his wife. From foolish colleagues. From inquisitive acquaintances. How are things going?

Nevertheless, he cleared his throat and said:

"Hi. How are things going?"

"We-ell," said Månsson. "When I've anything to tell you, I'll let you know."

Which was, naturally, the reply he deserved.

"Ask him if there are any further developments generally speaking," said Hammar.

"Are there any further developments generally speaking?" said Martin Beck.

"On Olofsson?"

"Yes."

Who's that mumbling away in the background?"

"Hammar."

"Uhuh," said Månsson. "So it's like that is it?"

"Ask him if he's taken the international aspect into consideration," said Hammar.

"Have you taken the international aspect into consideration?" said Martin Beck.

"Yes," said Månsson. "I've taken that into consideration."

There was a moment's silence. Martin Beck coughed embarrassingly. Hammar went out and slammed the door behind him.

"Yes. Listen, I don't really want—"

"Uhuh," said Månsson. "I'm used to that sort of stuff. About Olofsson . . ."

"Yes?"

"He was obviously not very well known down here. But I've a couple of bites. People who at least know who he was. They didn't like him. Say he was a big-mouth and all that. Think he was . . ."

Månsson fell silent again.

"Yes?"

"The usual damned snotty Stockholmer," said Månsson emphatically, in tone of voice which implied that the expression to some extent met with his approval.

"Did they know what he was up to?"

"Yes and no. You see, among all my contacts, I've only found two who knew Olofsson by name and who admit that they've met him a few times. They say he smuggled drugs, but not on a large scale. He appeared down here now and again and they met him only sporadically. They got the impression that he was usually coming from Stockholm when he came here. He was driving a new car and shot his mouth off a lot, but didn't seem to have all that much money. He was seldom in Malmö more than a day or two, but he might appear for several days in a row. None of these guys seems to have met him the last time. One of them was inside anyhow last winter and didn't come out until Spril."

Silence. Martin Beck said nothing. At long last Månsson began to speak again.

"Well, this isn't by any means cleared up yet, so it's hardly worth telling you what little I know. I've got a bit of information, but none of it hangs together. Some of it I got from these two contacts and some I've rooted out for myself."

"Yes, I understand," said Martin Beck.

"He often went to Poland," said Månsson. "That's clear. The suit he was wearing came from there, by the way."

"Which means he presumably sold the cars there?"

"Yes, possibly," said Månsson. "But the question is whether we're any the wiser for that. More important is . . ."

He stopped.

"What?"

"That Malm and Olofsson met here on different occasions seems to be a fact too. Anyhow, they were seen together here."

"Oh, yes."

"Yes, but not this year. Malm was better known here than Olofsson. And people liked him better. Both my informers have met them together at least once or twice and they got the impression they were working together. . . . Well, that wasn't what I meant. Which was important, I mean."

"Wasn't it?"

"There's a lot that's obscure," said Månsson hesitantly. "For instance, Olofsson must have lived somewhere while he was here. Either rented a room or lived with someone. But I haven't been able to find out where or with whom."

"No, it won't be that easy."

"Oh, well, I'll find out, I expect. In time. Where Malm hung out when he was here, I do know. He used to stay at small flop houses down on the west

173

side. Round about Västergatan and Mäster Johansgatan, you know."

Martin Beck did not know Malmö well and the places meant nothing to him.

"Good," he said, for lack of anything better to say.

"Oh, that was easy," said Månsson. "I don't think it's important. This other thing, on the other hand."

Martin Beck began to feel slightly irritated.

"What other thing?"

"Well, where Olofsson lived."

"Perhaps he stayed a few hours, now and again. On his way through, or to meet up with Malm."

"We-ell," said Månsson. "I don't think so. He had a lair somewhere. But where?"

"How the hell would I know? And how do you know, anyhow?"

"He had a dame here," said Månsson.

"What? A girl?"

"Yes. Exactly. He's been seen with her several times, on widely different occasions, timewise. First time at least eighteen months ago, and last time that I know of just before Christmas."

"We must find her."

"That's just what I'm doing now," said Månsson. "I know a bit about her, what she looks like and all that, but I don't know her name or where she lives."

He was silent for a moment. Then he said:

"Strange."

"What is?"

"That I can't find her. If she's around here in town, then I ought to be able to get hold of her."

"I can think of plenty of explanations," said Martin Beck. "Perhaps she's not from Malmö. A Stockholm girl, for instance. Perhaps she's not even Swedish."

"We-ell," said Månsson. "I think she's from here. Well, we'll see. I'll get hold of her."

"D'you think so?"

"Yes, sure. But it may take some time. I'm going on vacation in June, by the way."

"Oh, yes," said Martin Beck.

"Yes. But after that I'll go on looking for her, of course," said Månsson quietly. "When I find her, I'll let you know. That's it for now."

174

"Bye," said Martin Beck automatically.

He remained sitting with the telephone receiver in his hand for a long time, although the other man had already hung up. He sighed and blew his nose.

Månsson was clearly a person it was wise to leave alone to do things his own way.

26

On Saturday the first of June, Månsson flew to Rumania with his wife. He had marked down his three-week vacation with great care and did not come back until after the Midsummer holiday, on Monday the twenty-fourth, to be exact.

He must have taken his knowledge of the case of the drowned man with him, as well as his thoughts and possible theories on Olofsson's life and miserable activities, for in general nothing much was heard from Malmö, and literally nothing of interest to Martin Beck.

Månsson was by no means the only person on leave in June. Despite diverse obscure intimations that the police ought not perhaps to take their vacations until after the elections, the force had thinned out, or at least those in command had, with astonishing swiftness. General elections were to be held in September, so July and August could be expected to be trying months and most policemen attempted to transform their regulation holidays from theory into practice. Melander retreated to his cottage on Värmdö and Gunvald Larsson and Rönn discreetly disappeared to Arjeplog where they allowed themselves to be illuminated by the midnight sun and spent the fine summer nights fishing.

They talked mostly about grayling and salmon-trout and different kinds of flies and bait. Now and again Rönn's face might suddenly cloud over and he did not reply when spoken to. On these occasions, he was thinking about the fire engine that had disappeared, but he never mentioned it.

Hammar just thought about his coming retirement and that nothing must happen before that.

Martin Beck meditated on the fact that he was even indifferent to whether he had a vacation or not. He sat out in Västberga and filled his day with routine work, devoting his free time mainly to trying to think out how he could manage to avoid celebrating the Midsummer holiday with his wife and brother-in-law.

Kollberg was Acting Chief Inspector and had been transferred to the Stockholm Homicide Squad and was enjoying both situations equally little. He hated the ovenlike office in Kungsholmsgatan and sweated and swore—in between times thinking about wanting to be at home with his wife and that that was the only thing he enjoyed nowadays.

Melander was outside his summer cottage, chopping wood and thinking lovingly of his plain wife, who was lying naked sunbathing on a blanket behind the outhouse.

In Euphoria on the Black Sea, Mansson was looking dully at the dove-gray Potemkin horizon and wondering how they had been able to achieve socialism and manage their five-year plan in three years in a country where it was 104 degrees in the shade and they did not have grape soda.

Eighteen hundred miles farther north, Gunvald Larsson was putting on his boots and sports jacket and glancing sourly at Rönn's machine-knitted woolen sweater, which was red and blue and green and awful and had elks on the front.

Rönn did not notice, as he was occupied thinking about that fire engine at the time.

Benny Skacke was sitting in his office checking a report he had just written. He was wondering how long it would take him to become Chief of Police and where in that case he would be.

Everyone was thinking his own thoughts.

No one was thinking about Malm or Olofsson or the fourteen-year-old girl who had been roasted alive in the attic of the house in Sköldgatan.

At least, it did not seem so.

On this Midsummer Eve, Friday the twenty-first of June, Martin Beck did something which made him feel actually criminal for the first time since he was fifteen and had forged his mother's signature on a sick-excuse note in order to be able to play truant from school and go to look at Hitler's pocket-battleship which was on a visit to Stockholm.

What he did was reasonably insignificant and would to most people have seemed wholly natural. In actual fact, it was not even criminal, as it is not a crime to tell a lie, as long as one does not first put one's hand on the Bible and promise to tell the truth.

He quite simply told his wife that he could not come with her and Rolf because he had been given an assignment which obliged him to be on duty over the holiday.

This was an outright lie and he had told it in a loud and clear voice while looking his wife straight in the eye. In the summer sun, on the longest and most beautiful day of the year. On top of this, the lie was the result of conspiracy and plot, insofar as another person was involved and had promised to keep quiet if there were any awkward questions.

This person was the Acting Chief Inspector.

His name was Sten Lennart Kollberg and his role as investigator was too obvious even to be called ambiguous.

The background to the plot could be said to be divided into two parts: First, Martin Beck's profound distaste in face of the prospect of two or at worst three loathsome days with his wife and his tippling brother-in-law, days which seemed even more intolerable as his daughter Ingrid was in Leningrad on some kind of language course, and so would not be on hand to lighten his mood. Second, Kollberg had free access to his in-laws' summer cottage in Sörmland and had already transported considerable quantities of food and life-giving drink out there.

Although he thus had good, anyhow justifiable, reasons for his behavior, Martin Beck took his lie very much to heart. He realized that he did not usually behave badly and so was singularly unfamiliar with the situation. Long afterward he would also see that this moment contained the origins of a belated change in his whole life. This had nothing to do with the fact that he was a policeman, as there is nothing to indicate that policemen in general lie any less than anyone else, or Swedish police any less than foreign ones. Available data, in fact, point to the opposite being true.

For Martin Beck it was entirely a question of personal ethics; he was taking a stand and justifying it to himself, and thus he had upset certain fundamental personal values. Whether that would entail a profit or loss in his own private balance sheet, only the future would tell.

Anyhow, for the very first time for a very long time, he had an enjoyable and almost trouble-free holiday weekend. The only thing that troubled him was the lie, but without much difficulty he allowed it to fade into the background for the time being.

Kollberg was outstanding as an organizer and conspirator and the company was extremely well chosen. The word *police* was not mentioned many times and their daily work, the detestable and all-overshadowing Service, was largely banished from the festive scene.

Except on one occasion when Martin Beck was sitting in the grass in the slow soft dusk, together with Åsa Torell and Kollberg and some others, looking at the maypole which they had erected and even danced around. They were somewhat exhausted and thoroughly bitten by midges by this time and Martin Beck's thoughts wandered.

"Do you think we'll ever find out who that guy in Sundbyberg really was?" he said.

And Kollberg said, very definitely: "Nix."

And Åsa Torell: "Which guy in Sundbyberg?"

She was an alert young lady, with varying qualities and inquisitive about most things.

And Kollberg said suddenly:

"Yeah—you know what I think? I think this whole case will explode in our faces. Just as it began."

He drank deeply from his wine glass, threw out his arms and said:

"Like that. Boom! Just as it began and then everything'll be over."

And Åsa Torell said:

"Oh that. Now I know what you're talking about. Right in the face of whom?"

"Me, of course," said Kollberg. "I'm the only one who is totally uninterested in it. Anyhow, I'll shoot you dead if you begin talking about policemen."

She was in fact going to join the police.

On another occasion, she and Martin Beck exchanged a few remarks on that particular subject.

He asked: "This business of joining the force, was it an idea you had because Åke was killed?"

She twirled her cigarette thoughtfully between her fingers and said:

"Well, not exactly. I just want to get a different job. A new kind of life. And I also think they're needed."

"What? Girls who join the police force?"

"Sensible people who want to do so," she said. "Think of all the fools there are in the force."

Then she shrugged her shoulders, smiled swiftly and went away, padding barefoot through the grass.

She was a slenderly built woman with large brown eyes and short dark hair.

Nothing else of interest happened, and on Sunday Martin Beck went home, still with a slight hangover, but contented and without too much on his conscience.

The plane which dispatched Per Månsson from the roasting-hot airport in Constanta to the considerably more airy Bulltofta in Malmö was a shining silver Ilyushin 18 turbo-prop plane from Tarom. As the wind was in the southeast and quite strong, the plane flew in a wide circle out over Öresund before it began to descend, finally to flatten out over Swedish country. It was a lovely summer's day and from his window seat he could see Saltholm and Copenhagen quite clearly, and no fewer than five passenger steamers which appeared to be standing still with their white bow waves petrified along the busy route between Malmö and Denmark. A little later he saw Industrihammen, out of which he had been involved in hauling an old car and a corpse nearly three months earlier, but as he was not yet on duty, he stopped thinking about that.

That he was looking so fixedly out of the window was mainly due to the fact that he did not want to look at his wife. He had in fact fallen in love with her again after the first rollicking days, but now, after three weeks of being together daily, they were sick of each other and he felt the strong draw of his bachelor apartment in Regementsgatan, of lone evenings with a toothpick in the corner of his mouth and a frosty Gripenberger within reach. Neither was it untrue that he was looking forward to the dismal view out over the asphalt lot of the police station.

Malmö was not in any way so idyllic and quiet as it may have appeared from the air. On the contrary, it seemed to Månsson that even in his first week on duty he was being drawn into a veritable whirlpool of crime, every imaginable offense from political disturbances and knife-fights to a formidable bank raid, which had been planned in Malmö and had the police forces of half the country up to their ears until it had been tied up.

He had a great deal to do, and so it was not until the third Monday in July that he seriously came to think about Olofsson again. Late in the evening on that day, he drew on the consequences of what he had seen during his landing in Malmö and completed a chain of thought which obscurely and unconsciously had already begun on the plane.

It was very simple and appeared almost self-evident now that he had at last succeeded in linking it together.

It was half-past eleven at night and he had just mixed himself a drink. Without thinking about what he was doing, he drank it down in one draft, got up out of his armchair and went to bed.

He was certain that within a short time he would find the answer to the question which had irritated him most in the whole Olofsson case.

27

The first half of July was cool and wet. Many vacationers, encouraged by the lovely hot June weather, decided to enjoy the fine Swedish summer instead of traveling to southern Europe, and then had sat dismally swearing and staring out at the rain through dripping tent-flaps and trailer doors, while dreaming of sun-drenched Mediterranean beaches. But when in the middle of the second week of the holidays, the sun rose quiveringly hot into the clear blue sky and the moisture from the rain steamed from the fragrant soil and vegetation, curses ceased raining down on the fatherland and proud Swedes put on their bright leisure clothes and prepared to conquer the countryside. Shining bright vehicles bowled along the roads, at the sides of which families with camping gear and picnic cases, thermos bottles and packs of food had moved out of their cars for a brief spell to settle among the roadside refuse. Smothered in dust and fumes, they listened to the unending wail of their transistors while commenting on the cars driving by, looking at the dusty and languishing vegetation on the other side of the road and sympathizing with the poor people who had to remain in town.

Martin Beck did not need anyone's sympathy. At least, not because he had been forced to remain in Stockholm and work in July. On the contrary, this was the time he liked being in the city most. He usually avoided taking his vacation just then, for despite everything he loved his native city and liked being able to move around it without being hustled, or having to hurry, or being pushed about, or feeling threatened by the increasingly dominating traffic and half-suffocated by its poisonous fumes. He liked strolling around empty streets in the center of the city on a hot July Sunday or walking along the quays on a cool evening, feeling the evening breeze bringing with it the smell of freshly cut hay from some meadow by the Mälar or a breath of the sea and seaweed from the islands.

On Tuesday, the sixteenth of July, however, he was doing neither of these things, but was sitting in his shirtsleeves at his desk in Västberga feeling bored. During the morning he had completed a case of homicide that was as clear and unmistakable as it was sad and meaningless. A Yugoslav and a Finn had been drinking together on a camping-site; they had quarreled and the Finn had stabbed the Yugoslav with a sheath knife in front of a dozen or so bewildered witnesses. The Finn had managed to get away from the site of the crime, but had been caught the same evening in an empty railway car at Central Station. He had a long list of crimes behind him, both in Finland and in Sweden, and had also entered the country illegally, as only a month before he had been deported for two years.

After that, Martin Beck had cleared up a lot of routine work and was now sitting staring listlessly out of the window. Kollberg was still Acting Chief Inspector and had his temporary office in Kungsholmen. Skacke was out somewhere; Martin Beck himself had sent him on some errand, but he could not remember what. He heard steps in the corridor, doors slamming, the clatter of typewriters and voices from adjoining rooms and wondered for a moment whether to go and ask if anyone would like to come out for a cup of coffee, but then he didn't, as he really had no desire to.

Martin Beck lifted his blotter and picked up the list of things to remember that he kept there. He had in fact a very good memory, but sometime ago he had thought he noticed that it had begun to deteriorate and decided to note down anything that he was not able to tackle immediately, but which would have to be done later. The doubtful part of this method was that he kept forgetting the list existed and for long stretches of time it lay in its hiding-place without his giving it a thought.

All the items on the list except two had already been dealt with without his having to look. He picked up his ballpoint pen and crossed them out, while he tried to remember what the name placed at the top of the list meant. Ernst Sigurd Karlsson. At the bottom stood Zachrisson. Zachrisson anyway, was a policeman, whom he had thought of asking for a more thorough description of what Malm had done when he was being shadowed. The other man who had shared the job of trailing Malm had already reported in detail, but Zachrisson had only been questioned in passing soon after the fire. And now he was on leave.

Martin Beck lit a Florida, leaned back and blew smoke straight up at the ceiling.

"Ernst Sigurd Karlsson," he said half-aloud to himself.

At that moment he remembered who the man was. A man quite unknown to him had written his name on a pad before shooting himself. Martin Beck still did not know why. In itself it was not all that remarkable that people he did not know knew him. As a Chief Inspector and investigator into murders, he was often mentioned in the papers and he had several times been forced to appear on television.

He put the list back under the blotter. Then he got up and walked across to the door. A cup of tea would go down well after all, he thought.

On Monday, the twenty-second of July, Zachrisson came back from his vacation and Martin Beck had contacted him at once in the morning.

Now he was sitting in Martin Beck's room in Västberga, clearing his throat and reading aloud in a monotonous voice from a notebook. Times and places followed a somewhat tedious pattern. Now and again the man looked up and filled in with what he could remember seeing.

Göran Malm's last ten days were imprinted with melancholy and monotony. Most of the day he had spent in two beer cafés in Hornsgatan. He had nearly always gone home alone, half-drunk, and at about eight-o'clock. On two occasions he had bought liquor and had taken a prostitute with him. It was obvious that he had been very short of money. Olofsson's death must have left him in a difficult situation. The day before Malm died, Zachrisson had seen him standing outside one of his regular haunts for nearly an hour, begging money to be able to go in and have a beer.

"So he was quite broke?" mumbled Martin Beck.

"He tried to borrow some money the same day he died," said Zachrisson. "I think so anyhow. He went to someone in . . ."

He turned a page in his notebook.

"At nine-forty on the seventh of March he left Sköldgatan and went to number 4 Karlviksgatan."

"Karlviksgatan," said Martin Beck to himself.

"Yes, In Kungsholmen. He took the elevator up to the fourth floor and after a few minutes came out again. He looked nervous and peculiar, which was why I thought he'd been trying to borrow money from someone, who had either been out or had refused him."

Zachrisson looked at Martin Beck as if expecting praise for this effort of deduction. But Martin Beck was staring past him, and said:

"Number 4 Karlviksgatan. Where have I heard that before?"

Then he looked at Zachrisson and said:

"You've probably been through this before, haven't you?"

Zachrisson nodded.

"For Chief Inspector Kollberg at least," he said. "Because he told me to check the names of everyone who lived in the building."

"Yes?"

Zachrisson looked in his book.

"There weren't many," he said. "Seved Blom, A. Svensson, Ernst Sigurd Karlsson . . ."

Karlviksgatan is a short and not very well-known street running from Norr Mälarstrand to Hantverkargatan, quite near Fridhemsplan. It took Martin Beck ten minutes to get there by car.

He did not know what to expect, as Ernst Sigurd Karlsson had been dead for four and a half months.

Three flights up there was indeed SEVED BLOM and A. SVENSSON on two of the doors, but on the third was a new plate, with the name SKOG. Martin Beck rang the bell, but no one came to the door. He rang the bell next door.

As soon as Martin Beck had got rid of Zachrisson, he had called up the policemen who had been to Ernst Sigurd Karlsson's apartment on the morning after his suicide. From them he had, among other things, found out who had called the police.

Captain Seved Blom let Martin Beck in immediately and began to tell him how he had been sitting playing solitaire when he had heard the shot. He was clearly delighted to be able to relate his dramatic story all over again and described in detail everything that had happened. Martin Beck heard him out and then finally asked:

"What do you know about the dead man? Did you usually talk to him?"

"No. We greeted each other when we happened to meet, but nothing more. He appeared to be a withdrawn person."

"Did you ever see any of his friends?"

Captain Blom shook his head.

"He didn't seem to have any. It was always quiet in there and no one ever came to visit him. Yet, strangely enough, someone he knew came to see him the same morning. That morning. A seedy little man. I was just taking the garbage out, the ambulance had gone and all the policemen had left too. Well, then, there was that man standing there, ringing the bell. I asked him who he was looking for and all that, and when I realized he was a

184

close acquaintance of his, I told him what had happened. And that he could go to see the police if he wanted to know anything more."

"Did you tell him Karlsson had committed suicide?"

"We-ell ... I said he was dead, anyhow, and that the police had been there."

When Martin Beck got back to Västberga, he sat smoking and thinking for a long time before calling up Hammar.

"This is getting crazier and crazier," said Hammar. "It would be a good thing for once if you could find someone involved in this case who is alive. What are you going to get out of all this? And why did the man write your name down before killing himself?"

"I think that Karlsson and Olofsson and Malm belonged to the same—well, shall we call it gang? And Karlsson for some reason wanted to get out. He thought of calling up the police and had perhaps heard of me and so wrote down my name. Then he changed his mind. I don't know what part he played in the gang. How do you think that sounds?"

"I think the whole mess sounds like a schoolboy's story," said Hammar. "Now we've three dead men, one murdered, one both murdered and committed suicide and one who only committed suicide. How do you explain this suicidal psychosis?"

Martin Beck sighed.

"I presume Malm began to get nervous and finally looked up Karlsson to ask him if he knew where Olofsson had got to. When he heard that Karlsson was dead, then he felt impelled to take his own life."

There was a moment's silence.

"Yes," said Hammar. "It could have been like that. But I've never been on a case with so many ifs and buts and perhapses and presumablys. We don't know much for certain. We'll have to have a meeting soon. I'll call and get it fixed."

He put the receiver down.

Martin Beck sat for a moment with his hand on the telephone receiver, trying to imagine what Kolberg would say. Before he had time to lift the receiver, the telephone rang.

"Bingo!" said Kollberg.

"What?" Martin Beck asked.

"Reply from Interpol. Lasalle's fingerprints."

"Oh, hell. Well?"

"Well, they recognize that thumb, but not the name Alfonse Lasalle."

"Whose thumbprint is it then?"

"Just a moment, will you? The man with the thumb has many aliases. The French police know him as the following: Albert Corbier, Alfonse Benette, Samir Riffi, Alfred Laffey, Auguste Cassin and Auguste Dupont. They're sending more names later. They don't know who he is but think he has Lebanese citizenship and that he's spent most of his time lately in France and North Africa. They think it is evident that he was a member of the OAS earlier. He's suspected of a whole string of crimes or complicity in crimes. Drug-trafficking, currency-smuggling and plenty more, murder among them."

"Has he never been caught?"

"Apparently not. Sounds a slippery devil. He obviously changes passports and names and nationality more often than his underpants and they've still got no real evidence against him."

"Description then?"

"Well, it's not all that clear. They've sent one, but say it need not necessarily fit. Nice of them. Let me see, now. Yes, age about thirty-five, height five ten, weight hundred and sixty, black hair, good teeth, wait . . . this is in French and I've not had time to translate it yet . . . straight hair-line, thick straight eyebrows, slightly hooked nose with a three-quarter-inch, scarcely visible scar on the left nostril, otherwise no known physical defects or special marks of recognition."

"Yes, that fits well with Lasalle. They don't know where he is, of course?"

"No. I'll call back in a while. Must get this translated and written down."

Martin Beck remained sitting with the silent receiver in his hand. As he put it down, he remembered that he had not had time to tell Kollberg about Ernst Sigurd Karlsson.

28

Månsson went to Copenhagen on Tuesday morning, the twenty-third of July. As he considered speed essential, he took one of the hovercraft ferries. It was called *The Flying Fish* and covered the stretch across the strait in exactly thirty-five minutes. Otherwise, it was no fun at all. One sits there, shaking in an airplane seat and without a window seat, the prospects of catching even a passing glimpse of the water are remote.

As far as Denmark was concerned, Månsson's international connections were excellent. He slipped past all ordinary obstacles and interstate complications and walked straight up to a police inspector named Mogensen and said:

"Hello. I'm looking for a woman. I don't know her name."

"Hello, yourself," said Mogensen. "What does she look like?"

"She's got short curly fair hair and blue eyes. Strong features, wide mouth, good teeth and a dimple in her chin. About five feet eight, broad shoulders and hips, narrow waist. Strong short legs and well-shaped calves. She's about thirty-five. Swedish. Certainly from Skåne, probably from Malmö."

"Sounds delightful," said Mogensen.

"I'm not sure about that. She usually wears long dark knitted sweaters and long trousers or short checked skirts, the latter probably, at this time of year. She wears very wide belts, which seem to be pulled very tight around her waist. It's not out of the question that she takes drugs. She may have some kind of artistic connection. People who have seen her say that she's always got paint or something like it on her hands."

"Good," said Mogensen.

And that was that.

Månsson's good relationship with this man went far back in time. They had known each other since the end of the war, when Mogensen had gone to Trelleborg from

Germany. He was one of approximately two thousand Danish policeman arrested by the Gestapo during the great raid on the nineteenth of September, 1944, and taken off to German concentration camps.

They had kept contact ever since then; their connection was informal and practical and useful on both sides. What would have taken Mänsson six months to find out if he had gone through the usual channels, Mogensen could arrange in a day. And when Mogensen wanted something definite in Malmö, Månsson generally managed to find it in a couple of hours. The time-difference was due to the fact that Copenhagen is actually four times the size of Malmö.

It is part of good Scandinavian relations to say that cooperation between the Swedish and the Danish police is extremely good. In practice, however, it is otherwise, to some extent due to language difficulties.

That Swedes and Danes understand each other's languages with the minimum of effort is a truth which over the years has been carefully cherished at high levels in both countries. But this is often a truth with modification, and even more often something much more serious, an attack of wishful thinking, for instance, or an illusion. Or to put it bluntly, a lie.

Two of the many victims of this wishful thinking were Hammar and a prominent Danish criminologist, who had known each other for many years and wrestled together at numerous police conferences. They were good friends and each used to make high-sounding statements on how they both mastered each other's language with the greatest of ease, which any other normal Scandinavian ought to be able to do anyhow, a sarcastic addendum they seldom neglected to make.

This was so until, after a decade of hobnobbing at conferences and other high-level meetings, they met for a weekend at Hammar's country cottage, when it turned out that they could not even communicate with each other on the simplest everyday matters. When the Dane asked to borrow a map, Hammar went and fetched a photograph of himself, and then it was all over. Part of their universe had collapsed and after celebrating formal orgies of foolish misunderstandings for a few hours, they went over to speaking English and discovered that they did not really like each other at all.

Part of the secret of the good relations between Månsson and Mogensen was that they did in fact understand each other. Neither of them was sufficiently presumptuous to think that he would understand the other's language just like that, and consequently they spoke to each other in so-called Scandinavian, a homemade mixture which they were almost the only ones to understand. In addition, they were both good policemen and neither of them was of a disposition to complicate matters.

At half-past two in the afternoon, Månsson went back to the police station in Polititorvet in Copenhagen and received a paper on which was typed a name and address.

A quarter of an hour later, he was standing outside an old apartment block in Læderstræde, comparing the words on the piece of paper with the faded number above a narrow dark entrance. He went through it, continued up an outside wooden staircase, which sagged precariously under his weight, and finally arrived at a peeling door with no name plate.

He knocked on the door and a woman opened it.

She was small and sturdy, but well built, with broad shoulders and hips, narrow waist and good strong legs. About thirty-five years old, with fair curly hair cut short, wide sensual mouth, blue eyes and a dimple in her chin. She was bare-legged and barefooted and was wearing a paint-smeared coverall which had once been white. Under the coverall, she was wearing a black pullover sweater. More than that he could not see, as the coverall was tightly drawn at the waist by a broad leather belt. Behind her he could just see a kitchen. It was dark and very small.

She stared inquiringly at him and then said in typical Malmöese:

"Who might you be?"

Månsson did not answer her question.

"Is your name Nadja Eriksson?"

"Yes."

"Did you know Bertil Olofsson?"

"Yes."

Then she repeated her first remark.

"Who might you be?"

"Sorry," said Månsson. "I just wanted to check that I'd come to the right place. My name is Per Månsson and I work for the police in Malmö."

"The police? What are the Swedish police doing here? You've no right to push your way in here."

"No, you're quite right. I've no warrant or anything like that. I just want to talk to you for a moment. And I only wanted to tell you who I was. If you don't want to talk, then I'll go away again."

She looked at him for a moment, thoughtfully poking her ear with a yellow pencil. Finally she said:

"What do you want?"

"Just to talk, as I said."

"About Bertil?"

"Yes."

She wiped her forehead with the sleeve of her coverall and bit her lower lip.

"I'm not that keen on the police," she said.

"You can regard me as—"

"What?" she interrupted. "A private person? The neighbor's cat?"

"Whichever you like," said Månsson.

She laughed huskily and suddenly.

"Go ahead," she said. "Come on in."

Then she turned around and crossed the minute kitchen. As Månsson followed, he noticed that her feet were dirty.

Beyond the kitchen was a large studio with slanting windows, which could not truthfully be called unclean. Pictures, newspapers, tubes of paint, paintbrushes and clothes lay scattered all over the place. The furniture consisted of a large table, a few wooden chairs, two large cupboards and a bed. On the walls hung posters and pictures, and on pedestals and stands stood pieces of sculpture, of which several were wound around with wet cloths, and one clearly just being created. On the bed lay a small dark-skinned youth wearing a string undershirt and underpants. He had curly black hair on his chest and a silver crucifix on a chain around his neck.

Månsson looked around at the disorder. It was untidy, but it appeared singularly lived in. He threw an inquiring look at the figure on the bed.

"You don't have to bother about him," said the woman.

"He can't understand what we say anyhow. For that matter I can get rid of him."

"Not for my sake," said Månsson.

"You'd better run along, baby," she said.

The young man on the bed got up at once, picked a pair of khaki trousers up off the floor, pulled them on and left.

"Ciao," he said.

"He's queer," the woman said laconically.

Månsson looked timidly at the sculpture. As far as he could make out, it represented an erect penis, stuck through in all directions with old screws and rusty bits of iron.

"This is just a model," she said. "It should really be three hundred feet high."

She frowned thoughtfully.

"Isn't it awful?" she said. "Do you think anyone will buy it?"

Månsson thought about the public works of art which ornamented his native city.

"Yes, why not?" he said.

"What do you know about me?" she said, thrusting another bit of iron into the sculpture with a glint of sadistic enjoyment.

"Very little."

"There isn't much to know," she said. "I've lived here for ten years. I do this sort of thing. But I'll never be famous."

"You knew Bertil Olofsson?"

"Yes," she said calmly. "I did."

"Do you know he's dead?"

"Yes. The newspapers had a bit about it a few months ago. Is that why you're here?"

Månsson nodded.

"What do you want to know?"

"Everything."

"That's rather a lot," she said.

There was a moment's silence. She picked up a wooden club with a short handle and thumped the sculpture a few times with no noticeable effect. Then she scratched her curly blonde head and frowned, standing with her head bowed, gazing at her feet. She was quite nice-looking.

191

There was a kind of confident maturity about her which appealed very much to Månsson.

"Do you want to sleep with me?" she said suddenly.

"Yes," said Månsson. "Why not?"

"Good. It'll be easier to talk afterward. If you open the cupboard over there you'll find a pair of clean sheets on the top shelf. I'll lock the outer door and get washed. Especially my feet. Toss the dirty linen into the bag over there."

Månsson fetched the newly laundered sheets and made the bed. Then he sat down on the bed, threw his chewed toothpick onto the floor and began to unbutton his shirt.

She walked through the room wearing black clogs, a towel flung over her shoulder. So far as he could see, she had no scars on her arms or on her thighs, and in general no special markings on her body.

She sang as she showered.

29

The telephone rang at three minutes past eight on Friday the twenty-sixth of July. It was the middle of the summer and very hot. Martin Beck had taken off his jacket and begun to roll up his shirtsleeves the moment he entered the office. He picked up the receiver and said:

"Yes. Beck."

"Månsson here. Hi. I've found that girl."

"Good. Where are you now?"

"In Copenhagen."

"Yes."

"And what have you found out?"

"Quite a lot. For instance, Olofsson was here on the afternoon of the seventh of February. But there's too much to tell you over the phone."

"You'd better come up here."

"Yes, I thought that too."

"Can't you bring the woman with you?"

"Should hardly think she'd come. And it's not necessary. But I can always ask her."

"When did you find her?"

"Last Tuesday. I've had time to talk to her quite a bit. I'm going up to Kastrup now and asking for a standby flight. I'll take the first plane to Arlanda."

"Good," said Martin Beck, replacing the receiver.

Thoughtfully, he stroked his chin. Månsson had seemed strangely confident, and he had also voluntarily offered to come to Stockholm. He really must have found something.

Månsson arrived at the police station in Kungsholmsgatan just before one, sunburned, calm, pleased, and casually dressed in sandals, khaki trousers with a checked shirt hanging outside them.

He had no lady accompanying him, but he did have a cassette tape recorder which he placed on the table. Then he looked around and said:

"Helluva great crowd here. ... Hi! ... Good afternoon."

Since he had called from Arlanda half an hour earlier, an illustrious gathering of detectives had collected. Hammar and Melander and Gunvald Larsson and Rönn. Plus supporting troops from Västberga, i.e., Martin Beck, Kollberg and Skacke.

"Aren't you going to applaud as well?"

Martin Beck was suffering dreadfully in the crush. He wondered how the hell Månsson, a man two or more years older than himself, could appear so fit and contented.

Månsson laid his hand on the tape recorder and said:

"It's like this. The woman's name is Nadja Eriksson. She is thirty-seven years old and a sculptress. Born and bred in Arlöv, but lived in Denmark for more than ten years. Arlöv is a place just outside Malmö. Now we'll hear what she has to say."

He switched on the tape recorder and it sounded slightly odd to hear himself speaking.

"Conversation with Anna Desirée Eriksson, born on the sixth of May 1931, in Malmö. Sculptress. Unmarried. Known as Nadja."

Martin Beck pricked up his ears. That Rönn had sniggered was quite clear, but had Månsson not sniggered too, on the tape? Well, anyhow, he continued by saying:

"Shall we summarize all this about Bertil Olofsson?"

"Yes, of course. Wait a moment, though."

The woman spoke with a Skåne accent, but not in a whining manner. Her voice was deep and clear and resonant. There was a rustle on the tape. Then Nadja Eriksson said:

"Well, I met him almost two years ago. The first time in September 1966 and the last time at the beginning of February this year. He came here regularly, mostly once at the beginning of each month, staying one or two days. Never more than three. He used to come about the fifth and go again on the seventh or eighth. When he was here in Copenhagen, he lived with me, never anywhere else, as far as I know."

"And why did he come so regularly?"

"He had a kind of timetable which he had to stick to. Every time he was here he came from abroad, usually via Malmö. Sometimes he might come by air or on one of the ferries from the Continent. And then he stayed a couple of days. He came here to meet someone . . . he simply had time to fill up once a month."

"What did Olofsson do?"

"He called himself a businessman. And he was in some ways. Thieves are businessmen too, aren't they? For the first six months that I knew him, he said nothing about what he did or where he came from. But then he began to talk. It seemed to come out then. He was the kind of person who simply couldn't keep his mouth shut. He boasted. I'm not an inquisitive person and I think it was just the fact that I never questioned him which made him shoot his mouth off. Finally, as I said nothing, he got to the bursting point. Shall I go into all that about . . . God, it's hot . . ."

Månsson turned his toothpick over with his tongue, unashamedly scratched himself in the crotch and said:

"There's a brief interruption here. Technical fault."

After thirty seconds' dead silence, the woman's voice came back:

"Yes, Bertil was a poor bastard. He had a peasant's shrewdness but generally speaking he was stupid and boastful. I understood him to be a person who couldn't take success. He was that kind of person—the most insignificant success went to his head. For instance, if he earned a little money or found out something that he thought no one else knew. He always had tremendous plans, prattling about the big break that was coming his way and so on. Besides, he overestimated his own intelligence that way, and by no means modestly either. When he once realized that I more or less understood what he did and what sort of businessman he was, he grew inclined to make himself out to be a real big-shot gangster and began talking about million kronor deals and killing people with bicycle chains and that sort of thing. In actual fact, he wasn't all that successful, as I said."

"If we try to consolidate what he did and presume that . . ."

Månsson left the words hanging in the air and a few seconds elapsed before she replied . . .

"I think I know exactly what he was up to. He and two other men worked at getting hold of stolen cars in Stockholm. Some they stole themselves and the rest they bought off other thieves for some piddling sum. Then they fixed those cars so that no one would recognize them and drove them to the Continent, mostly to Poland, I think. The person who received the cars didn't pay them in money, but with something else. Mostly jewelry or loose stones, diamonds and so on. I know that, because Bertil even gave me one, last autumn, when he thought he was going to become a millionaire and was splurging a bit. But this business wasn't their idea at all. They were just underlings. The firm's Stockholm branch, he used to say, the fool. That was why he had to come here to Copenhagen once a month. He was to hand over the valuables he got for the cars to someone who gave him money instead. The guy who came with the money was a messenger too. He came from Paris or Madrid, or somewhere like that. I don't really know much about that side of it, because I never met him. Even Olofsson had that much sense. He never let me even see the guy with the money and he never told anyone where he lived. He was darned keen on that, keeping me out of that part of the affair. I think it was a sort of reverse outlet for him. He'd got himself somewhere to live which no one knew about except him. I never introduced Bertil to anyone, in fact, and I didn't let a single person in when he was here. In Copenhagen, into my apartment, I mean. No one, not even the pol—"

The voice was cut off.

"That recorder's a bit tricky," said Månsson, unmoved, "I borrowed it off the Danes."

When the woman came back on the tape, her voice sounded different, but it was not easy to say in what way.

"Where was I? Yes, not even the police would have a chance of finding me if Bertil hadn't dragged me over to Malmö a few times. He was forced to go there to meet his partner, as he called him, some poor guy called Girre or something. Malm, his name was, I think. He drove the cars too, from Stockholm or Ystad or Trelleborg and then over the border. In between times he worked in a garage somewhere and resprayed the cars and fixed them up with false license plates. So I went to Malmö four or five times, mostly because I was curious. Anyhow, it was just as deadly each time. They sat in some room and drank and boasted and played whist with different so-called business friends and I sat there yawning in a corner. The reason why Bertil had to go there, as far as I could make out, was that Malm was broke and had to have money to get back to Stockholm. And that he was stupid enough to drag me with him was because he wanted to shoot his mouth off a little discreetly to his buddies. Do you think . . ."

Another break. Månsson yawned and changed toothpicks.

"To show that he had a broad, my God! Now, Bertil wasn't the type of . . . man who needed girls. As girls, I mean. Malm was the only one of those three at the so-called Stockholm branch. The third man I never met. He was called Sigge. It was he who organized the false papers, I think."

Sigge. Ernst Sigurd Karlsson, thought Martin Beck.

A short pause, not mechanical this time. The woman appeared to be thinking and nothing was heard from Månsson, neither on the tape nor in reality.

"Now you must understand that this is just what I myself thought. But I'm sure it's right. Bertil could not keep his mouth shut and it was impossible to misunderstand much of what he and Malm talked about together. Well, ever since some time last summer, Olofsson began to become more and more bigheaded every time I saw him. He began to talk about the so-called head office making enormous profits. He went on about it every time he had been there. Said that the Stockholm branch and most of all he himself did all the work and took all the risks, while the head office took most of the profits. But he himself didn't even know where this much talked-of head office was. If he and those other two guys took over the business and ran the Stockholm branch themselves, then they'd earn a helluva lot of money, he said. I think all that went to his head in the end. And in December he did something unbelievably stupid . . ."

"What?" asked Gunvald Larsson, astonishingly enough, just like a seven-year-old at a children's film matinee.

". . . As far as I could make out, he followed the guy who brought him money. Where to I don't know, Paris perhaps, or Rome. I think he'd already found out where this courier used to fly to, and that immediately after their meetings he took the first plane back to wherever it was, and then Bertil waited for the courier and followed him to see where he went. When he came here on the fifth of January this year, anyhow, he was extremely coarse and said that he had investigated the situation and was to go to France, yes, of course, he did in fact say France that time. But perhaps he was lying. He could lie too, if he wanted to. Well, anyhow, he was to go to the Continent and find out exactly what the situation was, he said. He also said that he and Malm and the third man were now in a position to set conditions and he was reckoning on at least tripling their income very soon. I think he really did take that trip, because the next time he came here he was awfully twitchy and nervous. He said that head office had agreed to send up a negotiator. When he talked, it was always in those sort of terms, as if it really were some ordinary business affair. Strangely enough, he did this to me too, although he knew that I understood what it was all about. On the sixth of February, he came here. He went out at least ten times that day to find out if the negotiator had come to his hotel. I haven't got a telephone, you see. He implied that it was to be a decisive meeting and that Malm was sitting waiting for news in Malmö. At about three the next day, that was Wednesday, I remember, he went out for the third time that day. And he never came back. Full stop. The end."

"Hm. Perhaps we should discuss your relationship to him too."

The woman replied without a trace of hesitation.

"Yes. We had an agreement. I use drugs insofar as I smoke hash sometimes, and regularly use Spanish phenedrine tablets when I work, Simpatina and Centramina. Excellent, both of them, and completely harmless. Now owing to this darned frenzy about drugs, those tablets are hard to get hold of and the price has doubled five or ten times. I simply can't afford them. When I met Bertil Olofsson quite by chance down in Nyhavn, I asked him if he had any to sell, just as I asked practically everyone I came into contact with. It turned out that he had access to what I wanted and I had something he needed, a place to stay which no one knew about, two nights a month. I hesitated, because he wasn't all that great shakes. But then it turned out that he didn't care a fig for girls and that settled the matter. We made an agreement. He stayed that night, or sometimes a little longer, at my place. Every month. And every time he came I got my monthly supply. Then he disappeared and I haven't had any tablets since. They're too expensive to buy on the black market, as I told you, and the result is my work gets worse and slower. From that point of view, it was a pity they killed him."

Månsson stretched out his hand and switched off the tape recorder.

"Uhuh," he said. "That's it, then."

"What the hell was all that?" said Kollberg. "Sounded rather like a radio play."

"Extremely skillful interrogation," said Hammar. "How did you get her to talk so freely?"

"Oh, no difficulty," said Månsson modestly.

"Please, may I ask something," said Melander, pointing at the tape recorder with the stem of his pipe. "Why didn't that woman go to the police of her own accord?"

"Her papers aren't entirely in order," said Månsson. "Nothing serious. The Danes don't bother about it. And also she really didn't care a bloody fig for Olofsson."

"Brilliant interrogation," said Hammar.

"That's really only a summary," said Månsson.

"Here, can one rely on that dame?" Gunvald Larsson asked.

"Absolutely," said Månsson. "And what's more important . . ."

He fell silent and waited until all the others had done so too.

"What's more important is that we now have evidence to show that Olofsson went from his temporary living-quarters with ... in Copenhagen at three o'clock on Wednesday the seventh of February. He went to meet someone. And this someone most likely took him across Öresund presumably on the excuse of meeting Malm, killed him and put him in an old car and pushed the whole contraption into the harbor."

"Yes," said Martin Beck. "That leads automatically to the question of how Olofsson got to Industrihammen."

"Exactly. We now know that the Prefect was not drivable and that the engine hadn't run for years. We also know that people saw it standing about out there for one or more days, but as there are scrap cars all over the place, no one gave it another thought. The crate was thus in place."

"And who had arranged it?"

"I think we know roughly who arranged it," said Månsson. "Who in actual fact put the car there is harder to say. It could have been Malm, quite simply. He was in Malmö at the time and could be contacted by phone."

"Well, how did Olofsson get to the harbor?" asked Hammar, impatiently.

"By car," said Martin Beck, more or less to himself.

"Exactly," said Månsson. "If he met the guy who killed him in Copenhagen that means they must have gone together from Copenhagen to Malmö, and that you do by boat, unless you're crazy or a long-distance swimmer."

"Or a transit passenger by air," said Kollberg.

"Yes, but that seems unlikely. As it's illegal to transport corpses on those boats, then Olofsson must have been alive during the crossing. And also to have gone on a boat that carries cars. As far as we can make out, the person who killed Olofsson must have had a car at his disposal and it is likely that he had it with him from Copenhagen."

"No, I don't follow this," said Gunvald Larsson. "Why must he have had a car?"

"Wait a minute," said Månsson. "I'll try to get through this quickly. It's actually all quite clear. Both of them, Olofsson and the man who killed him, went from Copenhagen to Malmö that evening, the seventh of February, I mean. What I was trying to tell you was how I found out about it."

"How you found out?" said Gunvald Larsson.

Månsson threw him a tired look and said:

"If he didn't kill Olofsson either in Copenhagen or on the boat, then he must have done it here in Malmö. Where in Malmö? Presumably out at Industrihammen. How did he get to Industrihammen? By car, because there's no other way to get there, for Christ's sake. Which car? Well, the car he had brought over from Denmark. Why? Because if he'd been stupid enough to take a taxi or some other car in Malmö, then we'd have found out about it."

Calm was restored. Everyone stared in silence at Månsson. He slowed down the tempo somewhat.

"This made me take two measures. First, I had two men check the ferries which ran in the afternoon and evening of the seventh of February. It turns out that indeed a steward on the train ferry *Malmöhus* recognizes Olofsson from a photograph and also can give quite a good description of the person who was with Olofsson. With this witness as a starting point, my two boys then find two supporting witnesses, one another steward and the other a seaman who was responsible for the arrangement of automobiles and railway cars on the vehicle deck. So we know with absolute certainty that Olofsson went from the free port of Copenhagen to Malmö on the train ferry on the evening of the seventh of February this year. On its last trip, the ferry left Copenhagen at a quarter to ten and got into Malmö at quarter past eleven. It does that every day, anyway, and has done so for many years. We also know that Olofsson was with a man whose description you'll hear shortly."

Månsson slowly changed toothpicks. He looked at Gunvald Larsson and said:

"We also know that they both traveled first class, that they sat in the smoking room and drank beer and ate two sandwiches containing cold beef and cheese, which agrees with the little that remains of the contents of Olofsson's stomach."

"That's obviously what he died of," mumbled Kollberg. "Swedish Railway's sandwiches."

Hammar threw him a murderous look.

"We even know which table they sat at. Furthermore, we know that they were in a Danish-registered Ford Taunus. Further investigations showed exactly which car it was, and that it was light blue."

"How . . . ?" said Martin Beck, and then fell silent. "Of course," he said. "A rented car."

"Exactly. The man who was with Olofsson did not bother to drive from God knows where to Copenhagen. Naturally he flew and rented a car when he got to Kastrup; at the car-rental firm he said his name was Cravanne and he produced a French driving-license and a French passport. He returned the car on the eighth and thanked them very much. Then he flew from there. Where to and under what name, we do not know. On the other hand, I think I know where he stayed, namely at a scruffy little hotel in Nyhavn. There, however, he produced a Lebanese passport and said his name was Riffi. If it's the same man. I'm not quite sure, as I mentioned. A person with that name, anyhow, was there from the sixth to the eighth. People in Nyhavn don't like the police."

"And the conclusion," said Martin Beck, "is that this person came to Copenhagen to do away with Olofsson. They met on the seventh, went to Malmö in the evening and . . . you said you'd investigated something else, didn't you?"

"Had it investigated," said Månsson lazily. "Yes, another look at the car, the Prefect, I mean, to find out how it got into the water. You know, it's always good to know what you're looking for. Then you find it more easily."

"What?" said Melander.

"The marks. A moment ago I said that the Prefect couldn't move under its own steam. How did it get into the water then? Well, the gear was put into neutral, then the car was pushed out into the water by another car, at quite a speed. Otherwise it wouldn't have landed so far out from the wharf. From behind, bumper to bumper, so to speak. The marks are there. There are corresponding marks on the other car, too."

"But who drove the Prefect to that miserable harbor, whatever it's called?" asked Gunvald Larsson.

"It must have been towed there. From some scrapyard. Personally I think it was Malm. He was staying at his usual place on the west side of Malmö, having already gone there on the fourth of February."

"But then it might as well have been Malm who . . ." said Hammar, and then he fell silent.

"Nix," said Månsson. "Malm had more sense of self-preservation than Olofsson. He left Malmö at top speed on the morning of the seventh and scuttled up here to Stockholm. That's proved. My belief is that Malm had orders to get a car that could not be identified to a definite place. By telephone from Copenhagen from that Cravanne or Riffi. Malm did so, but realized at the same time that they had gone too far and the game was up. By the way, someone who spoke bad Swedish was looking for Malm on the telephone at midday on the seventh. The people at the hotel then said he'd gone. Do you want to hear the description now? I've taped a summary here to get everything in."

He changed tapes and pressed the starting switch.

"Cravanne or Riffi looks between thirty-five and forty years old. He is at least five foot eight and at most five foot ten, rather above average in weight for that height, because of his squat and powerful build. He is not fat, however. His hair is black, as well as his eyebrows, and his eyes dark brown. He has good white teeth. His forehead is rather low, and hairline and eyebrows make two parallel lines. His nose is rather hooked and he might have a scar or a scratch on one nostril which has perhaps gone by now. He has a habit of running his forefingers over the place where the scar or scratch is. He is well and soberly dressed, suit, black shoes, white shirt, tie, and his behavior is quiet and polite. His voice has a deep note and he speaks at least three languages: French, which is presumably his native language, English very well but with a French accent, and Swedish quite well but with an accent."

The spool stopped whirring.

"Uhuh," said Månsson, with bovine calm. "Does that tell you anything?"

They stared at him as if they'd seen a ghost.

"Well," said Månsson. "That's about it. For the moment. Have you fixed up a room for me? Christ, it's hot. Excuse me a moment."

He went out into the corridor.

Rönn rose and followed him. For most of the time he had been sitting thinking about something else besides Olofsson and his accomplices, namely that Månsson was an expert in house-searches. He caught up with Månsson and said:

"Say, Per, would you like to come back and have dinner with us tonight?"

"Of course," said Månsson. "Very much indeed."

He seemed both delighted and surprised.

"Good," said Rönn.

It was now over three months since the fire engine that Mats had been given for his fourth birthday had disappeared, and although the boy hardly bothered to ask after it any longer, Rönn could not help wondering how it had disappeared so completely. He still hunted for it now and again, but was convinced that there was not a square inch of the apartment that he had not covered.

When Rönn, sometime back, had lifted the lid of the water-tank behind the toilet for the fiftieth time, a remark of Månsson's had come back to him. Nearly six months ago, an important page from a report had been missing and Martin Beck had asked if anyone was an expert at searching. Månsson, who at the time had come up from Skåne to take part in a case of multiple murder, had replied: "I'm good at looking for things. If there's anything to find, then I'll find it." He had indeed also found the page of the report.

So it was this speciality of his that Månsson had to thank for the fact that instead of a dismal and lonely dinner at some cheap eating-place, he was given the opportunity of enjoying Unda Rönn's excellent cooking. Månsson liked food very much, but he was also fastidious and knew how to appreciate a well-prepared meal.

By the time he had eaten the crisply fried venison slices with scrambled eggs as creamy as he himself usually made them, he was sighing with pleasure, and when a dish of golden brown grouse was placed on the table, he leaned forward and drew in the aroma through his nostrils.

"Now this really is quite something," he said. "Where does such wonderful grub come from at this time of the year?"

"We got them from my brother in Karesuando," said

Unda. "He goes shooting quite a bit. He's the one who keeps us in venison, too."

Rönn passed the bowl of cloudberry jelly and said:

"We've a whole reindeer in the freezer. From the autumn culling."

"Not horns and all, I suppose," said Månsson, and Mats, who had begged to be allowed to sit at the table, burst out laughing:

"Ha-ha! You can't eat the horns. You chop them off first."

Månsson ruffled the boy's hair and said:

"You're a clever boy. What are you going to be when you grow up?"

"A fireman," said the boy.

He jumped down from his chair and vanished through the door, wailing like a fire engine.

Rönn grasped the opportunity to tell Månsson about the disappearing fire engine.

"Have you looked under the reindeer?" asked Månsson.

"I've looked everywhere. It's simply gone."

Månsson wiped his mouth and said:

"Oh, no. We'll probably find it."

When they had finished their meal, Unda shooed them out of the kitchen and carried the coffee into the living room. Rönn got out a bottle of brandy.

Mats was lying on the floor in his pajamas in front of the television set, watching with interest a group of solemn people sitting on a semicircular sofa, discussing something. A young man with an important expression on his face said:

"I consider that divorce in marriages where there are children should as far as possible be prevented or made difficult by society, as children of lone parents become more insecure than others, and with that more disposed to succumb to alcohol and drugs," . . . and disappeared into a shining dot as Rönn switched off the set.

"Load of shit," said Månsson. "Look at me for example. I didn't meet my father until I was over forty. My mother brought me up on her own from when I was a year old, and there's nothing wrong with me. Nothing seriously wrong, that is."

"Did you look up your father after so many years?" said Rönn.

"Christ, no," said Månsson. "Whatever for? No, we met by chance at the liquor store in Davidshallstorg. I was a sergeant at the time.

"What did it feel like?" said Rönn. "Meeting your father like that?"

"Nothing special. I was standing there in line and in the next line there was this big guy, gray-haired, as tall as I am. He came up to me and said: 'Good-day. I am your father, sir. I've been meaning to speak to you many a time when I've seen you in town, sir, but it never came off.' Then he said: 'I've heard things are going well for you, sir.'"

"What did you say?"

"I didn't really know what to say. Well, then the old man stuck out his hand and said, 'Jönsson.' 'Månsson,' I said and we shook hands."

"Have you met since?" asked Rönn.

"Yes, we run into each other occasionally, and he always greets me just as politely."

Unda came in and fetched Mats, who was falling asleep on Rönn's knee. After a while, she came back and said:

"He wants you to go and say goodnight."

The boy was already asleep when they went into the room. Månsson looked round with expert eyes before tiptoeing out and closing the door.

"I presume you've looked in there?" he said.

"Looked," said Rönn, "I've turned the whole room upside down. The others too, for that matter. But you can look around. Perhaps I've overlooked something."

He had not done so. They went together through the whole apartment and Månsson could not find a cranny where Rönn had not already searched several times. They returned to their coffee and cognac and Unda.

"Yes, it is strange, isn't it?" she said. "It was quite a big one, too."

"About a foot long," said Rönn.

"You said that he hadn't been out for several days after he was given it," said Månsson. "Might he have thrown it out the window?"

"No," said Unda. "As you see, we have safety chains on

205

every window so that he can't open them himself. And we never have the windows open when Mats is around."

"And when you open them with the chain on, the gap is too small for the fire engine to get through," said Rönn.

Månsson rolled his cognac glass between his palms and said:

"The garbage bag then? Might he have put it in that?"

Unda shook her head.

"No, it's the same cupboard as the soap powders and that sort of thing and we've got a kind of bar on the door which he can't open."

"Uhuh," said Månsson, sipping his cognac thoughtfully.

"Have you an attic storage room here?" he said.

"No, one down in the basement," said Rönn. "Have you taken anything down there since the fire engine disappeared?"

Rönn looked at his wife, who shook her head.

"Neither have I," said Rönn.

"Can you think of anything that has been moved out of here? Something that has been sent for repair, or something like that? Or laundry? It might have gone with the dirty laundry."

"I wash everything myself," said Unda. "We've a laundry down in the basement."

"And he's had no friends here who might have taken it with them?"

"No, he'd had a cold for quite a long time, so no one had been here during the time," said Unda.

They sat in silence for a while.

"Has anyone else been here who might have taken it with him?" asked Månsson.

"I've had some of my friends here once or twice," said Unda. "But they don't steal toys. Anyhow, it was not until after that that we discovered it was missing."

Rönn nodded gloomily.

"This is as bad as police interrogation," said Unda with a laugh.

"Just you wait until he gets out his stick and starts third-degreeing you," Rönn said.

"Think now," said Månsson. "Has anyone else been here, someone who came to fetch something, or to read the meter, or a plumber or another workman?"

"No," Rönn said. "Not as far as I know. Do you mean that someone might have stolen it?"

"Well, why not?" said Månsson. "People steal a lot of strange things. In Malmö, we had a guy who went around to houses pretending to be from Anticimex exterminator company and when we got hold of him he had a hundred and thirteen pairs of ladies' panties in a box at home. That was the only thing he stole. But I was thinking that the fire engine had more likely gone with someone by mistake."

"You ought to know that, Unda," said Rönn. "You're at home in the daytime."

"Yes, I was just sitting here thinking about it. I can't remember having any workmen here. That man who put in the new windowpane was much earlier, wasn't he?"

"Yes," said Rönn. "That was in February."

"Yes," said Unda.

She bit the knuckle of her forefinger thoughtfully.

"Yes," she said. "The janitor was here letting the air out of the radiators. That was a few days after Mats's birthday, I'm sure."

"Letting the air out of the radiators?" said Rönn. "I didn't know that."

"I probably forgot to tell you," said Unda.

"Did he have his tools with him?" said Månsson. "He must have had a wrench. Do you remember whether he had a tool kit with him?"

"Yes, I think so," said Unda. "Though I'm not sure."

"Does he live in the building?"

"Yes, on the ground floor. Svensson's his name."

Månsson put down his cognac glass and got up.

"Come on, Einar," he said. "Let's go and visit your janitor."

Svensson was a small sinewy man of sixty or so. He was wearing well-pressed dark trousers and a brilliantly white shirt with sleevebands.

Månsson had already spotted a tool kit standing on a shoe-shelf in the hall, when the janitor said:

"Good evening, Mr. Rönn. Can I help you with anything?"

Rönn did not really know how to begin, but Månsson pointed at the tool kit and said:

"Is that your tool kit, Mr. Svensson?"

"Yes," said Svensson in surprise.

"How long is it since you last used it?"

"Well, I don't really know. It's quite a while now. I've been in the hospital for several weeks, so Berg at number 11 has been looking after the block for me in the meantime. Why, if I may ask?"

"May we look inside it?"

The janitor picked up the tool box.

"Please do," he said. "Why . . ."

Månsson opened the bag and Rönn saw how the janitor stretched his neck and looked down into the bag with undisguised astonishment. He stepped forward himself and there, among the hammers, screwdrivers and wrenches, lay the fire engine, red and shining.

Several days later, Tuesday, the thirtieth of July to be exact, Martin Beck and Kollberg made a private summary of the case as they sat out at Västberga, sipping coffee.

"Has Månsson gone home?" asked Martin Beck.

"Yes, he went off on Saturday. Doesn't think much of Stockholm, I guess, that man."

"No, he probably had enough of it last winter, after the bus murder."

"Damned good job he's done," said Kollberg. "I'd never have expected it of that slow-poke. And yet, I keep wondering . . ."

"What?"

Kollberg shook his head.

"There's something fishy about that interrogation. The girl, you know . . ."

"Why do you think that?"

"I don't know really. Well, anyhow, the whole thing seems all tied up now. Olofsson and Malm and that guy Karlsson, who was their forger, thought of getting off and opening their own . . ."

"Apropos Karlsson, by the way, we went up and had a look at the insurance company where he worked. All the things he used for the forgeries were there. Stamps and papers and so on," said Martin Beck. "He had them in a cupboard there and his head of department had packed them all up in a box without knowing what they were. It's at Kungsholmsgatan now, if you want to look at it."

"He wasn't a bad forger," said Kollberg. "Well, those

three guys knew too much and so that Lasalle-Riffi-Cravanne whatever we're to call him was sent over."

"Call him Whatshisname."

"Yes, Whatshisname'll do fine. He went to Copenhagen and then on to Malmö and knocked off Olofsson. But Malm got scared and scrammed. Then Malm got nabbed by the police and ..."

"Yes," said Martin Beck. "Both he and Sigge Karlsson had lost their livelihoods. They knew or had some idea of what had happened to Olofsson. They were broke and desperate and finally Malm took a car which he thought of driving down and selling on his own accord, to get some money somehow. And got caught at once."

"And then he was released and that didn't make things any better. He and Sigge Karlsson were just waiting for this Whatshisname or someone else to appear and finish them off for good. They were living on borrowed time, so to speak."

"And Whatshisname did indeed arrive like a letter in the mail. He must have made his presence known in some way, presumably by telephone, or perhaps they caught sight of him when he was checking on their addresses. Sigge Karlsson gives up altogether and shoots himself, first having had a moment of clarity and considered calling you, but that obviously passed very quickly."

Martin Beck nodded.

"Malm is now in such a fix that he quite openly visits Sigge Karlsson, although he probably knows he is being tailed. Then he hears that Karlsson is dead."

"So he buys a beer with his last penny and goes home and turns on the gas. But before that, Whatshisname, who is in town to do a job and wants it done quickly, has been there and put his jolly little contrivance into Malm's bed. The day after, Whatshisname takes a plane to Whats-itcalled. And left behind are we. The Keystone Cops. The Flatfoots. It seems idiotic that a crowd of people like you and me and Rönn and Larsson have been stumping round for five months, hunting for a guy who was dead a month before we began, and for a guy whose name we don't know and was also far out of reach from the very beginning."

"Perhaps he'll come back," said Martin Beck thoughtfully.

"Optimist," said Kollberg. "He'll never set foot in the place again."

"Hm," said Martin Beck. "I'm not so sure. Have you thought about one thing? He's got an important asset for doing jobs here, namely, that he speaks Swedish."

"Yes, where the hell did he learn that?"

"Worked in Sweden some time or been here as a refugee during the war. Anyhow, he must be extremely valuable if the firm decides to build up its Stockholm branch again. And also, he has no idea that we even know of his existence. He may very well appear again."

Kollberg tilted his head to one side and looked doubtful.

"Have you thought about another thing?" he said. "Even if he does come back and perhaps even voluntarily steps in here, then what can we prove? It isn't illegal for him to have been in Sundbyberg."

"No, we can't blame the fire on him, but he's pretty well tied to this affair in Malmö, the murder of Olofsson."

"True. But that's not our headache. Anyhow, he won't ever come back again."

"I'm still not convinced of that. I'll ask Interpol and the French police to keep their eyes open. And notify us if he appears."

"You do that," said Kollberg yawning.

30

Just over a month later, Lennart Kollberg was sitting in his office in Västberga puzzling over where a seventeen-year-old girl had got to. People were constantly missing, especially girls, and mostly in the summer. Nearly all of them appeared again, some having hitched to Nepal to sit cross-legged smoking opium, others having earned a little extra posing naked for German pornographic magazines, and others having gone with friends to the country and simply forgotten to telephone their families. But this one seemed to have genuinely disappeared. The girl in the photograph lying in front of him was smiling and he thought gloomily that she would probably reappear in somewhat less good shape, out of the Channel, for instance, or out of some pond in Nacka national park.

Martin Beck was on leave and Skacke unobtainable, although he ought to have been somewhere in the vicinity.

It was raining outside, fresh clean summer rain, which sluiced the dust off the leaves and spattered cheerfully against the windows.

Kollberg liked rain, especially this fresh kind of rain after oppressive heat, and he looked with pleasure at the heavy banks of gray clouds which occasionally opened up and allowed the sun to sift through in ragged patches, and then he thought about how he would soon be going home, at the latest half-past five, and that was late, for it was Saturday.

And then, of course, the telephone rang.

"Hello. It's Strömgren."

"Uhuh."

"I've got something on the Telex which I can't really make out."

"What?"

"From Paris. Just got a translation. It just says this: Lasalle inquired about probably en route from Brussels to Stockholm. Extra-flight SN X3 estimated at Arlanda eighteen fifteen hours. Name Samir Malghagh. Passport Moroccan."

Kollberg said nothing.

"It's for Beck, but he's on leave. I can't make it out at all. Can you?"

"Yes," said Kollberg. "Unfortunately. How many people around your place?"

"Here? Practically none. Except me. Shall I ring Märsta station?"

"Don't bother," said Kollberg wearily. "I'll fix it. Did you say quarter past six?"

"Eighteen fifteen hours. That's what it says."

Kollberg looked at the time. Just past four. Plenty of time, relatively.

He depressed the knobs on the telephone and dialed his home number.

"It looks as if I'll have to go out to Arlanda."

"Hell," said Gun.

"Couldn't agree more."

"What time'll you be back?"

"No later than eight, I hope."

"Hurry."

"Bet your sweet ass. Bye."

"Lennart."

"Mmm."

"I love you. Bye."

She replaced the receiver so quickly that he had no time to say anything. He smiled, got up, went out into the corridor and yelled:

"Skacke!"

The only thing he could hear was the rain, and in some way or other it was no longer pleasant.

He had to go practically through the whole floor before he found a living soul. A policeman.

"Where the hell is Skacke?"

"He's playing football."

"What? Football? On duty?"

"He said it was a very important match and that he'd be back before half-past five."

"What team is he playing in?"

"The Police."

"Where?"

"At Zinkensdamm. He's off duty until half-past five, anyway."

This was true and did not improve matters. It was not an attractive prospect to have to go out to Arlanda alone, and also Skacke was in on the case and could take over as soon as Kollberg had shaken hands with Mr. Whatshisname. If it came to that even. So he put on his raincoat, went down to the car and drove to Zinkensdamm.

The posters outside were white with green lettering: SATURDAY 15:00 HOURS POLICE SPORTS CLUB VERSUS REYMERSHOLM SPORTS CLUB. Over Högalid church curved a magnificent rainbow and over the green sports stadium only light misty rain was falling now. On the churned-up field were twenty-two soaked players and round about stood a hundred or so spectators. The atmosphere seemed numb.

Kollberg was not in the least interested in sports and after sweeping a look over the field, he went to the far side where he caught sight of a policeman in mufti stand-

212

ing quite alone by the railing, nervously scratching his palms.

"Are you some kind of manager, or whatever it's called?"

The man nodded without taking his eyes off the ball.

"Get that creature in the orange shirt off at once, the one who's just tripping over the ball there."

"Impossible. We've already put in our twelfth man. Quite out of the question. Anyhow, there's only ten minutes left."

"What's the score?"

"Three-two for the Police. And if we win this match, then ..."

"Yes?"

"Then we can go up into ... no ... oh, thank God ... into the third division."

Ten minutes was not the end of the world and the man looked so agonized that Kollberg decided not to add to his burdens.

"Ten minutes isn't the end of the world," he said good-naturedly.

"A lot can happen in ten minutes," said the man pessimistically.

He was right. The team in green shirts and white shorts scored two goals and won, amid ragged applause from the alcoholics and other veterans who appeared to form the majority of the spectators. Skacke got kicked in the legs and fell flat into a muddy puddle.

When Kollberg managed to get hold of him, he had mud in his hair and was panting like an old steam engine going up hill. He also looked completely crushed.

"Hurry, now," said Kollberg. "That Whatshisname's coming to Arlanda at six-fifteen. We've got to go and meet him."

Skacke vanished like lightning into the dressing room.

A quarter of an hour later, he was sitting beside Kollberg in the car, newly showered, hair brushed and trim.

"That's a hell of a thing to do," said Kollberg. "Go and get beaten like that."

"We've the crowd against us," said Skacke. "And Reymers is one of the best teams in the league. What are we going to do with this Lasalle?"

"We'll have to have a chat with him, I suppose. I

213

reckon our chances of getting him are minimal. If we take him with us, he'll probably set up such a damned row that we'll have the Foreign Office on our necks and in the end we'll have to apologize and say goodbye and thanks very much. The only possibility is if we can disconcert him so that he reveals himself in some way. But if he's as smart as they say, he won't get had that way. If it is him at all."

"He's very dangerous, isn't he?" said Skacke.

"Yes, he's said to be dangerous. But hardly to us."

"Wouldn't it be a better idea to tail him and see what he's thinking of doing? Had you thought of that?"

"I'd thought of that," said Kollberg. "But I think this way's better. There's a faint chance that he'll blunder. If nothing else, perhaps we can scare him away."

He sat in silence for a moment. Then he said:

"He's smart and ruthless, but probably not all that bright. And that's where our chance lies."

A little later he added maliciously:

"Of course, most policemen are not all that bright either, now, so in that respect the odds are even."

The traffic on the highway north was fairly light, but they had plenty of time and Kollberg maintained a moderate speed. Skacke was fidgeting about. Kollberg glanced suspiciously at him and said:

"What are you up to?"

"I don't like this shoulder holster."

"Have you got your pistol on you?"

"Of course."

"When you go to play football?"

"I had it locked up during the match, of course."

"Fool," said Kollberg.

He himself went unarmed and had done so for as long as he could remember. He was one of those who urged that all policemen should be disarmed completely.

"Gunvald Larsson's got one of those clips you fasten into your trouser belt. I wonder where he got it from."

"Mr. Larsson would probably prefer to go round carrying a nickel-plated Smith and Wesson 44-Magnum with a butt of grooved Gonçala Alves and an eight and three-eighths inch barrel and a nameplate in chased silver."

"Are there such things?"

"Oh, yes. Cost more than 1,000 kronor and weigh about three pounds."

They continued in silence, Skacke sitting rigid and tense, licking his lips now and again. Kollberg nudged him with his elbow and said:

"Relax, kid. Nothing special is going to happen. You know the description, don't you."

Skacke nodded hesitantly and then guiltily sat mumbling to himself for the rest of the way.

The plane was a Sabena Caravelle and landed ten minutes late, by which time Kollberg was already so tired of both Arlanda and his earnest colleague that he had nearly yawned his jaw out of joint.

They were standing on each side of the glass door, watching the plane taxiing toward the airport building. Kollberg was standing just by the door and Skacke about five yards inside the airport lounge. This was a routine safety precaution which they had taken without discussing the matter.

The passengers filed out and approached in a straggly line.

Kollberg whistled to himself. Clearly it was not just anyone who had come on this extra flight. First in was a squat, dark-haired man, impeccably dressed in a dark suit, snow-white shirt and highly polished black shoes.

This man was a prominent Russian diplomat. Kollberg recognized him from the State Visit five years earlier and knew that nowadays he was a key man in Paris or Geneva, or somewhere. Two yards behind him came his beautiful wife and another four yards behind her, Samir Malghagh or Lasalle or whatever his name was. The description fitted anyhow. He was wearing a felt hat and a blue shantung suit.

Kollberg let the Russian pass and involuntarily glanced at his wife, who really was a good-looker, a mixture of Tatjana Samojlova and Juliette Greco and Gun Kollberg.

That glance was the most fateful mistake Kollberg had made in his life.

For Skacke misinterpreted it.

Kollberg immediately turned his head back, looked at the much-discussed Lebanese or whatever he was, raised his right hand to his hat, took half a step forward and said:

"Excusez moi, Monsieur Malghagh . . ."

The man stopped, smiled toothily and inquiringly, and also raised his right hand to his hat.

And just at that very moment, Kollberg saw the unheard-of thing happening, diagonally behind him, out of the corner of his eye.

Skacke had taken a step forward and placed himself in front of the prominent diplomat, and the Russian had routinely raised his right arm and swept him away, no doubt in the belief that the man was an impertinent reporter, for the Czechoslovakian crisis was on and all that, and Skacke tottered backward and stuck his right hand inside his jacket and pulled out his Walther 7.65.

Kollberg turned his head and yelled:

"Skacke, for Christ's sake!"

The moment Malghagh saw the pistol, his face changed and grew taut and strained, and for a fraction of a second his brown eyes expressed only surprise and fear. Then he had a knife in his hand, which he must have had up his sleeve, Kollberg had time to think, a sharp terrible weapon with a blade at least nine inches long and no more than half an inch wide.

Kollberg had nothing but his training and speed of reaction to thank for the fact that he realized that the man intended to cut his throat, and he had time to raise his left arm to parry the knife thrust. But the other man turned with lightning and masterly speed and stabbed from below upward, and Kollberg, still off balance and some of his attention drawn in the wrong direction, felt how the blade went in just below his ribs on the left side of his diaphragm. Like a hot knife through butter, people say, thought Kollberg, and that's exactly what it feels like, and he doubled up over the knife, still quite conscious of what he was doing and why he was doing it. He knew that it would delay the other man for a few seconds. How many? Perhaps five or six.

All this happened while Skacke was still standing, utterly bewildered, about to raise his pistol and press down the safety catch with his thumb.

Then Malghagh or whatever his name was got the knife free and Kollberg fell doubled over, his head down to protect his carotid artery, and the knife went up again and at that moment Skacke fired.

The bullet hit Lasalle or whatever his name was in the center of his chest and threw him violently backward, the knife flying out of his hand as he landed on his back on the marble floor.

The scene was completely static. Skacke was standing there with his arm outstretched, the barrel of his pistol still pointing diagonally upward after the recoil; the man in the shantung suit was lying flat on his back, his arms outstretched; and between them lay Kollberg doubled up and half on his side, with both hands pressed against the left side of his diaphragm. Everyone else was standing absolutely still and no one had time to scream.

Then Skacke ran up to Kollberg, knelt down, the pistol still in his hand, and said breathlessly:

"How is it?"

"Bad."

"Why did you wink at me? I thought—"

"You were just about to arrange a third world war," whispered Kollberg.

And then, as things should be, panic and chaos broke out, with screams and running hither and thither, as usual, when everything is over.

But everything was not over for Kollberg. In the wailing ambulance on its way to Mörby Hospital, he was at first immensely scared of dying. Then he looked at the man in the shantung suit lying on a parallel stretcher only a yard away from him. The man had his head turned to one side and he was looking at Kollberg with eyes that were rigid with pain and terror and rapidly approaching death. He tried to move his hand, perhaps to make the sign of the cross, but all he could manage was a slight jerk.

"Ha, you're going to die before you get the last rites, or whatever it's called," thought Kollberg impiously.

He was right. The man did not even survive as far as the emergency room. Just as the ambulance began to slow down, his lower jaw dropped and blood and filth began to pour out of him.

Kollberg was still immensely scared of dying.

And just before he lost consciousness, he thought:

"It's not fair. I've never been interested in this damned case. And Gun waiting . . ."

"Will he die?" asked Skacke.

"No," said the doctor. "Not from this, anyhow. But it'll be a month or two before he can thank you."

"Thank?"

Skacke shook his head and went over to the telephone. He had many calls to make.

About the Authors

PER WAHLÖÖ and MAJ SJÖWALL, his wife
and co-author, wrote ten Martin Beck
mysteries. Mr. Wahlöö, who died in 1975,
was a reporter for several Swedish newspapers and magazines and wrote numerous radio and television plays, film scripts,
short stories and novels. Maj Sjöwall is
also a poet.